CONNECTIONS

Jim Goldmann

This book is a work of fiction. Names, characters, places, and incidents are products of the author's imagination or are used fictitiously. Any resemblance to actual events or locales or persons, living or dead, is entirely coincidental

Chapter 1

At first, only pain invades his consciousness. Barely aware of his surroundings, he is unable to orient himself. Impenetrably dark. Numbingly cold. No frame of reference. Something is very wrong. He realizes he must have been unconscious as instinct takes over and he struggles to get his bearings. Though barely able to mentally voice the desperate questions: 'Where am I, how did I get here'; he knows there is no one to answer. And, in response to the unheard questions memory floods back, and with it, deepening dread.

§

He had been on his way home from work, late, but no later than usual. There had been better days, few worse. Michael frequently found gratification in his job as a hospital executive, but truth be told, the politics drove him nuts. This day had brought a succession of meaningless meetings in an attempt to make sure everyone was on the same page, which they weren't; or to get them to agree, which they wouldn't. The last meeting of the day had proven to be the most aggravating. The federal government had announced additional Medicare cutbacks and he knew the private insurance companies would quickly follow suit. In addition, the current recession saw far too many people out of work and unable to pay their medical bills. For four protracted hours the management team had been meeting to consider additional cost reductions. Michael had just voiced his challenge to the latest proposed cut.

"When are you going to get your head out of the sand?" came the typically insightful comment from the Chief Financial Officer. While tempted to reply, 'The view is much better from this position', in true diplomatic fashion Michael responded with a more reasoned comeback.

"Karl, do you even understand why we're here? If we close the breast cancer screening clinic, where are the women without insurance going to go? If we don't catch the disease in its earliest stages, they'll come back later, sick or dying, and their care will cost even more. Using your logic, we should close down all of our services and just manage our investments."

Preceding his comments with a sigh of barely concealed disdain, Karl replied, "You know what I'm talking about, Michael. We don't have the funds to continue providing care to those who can't pay for it. We have to cut services and staff if we're going to balance the budget."

"Look guys, we aren't going to get anywhere if we continue bickering," said Bill, the CEO whose only priority was to maintain his position in the balancing act between the doctors and the Board of Directors. "It's already past seven and a mess outside. We'll reconvene at three tomorrow. Come prepared with the targeted reductions for each of your areas. Is everyone okay with that?"

Emotionally and physically exhausted, they all agreed, picked up their mounds of paper, and headed to their offices; islands of sporadic solitude where each manager could find some peace, if only for a moment, before the phone rang again or some physician barged in with a life-or-death demand or inconsequential complaint. As the weary mob headed down the hall, Michael tried to strike up a conversation with Karl in an attempt to part on amiable terms but only found indifference in return.

Back in his office he looked at the papers overflowing his in-basket (and on every other surface in the office except the floor) and decided work could wait until morning. He had reached the point where he just wanted to get home and sit in front of the fire with the one person he knew he could count on to lift his spirits.

Michael grabbed his coat and scarf off the hook on the back of his door and headed down the hall exiting the executive suite; relieved he was finally going home and wanting nothing more than to avoid thinking about what would face him the next day. Karl didn't look up as Michael passed his door, working silently with only the light of a table lamp to illuminate his organized desk.

After several twists and turns down multiple hallways in the exceedingly lit rabbit warren through the back halls of the hospital he approached the corridor leading to the employee parking lot anxious to get home and recover without further delay.

No sooner had he rounded the corner near the back entrance, when, from the other direction came the chairman of the psychiatry department, Thomas Thomas.

"Michael, wait a minute," he called out.

Thomas routinely feigned friendship toward anyone with influence who would listen to him. As low man in the medical staff pecking order he needed all the help he could get. Momentarily he considered bolting in the opposite direction, but Michael instead stopped and waited wondering, *does he want something or does he only want to gossip?*

"Hi, Tom, what's up?" Michael asked.

"How was the budget meeting? I heard my sleep clinic might get the axe. Is that true?" Thomas stood so close Michael could feel his breath, smell the coffee.

The man has no boundaries, thought Michael.

"It hasn't even come up, yet" Michael replied emphasizing the last word, intending to put Thomas off guard and yet taking no joy in the gamesmanship.

"Well, I'm not concerned. I have an important donor coming by tomorrow and they've already told me there shouldn't be a problem. By the way, if there is anything I can do to help, please let me know".

"What are you talking about?" Michael asked, alarm bells ringing in his head.

Thomas stepped back in mock shock, "I'm sorry, I thought you knew. I don't know that I should say anything but word is out that there are going to be layoffs and your name is on the list. I wanted you to know I'm here for you if you need a reference or something."

The clanging in his head transformed becoming a cold, leaden stone in the pit of his stomach. Michael first thought to deny the truth of Thomas' statement but in his gut he knew it to be true, though he couldn't articulate why.

As he considered this news, denial turned to anger as thoughts entered his mind too quickly to process. *Why did I have to hear it from Thomas? Who else knew? No wonder Karl and Bill had been distant for the past couple of days. Why couldn't they just come out and tell me?*

Putting on a brave face to mask his confusion, Michael responded, "You know how rumors are. I'll believe it when it happens."

Michael turned toward the door, needing more than ever to escape, and called over his shoulder, "I've gotta run. I'll talk to you tomorrow."

He pulled on his gloves as he passed through the door leading to the employee parking lot; leaving the brightly lit, warm hallway seeking relief from the devastating news in the dark, winter night.

As the wind whipped him towards his car, Michael had difficulty gathering his thoughts. It had been sleeting for the past several hours. Encrusted with a glistening sheen of ice the remaining cars sparkled like misshapen jewels. Michael walked briskly through the parking lot navigating between the weather and his anxiety.

Using his remote key he unlocked the car door, sat down, started the engine, and turned on the front and rear defrosters. He reached into the glove compartment, grabbed his plastic ice scraper, got out, and set about clearing the windows. By the time he finished the car was warm enough to take out the chill, at least the one caused by the weather.

Michael pulled out of the parking lot driving cautiously on the slick but navigable city streets. Driving as fast as conditions allowed along the highway toward home, he started considering his options. By the time he reached the off ramp, he was already starting to feel a little better.

Truth be told, maybe this would be liberating; a chance to make a new start, he thought. He was considering what to tell his wife as he turned on the tree-lined, winding rural road leading to his house.

Though he took every precaution steering cautiously on the dicey blacktop; he couldn't help but be distracted. Exhausted from months working long hours coupled with the latest news all but assured he would be caught by surprise when a car lost control, crossed over the center line, and headed directly for him.

Michael swerved to avoid hitting the oncoming vehicle but his delayed reactions, coupled with his heavy coat restricting his movement caused him to twist the steering wheel too fast causing the car to fish tail.

Adrenalin coursed through his veins focusing all his attention on righting the car. He turned the wheel the other direction attempting to pull out of the skid but over-compensated. Forgetting all he had learned about driving on ice Michael slammed on the brakes sending the car into an uncontrolled spin.

Recovering his composure, he turned the wheel more gradually this time tapping the brakes, slowing the spin.

Though the whole episode took moments to unfold Michael felt as if he were in slow motion. He needed just a little more time, time to get control, time he didn't have.

He successfully avoided the other car; nevertheless Michael's eyes went wide as he glimpsed the obstacle looming before him.

Before he could turn again, his car slammed into an eighty year old oak tree with the crash of tearing, grinding metal.

But Michael never heard the sound. The airbags failed to deploy and only his seatbelt saved him from certain death.

No one would ever know who drove the car that evening causing Michael's vehicle to swerve off the road; its inebriated driver either too frightened or uncaring to stay behind and help.

Nor would anyone have been able to predict this one, seemingly random, accident be as one small pebble rolling downhill, gathering other stones in its wake, creating an avalanche such as mankind had never seen.

§

"I am in my car, I can't move. I can't feel my legs. Smell gasoline. It's hard to breathe. Heartbeat too fast, getting weaker. Am I dying? Why can't I move? Why can't I feel anything? How will anyone find me in time?"

From somewhere deep inside the scream of a wounded animal erupts with terrible force.

§

"Michael, wake up!"

Michael's wife shook him.

"You're dreaming".

She looked down at him with eyes which saw through pain to the man he had been not so very long ago.

Chapter 2

Gabriella sat up in bed. She watched his chest labor as he tried to control his breathing. Speaking soothingly she asked, "Was it the same one?" knowing the answer before he spoke.

"Yes", one word as he stared at the ceiling above him.

She looked at the bedside clock. "It's about time to get up anyway. Do you want to stay in bed or get in your chair?" she asked attempting to muster a positive attitude.

Gabriella sat there, half covered by the blanket, knees up, elbows resting on them, her head in her hands staring down at nothing. It seemed like an eternity had passed when he replied that he wanted to sit in the wheelchair.

Gabriella reached to her left and turned on the lamp on the night stand. She stood up, crossed over to the other side of the bed and helped him to swing his legs over and hoist himself into the chair. Helping Michael, at 5'10" and a solid build, coupled with his growing weakness presented a mounting physical challenge for his wife, a full head shorter than he.

"A few months ago and I could have easily done this myself", Michael admitted grudgingly. Almost four years had passed since the accident but over the last several months Michael had found himself progressively losing strength in his upper body. "At least I can still cook. Why don't you get ready for work and I'll have a gourmet breakfast for you to get your day off to a great start."

"I can't wait", she responded sarcastically. Breakfast was not Gabriella's favorite meal. As Michael wheeled himself out of the bedroom, she walked into the bathroom and turned on the shower. She brushed her teeth, laid out her clothes, undressed and stepped into the soothing rain. She often did her best thinking in the shower but this morning wasn't the best time to try and solve the myriad of issues bothering her. Instead she pondered the possible meanings of Michael's dream. Dreaming about the accident wasn't new, but the dreams had been coming more frequently and they appeared to be more vivid. She wondered whether it had anything to do with his progressive neuropathy.

"I've got to find a way to move faster. I'm getting close but I'm not there, yet. Right, and maybe I'm only kidding myself," she thought. But then caught herself: *"No, I'm his only hope. I have to come through."* Turning off the faucet Gabriella grabbed her towel and stepped out of the shower.

Twenty minutes later she stepped into the kitchen and sat down at the table. The room wasn't as functional as she would have liked. Gabby loved to putter and would have appreciated a kitchen with more counter and cabinet space, but the two bedroom wood frame bungalow, built in the forties, was all they could afford right now.

Michael placed a plate with a blueberry Pop Tart on the table in front of her. Gabby looked down and couldn't help but laugh.

"My favorite!" she remarked. "You shouldn't have gone to so much trouble".

Michael tried to muster a smile but failed. He knew the burden she carried and it was the little things he could do which lightened it. The big things, like hold down a real job, be a real man, be a father to the child he knew she wanted; he just couldn't do those anymore. He started to take the plate away and she grabbed his wrist.

"What do you think you're doing? You made it; I'm going to eat it."

Michael brought her another plate with half a banana and half an English muffin covered in peanut butter. Neither of them drank coffee but she did like her tea in the morning. She poured milk from the little pitcher on the table. She liked her tea English style, as she called it.

Michael sat facing her, dipping his spoon absently into his cereal. "My dreams are getting worse. They're more real, it's as though I'm reliving the accident over and over again."

He paused, "I saw my shrink yesterday".

It took a lot of trial and error, mostly error, but Michael had finally found a therapist who could help him deal with the depression and post-traumatic stress. He had been seeing this new therapist for over a year and Michael appreciated his style. He didn't ask Michael how he was feeling or if he hated his mother. He didn't put up with any rationalizations or cop outs, but zeroed in to the heart of Michael's conflicts.

§

"You think your dreams are telling you something: your paralysis is getting worse and it's only a matter of time until, what . . . you go into a coma, you die? Specifically, what are you worried about?" Dr. Booker challenged.

"Let me count the ways," Michael responded sarcastically.

"I know you use humor to deal, that's healthy, but don't let it mask what you're really feeling. What's eating at you now?"

"I'm worried about not being able to take care of myself, watching myself decline, spending years in a coma with others to take care of me. It's the whole loss of control burden thing."

"And what does Gabby say?" Gabriella, or "Gabby" as her friends called her, had attended a number of the sessions early on.

"We haven't talked about it, not in the last few months, not since I've been getting worse. I don't want to raise the issue because I know what she will say: 'For better or worse, in sickness and in health, you are not a burden.' I don't think she's brought it up because she's waiting for me to be ready. And I", Michael hesitated, "I don't trust her response."

"You might be right. But the longer you keep her out of this, the harder it'll be to reconcile your feelings later. You can't do this alone, Michael, no matter how noble your motivations. You need to include her."

§

"I've had a hard time bringing this up. I don't know if it's because I'm in denial or I just don't know what to do about it."

Michael hadn't eaten a bite of his cereal; he paused, looked up at Gabby and said, "I am worried about what's happening to me. I hate what this has done to us already. I hate that I'm a burden and will become more of one. I'm afraid of what it means for me and I hate that I'm thinking about me when the real burden is going to fall on you." Michael shrugged.

"Must have been a hell of a session. I've been waiting for this".

She paused biting her lower lip as she often did when dealing with an uncomfortable subject.

"I wish you had come to me sooner. I know you think you are becoming more of a burden but we're in this together. You sound like you want to give up. What makes you think it's going to get worse? You could stabilize; you might get better."

"Please, I can't take any false hope. I really don't need that. I need to talk about what to do, figure where we go from here."

"Look, I want to talk about this too. You've been holding it all inside. Did you think I wouldn't understand or are you afraid of how I'd react?

"Anyway, your timing is lousy. I've got to get to work. I've got a meeting with Bob in 45 minutes I can't miss. We'll talk tonight".

Gabby rose and headed for the door feeling for the keys in her purse. She didn't need her medical bag anymore and BioDigiTech didn't allow employees to take work papers home.

Michael called after her, "I want to talk."

Gabby turned, speaking to his back, "I know you do, I've wanted to for a while but I can't right now."

Michael loudly dropped his spoon into untouched bowl not turning around to face her.

"What, now you're mad at me?"

"I'm sorry. It was hard enough bringing this up. I don't know if I'll be in the mood tonight, or if I will even be here. Maybe I'll go out dancing."

Gabby smiled to herself knowing he always had to have the last word. Despite his petulance she understand his struggle,

As she pulled on to the tree-lined snake of a road in front of their house her thoughts took a different direction. *I don't dare say anything, not yet*, she admitted to herself.

Contrary to Michael's accusation she didn't want to create false hope. Rather than consider her very real hope, she thought about her dream from the previous night. She'd had the same one before. There were slight variations, but it was the same dream. Gabby never quite remembered how it began, but it always ended in the same way, except this time.

Chapter 3

She's walking on sand, not the kind at the beach.

Gabby loved the beach, the smell of seaweed and salt thick in the air; the juxtaposition of land, sea, and sky. The primal atmosphere coupled with her scientific training fired her imagination: she existed in some primordial vista witnessing as the first legged creatures walked, or squirmed, onto land heralding a new era in animal evolution.

It isn't that kind of sand. Instead, it begins as hard-packed sand.

She is running, now, moving swiftly. Around her it's light, no visible source; and the sound of her breathing. Michael is running ahead of her and gaining. She's losing him. As she runs, the sand becomes less compact, like the sand in an hourglass. She's working harder, gasping for breath, slowing down. She calls for him but knows he can't hear her.

That's where the dream usually ends.

But this time the sand transforms suddenly becoming slick pavement. It's the road not one mile from their house. It's dark, cold. She is about to round the corner, the one where Michael had his accident, and she hears him scream.

I must have heard his scream in my sleep prompting the change in my dream, she thought. *Now, I'm getting sucked into his nightmare.*

She grimly considered the irony: *which nightmare?*

She knew Michael was going through a rough patch. *Really, we both are,* she thought, *but we'll find a way out of it, we have to.*

Initially she had been attracted to him by his substance, an evenness of character which made her feel safe and comfortable. He possessed an indefinable core, like an immovable rock. Now he seemed so fragile. Ever since the accident, he had been struggling, not only with his depression, but trying to find some sense of purpose.

§

As luck would have it, Michael had been found by an off-duty police officer within minutes of colliding with the tree. Officer Jimmy McCardle had gone out to dinner with his family and was on his way home when he came upon the accident.

As he pulled off the road and came to a stop near Michael's ruined vehicle, he instructed his wife, "Pam, call 911 and keep the kids in the car".

He stepped out cautiously to survey the scene. Smelling gasoline he quickly determined there was no risk of fire; if there had been, further injury be damned, he would have pulled the victim from the wreckage.

While waiting for the ambulance he checked Michael for a pulse and found one, though it was weak. He didn't see any signs of bleeding. No way to take his blood pressure to know for sure.

The driver looked pretty banged up but that wasn't the worst. The airbags had failed to deploy and from the driver's position and blood-stained hair Officer McCardle surmised the unconscious victim had hit his head against the steering wheel pretty hard. The guy had been wearing his seat belt. With the force with which he slammed into the tree, he probably would have been dead without it.

"Poor sap might be better off if he had died", worried the officer.

The wail of the sirens in the distance foreshadowed the arrival of the rescue crew accompanied by a fire truck and squad car. While the firemen worked to extricate Michael from the wreckage, the police officers identified the car and thereby the driver as Michael Neumann, a local who lived only a mile or so up the road.

The paramedics immobilized their unconscious patient and carefully loaded him into the ambulance, jumped in, and with sirens crying headed for the hospital. The officers thanked Jimmy and headed off to the victim's house in the event there was someone at home to notify.

Gabby had arrived home a little past 7:30 to find the house dark and empty. Some nights, especially when she was on call, Gabby might get home much later than Michael. As an assistant professor of neurology at the medical school she spent more time in her lab than with patients but that didn't prevent her from staying late from time to time. Long ago they had agreed that the first one home start dinner.

It was a cold, snowy night so Gabby had grabbed a plastic container of chili out of the freezer. They usually made a large pot and saved the leftovers for nights just like this. Once Michael got home they would probably sit in front of the TV or fireplace, eat dinner, and unwind. She knew work had been getting to him more than usual and he needed to come home and decompress.

As she stood over the stove stirring the delicious concoction she heard sirens in the distance. The sound took her by surprise; they so rarely heard sirens where they lived. But Gabby didn't give it another thought until, several minutes later, the doorbell rang.

Walking to the door, she felt her stomach growl stimulated by the smell of the warming chili as it floated through the house. As she turned on the porch light and opened the door she realized how oblivious she had been.

There stood two police officers. With a barely perceptible intake of breath she remembered the sirens.

Before Gabby could speak, one of the officers asked, "Are you Ms. Neumann?"

"Yes." Her reply came out as a question, waiting for the shoe to drop.

"I'm sorry ma'am but your husband has been in an accident. He is in an ambulance on his way to the hospital. We can take you there if you like."

She asked about Michael's condition and the officers told her he was unconscious and nothing more. She knew it would be fruitless to question them further. She needed to see Michael and make her own assessment.

"I can drive myself. Hold on a minute and I'll get my coat."

Gabby went to the hall closet, grabbed her coat and picked up her purse from a table near the front door. Then she remembered the chili and backtracked to the kitchen to turn off the stove.

While she maintained a veneer of calm a storm raged in her mind. There were too many unanswered questions but as a physician accustomed to using objective data to make a diagnosis, she tried to quiet her seething concern and headed for the hospital.

She wasn't successful. Gabby couldn't stop her churning mind from raising all of the most horrible possibilities. She realized she couldn't remain objective with her whole life at stake.

The drive took ten minutes, ten long minutes. Gabby pulled her car into the parking area reserved for emergency patients and walked into the emergency room with the calm assurance of someone who knew the system.

She had only stepped foot in this emergency room once before. One Saturday morning Michael had been working in the garage and had cut himself badly enough to need stitches. Gabby recalled the hospital staff had been competent on that occasion. She hoped they would be equally skilled dealing with major trauma.

Gabby walked up to the nurse's station and identified herself. "My name is Gabriella Neumann. You have my husband, Michael. I am a physician. When can I see him?"

The nurse looked up from her computer but before she could respond, a doctor in scrubs introduced himself.

"Dr. Neumann? I'm Tom Carrigan, the physician taking care of your husband. Could you come with me, please?" He pulled her into a quiet corner. "Your husband is in radiology getting a CT scan. Did I hear you say you are a physician?"

"Yes, I'm a professor of neurology at the med school." Gabby found herself wondering whether being an insider would help her deal with Michael's situation or make it more difficult.

"Your husband has suffered a broken femur and appears to have a skull fracture. He was shocky but stabilized quickly. No apparent internal injuries but he's still unconscious. We are doing a head CT now. Why don't you have a seat in the staff lounge and I will come and get you when I know more."

As he escorted her to the emergency room staff quarters Dr. Carrigan told her "Look, I know you must be freaking out. It could have been a lot worse. We should know more shortly". He knew better than to offer guesses to a colleague.

"Thanks, Tom, I appreciate it." Gabby waited in the lounge alternately sitting and pacing, oblivious to the drone from the talking heads on news channel filling the room. Instead, she gnawed her lower lip and contemplated all the possible scenarios.

After about 40 minutes Dr. Carrigan opened the door and said "Come with me, please".

As she strode down the hall Gabby didn't ask any questions and Carrigan didn't offer any answers. When they arrived at the darkened radiology reading room she saw another physician sitting in front of a large viewer. Carrigan took Gabby over and introduced her.

The other physician rose, held out her hand and said, "Hello, I am Dr. Gandhi, I am the radiologist on call tonight. I understand you are a neurologist." Gabby noticed a slight Indian accent and a calm demeanor reminiscent of her famous namesake.

"Yes I am. My name is Gabriella Neumann. What can you tell me?"

Dr. Gandhi proceeded to show Gabby the images on the viewer while explaining that Michael had suffered an injury to the parietal lobe of his cerebrum. Of course, Gabby knew this was the portion of the brain associated with movement along with other functions.

Gabby analyzed the scans clinically as a physician but only distantly heard Dr. Gandhi's explanation. She thanked the radiologist as Carrigan took her arm and ushered her out of the room.

"I'm going to take you upstairs. Your husband has been admitted. There's really nothing else I can tell you but the next 48 hours should tell us what we are dealing with. They can make arrangements for you to stay in your husband's room, if you like".

When she arrived on the patient floor visiting hours were winding down. Gabby entered Michael's room as a nurse was coming out. "Are you the wife?" she asked.

Are you the wife? Gabby repeated silently. Referring to him as "the husband" seemed so impersonal. "He's Michael" she wanted to say, with all the word implied.

Instead she replied, "Yes, may I stay in his room tonight?"

"Certainly", responded the nurse with a gentle smile, "let me get you a pillow, some sheets, and a blanket. The chair folds into a bed of sorts."

Gabby spent the next 24 hours at Michael's side speaking with the various specialists, nurses, and other staff as they filed in and out tending to her husband. She fielded calls from concerned family and friends and on the morning of the second day Michael was lucid enough to talk about the accident.

Gabby explained what had happened. Michael had, in fact, suffered brain damage. His cognitive function appeared fine, but he had lost feeling and the ability to move from the waist down. That afternoon, the neurologist presented his prognosis to Michael while Gabby sat next to him holding his hand.

The specialist explained, "We haven't seen enough of these types of injuries to predict the long term effects of the damage to your cerebral cortex. However, I think it unlikely your condition will improve. It is possible you will further deteriorate. There is no reason for you to stay here any longer. I will be discharging you tomorrow with orders for physical therapy and regular scans to track your progress."

Gabby had anticipated what the neurologist was explaining to them. As soon as she understood the injury she went online to survey the latest medical journals. The first day she had thought of transferring Michael to another hospital, even hers, but learned their specialist was well-trained and the prognosis he offered, realistic.

The adjustments had been considerable since the accident but they had learned to cope. They began with months of grueling rehabilitation. Michael tried support groups to help him deal with his disability but they weren't for him; instead preferring one-on-one counseling.

Eventually, he had attempted to go back to his job at the hospital. His coworkers were supportive, even Karl, but in the space of a few months Michael found he didn't have the energy to keep up. They outfitted their home to accommodate Michael's limited mobility and bought a van he could use to get around.

Gabby made adjustments, as well. She left the med school and joined BioDigiTech six months after the accident in part because they couldn't afford to live on her assistant professor salary.

But the hardest part, for both of them, was the toll Michael's illness and recovery took on their relationship.

§

The drive to BioDigiTech usually took thirty minutes give or take depending on the traffic and this day had been nothing out of the ordinary; the inconsiderate drivers weaving in and out as if there was no one else on the road: a slow car in the left-hand lane, the woman putting on her makeup, the man talking on his cell and looking at something on the seat next to him. Gabby remembered a time when drivers were more considerate and respectful toward each other. Now it was war on wheels mirroring how people often treated each other at work.

I'd better get off this train of thought, or I am only going to get angrier and I don't want to start my day this way, she resolved.

Shortly after exiting inside the beltway, Gabriella arrived at the tree-lined, four-lane boulevard leading to BDT. Situated to the right of the drive sat a stone monument approximately four feet high. Centered on the stone there sat a single word, 'BioDigiTech' in light blue outlined with a white border alongside the company logo, a computer monitor screen with the DNA double helix rising out of it at a 45 degree angle. Gabby wasn't sure whether it meant that the DNA infected the computer or vice versa. And she figured no one else had even considered the connection.

The pastoral drive to the guardhouse belied the vista now before her: multiple white concrete and glass buildings connected with foot bridges. She stopped at the front gate.

"Good morning, Harriett," she said greeting the guard in the gatehouse who signed everyone in. "Good morning Dr. Neumann. It's a beautiful day, isn't it?"

"Yes it is," Gabby replied. She had asked Harriett on multiple occasions to call her by her first name, but the security guard protested being too much of a traditionalist. Gabby drove her car through the open gate navigating to her assigned parking space near the front of Building E. All employees at BDT had an assigned parking space.

She got out of her car and walked into the five story building falling in step with the others coming to work. As they entered, each stood in a line swiping their badges to gain access to the building. Gabby rode the elevator to the fourth floor and walked to her lab.

Chapter 4

Gabby's lab was only large enough for half a dozen benches, a few pieces of floor mounted equipment and a small, private office surrounded by glass. In one corner sat her pride and joy, the refrigerated tanks which held the viral specimens which she referred to as her "Garden".

Gabriella had a meeting, first thing, with Bob Arnold, her immediate supervisor. His assistant had called late the previous day to put the meeting on Gabby's calendar but uncharacteristically didn't inquire when she would be available, as she usually did.

Instead, Margaret said, "Mr. Arnold needs you for an 8:30 tomorrow morning." Gabby had asked what he wanted to talk with her about but Margaret confessed her ignorance.

Gabby offered a brief greeting to her lab techs, picked up her notebook and headed down the hall to her boss's office. Halfway there she caught him coming toward her.

His face brightened when he saw her. People naturally trusted Bob and sought him out as a friend or ally. A hair over six feet tall, he was a bear of a man: a teddy bear if he liked and respected you, a grizzly if turned upon. Gabby valued his support and friendship.

"Good morning, Gabby!" he exclaimed with his usual bravado. "Ready to tackle the world?"

Bob had played football for the State University and commonly used football metaphors. His jovial manner and love of the game lulled some into thinking him an intellectual lightweight. Instead, the former linebacker's large frame hid a prodigious intellect making him ideally suited to lead BioDigiTech's biology research division. The company had lured him away from a professorship with an Ivy League life sciences department with the promise of more money and freedom.

He swept Gabby up in his wake as he barreled down the hall toward the elevator. Gabby practically ran to keep up with him.

"I read your latest report. How hard is it going to be to have a demonstration to show the big boys in 90 days? You know we are under a lot of pressure."

"Bob, we've gone over this. What we are trying to do here is not leading edge, its bleeding edge. I know we have the Pentagon breathing down our collective necks but one small error could be catastrophic. You know what we are fooling with here. This *is* rocket science. If we're not careful even the smallest error might come back to bite you, me, the company, not to mention the targets of our work."

The two spoke in generalities as they walked through the complex. While much of the work at BioDigiTech was ultimately aimed at the consumer and business market, few knew that close to forty percent of its revenue came through government contracts. A few of the agencies, among them the Pentagon, required absolute secrecy. A third of the researchers in Bob's division, including Gabby, held high-level security clearance.

"Gabby, we walk a fine line. If we don't meet our deadline it could cost the company millions. You know this project is vital to national security. It has the potential to bolster our strategic position and enhance the safety of our troops."

"Bob, why are you telling me all of this?" she queried. Bob wasn't usually so direct and passionate.

"To prepare you", came his perfunctory reply.

Gabby, totally absorbed in the discussion, hadn't noticed they had crossed the campus and entered Building A, corporate headquarters. They were riding up the elevator with the fifth floor button pushed. The top floor was home to the Chairman and CEO of BioDigiTech, Arthur Paulson. She had never been to his office and had only spoken with him once, briefly, at a social gathering.

The buildings on the campus, including building A, impressed visitors and employees alike with their unremarkable similarity. While the company didn't skimp on facilities, no one would call them opulent, with the exception of the Chairman's suite. Gabby had heard rumors and despite the trepidation she felt visiting Mr. Paulson's office, she harbored no small excitement to see if they were true.

As they stepped off the elevator, Gabby and Bob emerged into an open expanse with numerous comfortable waiting areas adjacent to offices ringing the perimeter of the building. Halfway across the floor from where they exited the elevator, stood two massive teak doors. Only the BioDigiTech logo to the right of the doors and a small plaque announcing the "Office of the Chairman", etched in platinum beneath it, offered any hint where they were going.

Bob didn't break stride and, as he approached the doors, they miraculously swung open as if sensing his presence. As the two passed through the portal; she felt as though she had entered a different world. There was no assistant to greet them. They found themselves in a spacious but comfortable sitting area, the floor covered with what looked to be large and expensive Persian rugs.

Groupings of overstuffed chairs and sofas in various configurations were placed strategically around the room including one grouping in front of a darkened fireplace on the left. A well-stocked floor-to-ceiling bar filled one corner of the room next to a buffet. The back wall held two more wooden doors, which Gabby assumed lead to offices in the back. On that wall hung tapestries and if Gabby had asked, she would have learned they were indeed authentic hangings from the late middle ages. Gabby thought it ironic such a warm room would be decorated with artwork intended to mask the chill arising from the stone walls of medieval castles.

Shelves covered the wall from which they entered supporting books, awards for technical development and philanthropy, and various works of art. But the wall on her right captured her attention. Also paneled in dark wood two large windows of leaded glass reaching practically from the floor to the ceiling punctuated the wall. She saw nothing remarkable except Gabby had spent enough time on campus to know the buildings all looked the same from the outside. There should have been open glass on the wall to her right.

As she practically gawked at the view, Arthur Paulson entered the room through the doors on the far side looking every bit the corporate mogul the public believed him to be. Tall and thin, his rectangular face was framed by a full head of dark, almost black hair, gray runners streaking back from his temples and dressed as if fitted by his own Seville Row personal tailor.

"Pretty nifty, huh?" he said as he held out his right hand to Gabby. "It's actually an optical illusion utilizing holograms and other whiz-bang technology. I'm not really sure how it works and it cost me a pretty penny but is serves the atmosphere.

How have you been Dr. Neumann, and how is your husband doing?" he asked as he motioned for them to sit.

"We're both fine, sir". Gabby held her guard not sure what was to come.

"Please don't call me sir. Arthur's fine." Gabby nodded skeptically; while Arthur Paulson greeted her as a colleague, she wasn't sure the sentiment was genuine.

§

Arthur Paulson created BioDigiTech twenty-two years earlier when he was in his mid-thirties. Since the 1980's, computers had found their way into every aspect of daily life from telephones and cars to refrigerators and children's toys. Several years later, with the mapping of the human genome, made possible, in part, by those same computers, along with multiple additional discoveries and developments, the bioengineering field exploded in an abundance of development.

Arthur Paulson had seen the economic potential of both technologies, bringing together some of the best and brightest from both disciplines and forming BioDigiTech, referred to by many as BDT, as a means to capitalize on the commercial potential arising out of those same developments. Over the years Paulson had built one of the planet's most successful R&D companies second only to IBM in annual patents.

Located in a large Midwestern capital, BioDigiTech would have been a Fortune 20 company if it wasn't still privately held. The company had made Arthur Paulson one of the wealthiest men in world. He was known to support numerous worthy causes from famine relief to providing high cost drugs for next to nothing in developing countries. He was behind the corporate green movement earlier than many, saying the investment was good for business.

But this public persona belied a reputed dark side. His ambition led him to be ruthless with competitors. He believed in teamwork in the workplace only so long as his subordinates agreed with him. He had no real friends. He had been married once, briefly; and dated occasionally but not seriously. Articles in the tabloids alleged he bought off one of his previous conquests who sought to expose his emotional abuse.

§

"I'll get right to the point, Gabby." Arthur leaned back in his chair poking his finger in the air at her.

"Bob tells me you are making progress on Project Achilles. But at the rate you are going, I don't think we'll hit our targets and I don't want to disappoint the Pentagon. I am adding another resource to your team."

Taken aback, Gabby protested. "Excuse me sir, I mean Arthur," she stammered. "While I'm sure the Pentagon would appreciate a speedy conclusion the chances for error are considerable and adding another person to the team would be counterproductive at this point. My group works well together. Adding an outsider at this point might in fact slow us down rather than get the results you expect."

"I understand", inserted Paulson, shaking his head from side to side. "I'm not going to interfere in with your group. Instead, I am bringing in one of our top technology researchers, Peter Keyes. He is doing remarkable work in artificial intelligence. I don't expect him to work in your lab, I want you to brief him on the project and see what he can do to get this moving."

Paulson rose as a sign the meeting was over. "I appreciate your indulgence. You will find Peter to be a big help."

With that Paulson escorted them out into the waiting area. As they were leaving, another gentleman stepped off the elevator. Arthur introduced Gabby to Jules Allen. As tall as Paulson but not rail thin, Allen had a presence which filled the room.

Gabby stood in awe. Allen, who looked about the same age as Paulson was one of the original backers of BioDigiTech and its largest single shareholder.

"Dr. Neumann I am aware of your work. We are looking for great things from you. Hello Bob", he added officiously as he swept into Paulson's office.

"Does he come here often?" Gabby asked as they left the suite.

"I don't really know," Bob added thoughtfully. "I've only seen him here once or twice. He intimidates me more than Arthur."

"Speaking of intimidation, were you expecting that?" Gabby shot Bob an accusing look.

"I wasn't sure what to expect but bringing Peter Keyes on board isn't a bad idea. Once you get used to him he's a not a bad person."

Gabby wasn't sure what he meant but had already resigned herself to this new variable's involvement.

"One more thing, Gabby." Bob's face took on a serious cast. "I know you are working on another project on the side. I haven't asked you what it's about and I haven't interfered, but I can't afford for you to be distracted anymore. Project Achilles is your *only* interest until it's completed. Am I clear?"

"Absolutely," Gabby lied. "It will be my only focus."

She had no intention of turning her attention away from Project Ulysses for even one minute. And she was more than mildly curious how Bob might have known about her 'other project'.

"Good. Enough said. I know I can count on you." And with that they arrived at Peter Keyes' office in Building C.

Chapter 5

Gabby found it difficult hiding her shock as she entered Peter's lab. Where her's was full of living things; his was possessed by electronic components and circuit boards. Where her's was well-ordered and meticulously clean, his was a mess with wires running in every direction and piles of equipment askew in every nook and cranny.

Peter Keyes sat hunched over a circuit board while his head bobbed back and forth between the board and the oscilloscope in front of him. For some reason, Gabby expected him to be the prototypical geek portrayed the movies, tall, impossible thin, unruly black hair and thick glasses. In fact, Peter Keyes was in his early thirties, over six feet tall with close cropped blonde hair and no glasses. He remained focused on his work as Gabby and Bob approached.

"Hello, Bob", Peter said without looking up. "This must be Dr. Neumann. "Happy to meet you", he said without emotion.

"Before I leave you two, I want to remind you to use your discretion when you talk about what you're working on," Bob cautioned. "Both of you hold the same security clearance but I want to avoid the appearance of a breach. We are taking a big risk putting the two of you together." With that Bob left.

"I don't know how he expects me to help you if we can't talk about your project," Peter stated absently.

"Look, Peter, I'm not thrilled about this either. Could you please look at me when you talk?"

"Sorry," Peter said, finally looking up at her. "I'm not used to being disturbed especially when I'm in the middle of something. Tell me what you're up to Dr. Frankenstein. Please be brief."

"In twenty-five words, Project Achilles is a DOD project where we are attempting to alter brain function to improve the performance of a select group of our soldiers."

"I'm impressed. That was 25 words, exactly, although I'm not sure if DOD is one or three words." Peter looked away returning to his work.

"Anyway I'm pretty buried right now. How about we get together and debrief tomorrow. I'm free at about 5:30. I know an intimate place we can go and talk without being heard. Then maybe we can relax and get to know each other."

"Look Peter, I'm married," Gabby interjected indignantly.

"Good for you, but I'm not asking you on a date. As I said, I am buried. It's a Thai restaurant not too far from here."

Peter gave her the name and address. She knew it. From time to time Michael had met her there after work in their former life.

"That will work," Gabby responded.

"Then it's a date."

"Now, wait a minute."

"You really need to lighten up."

Gabby found herself thrown by the morning's events. While she had faith in her methodology, time was not on her side. Bob and Arthur Paulson had made that perfectly clear. But she was still working with animals. They were getting closer but trials on human subjects should be a long way off.

What bothered her even more was Bob's knowledge of Project Ulysses. Did he know the object of her research or did he only suspect that all of her time and attention was not focused on his priorities? She had taken great pains to try and hide what she was doing but having two lab assistants made covering up difficult.

Gabby arrived back at her lab to find her staff at their stations working away on their individual tasks. Rather than brief them on the meeting with Paulson, she decided she would wait until after she met with Peter Keyes to see if he could help. Gabby wasn't even sure if he was willing to support her, despite direction to do so. As she thought more about the exchange, she found she had mixed feelings about involving Peter. On the one hand, she was afraid his interference might expose her other project but, on the other hand, with the pressure from on top, if he could help, Project Ulysses might indirectly benefit from his collaboration.

And, she had to admit Peter had been right. Laughter used to come more easily. She blamed the pressures of her job and concern for Michael's illness.

This was the day she usually held her weekly meeting with her two lab assistants, Karen & Edgar. But first Gabby spent over an hour revising each step in her work plan in an effort to respond to the curve ball she caught this morning. Whether Peter could help or not she was on the hook.

Staff meetings were held in a corner of the lab. Gabby stood, leaning with her back against a bench top. Karen sat attentively on a stool facing Gabby, and Edgar stood at his station across the bench from them. He only half listened as he continued with what he was working on.

She began the discussion with a review of progress each had made with their particular tasks. They had a solid understanding of their individual roles but security concerns prevented Gabby from sharing the bigger picture with either.

Of the two, Gabby preferred working with Karen. Though not as quick-minded, she put in the necessary hours and took changes in direction well. Edgar, by contrast, could be a pain in the ass. He often asked more questions than were necessary and at the same time was quite resistant to modifications in the routine. Meticulous to a fault, Gabby was sure he thought he could do a better job leading the effort discounting her training as a physician for his as a PhD biochemist.

"So, I think if we each make the adjustments we just went over, we can get to the next stage in three weeks rather than four." Gabby paused. "Are you paying attention, Edgar?"

"Of course", he replied with apparent boredom. "I don't think it's possible. There are too many factors. I might get through my part in four weeks, but it could take longer. I'm not going to shortcut my work just so you can look good."

"This isn't about looking good", Karen interjected. "I'm sure there are valid reasons to alter the methodology. I don't have a problem with it. We'll make adjustments."

"At any rate, we've talked this issue to death and I've got a lot more to cover so, on to the next topic." Gabby proceeded to review a number of other items from personnel issues to supply requisitions.

The rest of the day passed uneventfully. But try as she might, Gabby's thoughts kept coming back to the meeting with Bob and Paulson filling her with anxiety. Despite Bob's encouraging words, she couldn't help but feel if she didn't deliver soon, they might find someone else to take control. And she knew her future, the one she cared about, depended upon the success of Project Ulysses. If Achilles was shut down or she was shut out, that would be the end of the project she truly cared about. As she thought further she found comfort in the fact that the powers that be had assigned Peter to assist her.

Assuming he was more than competent she resolved to make him her ally. Perhaps he could really help, she rationalized.

Gabby thoughts returned to the issue of how Bob knew about Project Ulysses. Questions without answers came fast and furious. How much did he know? Was he spying on her? Was he tracking her spending and supply requisitions? Was there a leak? Gabby wouldn't have been surprised to know Edgar was talking to Bob. He could use the information to feather his nest.

Hoping a brief distraction from her current turmoil would help her focus again, Gabby turned to her computer and the latest blog from Samsa. She had been reading his posts for the past several months and, while she struggled to appreciate his anger, she had to admit she agreed with him on a number of points.

And Gabby wasn't the only one. Samsa provided a voice and, ultimately, a forum for a rising discontent. He had tapped into a growing disillusionment among people worldwide who had lost faith, or were, at least, questioning the ability of many time-honored institutions to meaningfully address society's broader problems. Almost everyone she knew read him regularly and his blogs were often topics of conversation in public forums from the coffee bar to the self-anointed pundits on radio and television.

He had been posting for almost two years and his readership wasn't limited by national or cultural boundaries. Not long after he had first started writing his influence became apparent. Some credited him, at least in part, with fomenting a popular uprising in Myanmar bringing down that notorious regime. Ever since the Magwe Incident, named for the city in which the uprising began, totalitarian regimes attempted to block access to his writings with little success.

His reach may have been global but no one knew who he was; a politician who didn't want to be known for taking unpopular stands, an academic who wanted to avoid notoriety or simply a writer or journalist who didn't want the attention? Rampant speculation circulated since the blogs started but to no avail. This week's blog continued a trend of thought she had been reading for the past several weeks. *Is he leading to a conclusion or is this just his latest rant*, she wondered.

Pulling herself out of her reverie, Gabby got back to work recognizing the unspoken threat from Bob and Arthur Paulson. Time was getting short for both Project Achilles and Project Ulysses.

As she worked she speculated on how Peter might be able to help. Not knowing his area of expertise or familiarity with the neurosciences she was unclear about how she should position the discussion. She needed to tell him as much as possible without giving away her more closely guarded secrets.

She smiled to herself. *Who am I kidding?* she wondered. *I'm not good at playing games. He'll probably see through any misdirection.* Turning from her computer, Gabby redoubled her efforts and before long it was time to close up shop and go home for the evening.

Unbiased Opinions of the Clearly Confused

Today's Message

I stand at a crossroads; the way forward unclear. All before me is shrouded in fog, obscuring all paths. Maybe there are no paths. Maybe we are at a dead end.

I've been talking about the dichotomy, the yin and yang, of our current dilemmas. Our world has never seen greater material prosperity and yet profound poverty persists. We are linked together by networks of computers that wipe away ancient cultural barriers and yet, deep, wrenching conflict abounds.

We have believed in a basic principle of the Enlightenment and its response, the Romantic Movement; that our society continues to evolve to a greater and greater good, that progress is inevitable. We believe it's evidenced in the evolution of political systems. Absolute power has been replaced by the rule of law. And yet those laws are corrupted by political manipulation; the United States Congress and the Administration bought by lobbyists and political action committees. Activist courts interpret the law according to their political leanings, left and right.

We pride ourselves on our enlightened societies which take care of the less fortunate. But then why is it the most materially wealthy country on Earth has such a high infant mortality rate?

Capitalism has created great material wealth for societies and proven itself more dynamic and adaptive than the failed systems of socialism and its more extreme cousin, communism. And yet, capitalism has subjugated much of the world. The gulf between rich and poor grows.

Has capitalism replaced the absolute tyranny of the unaccountable monarch with the more subtle oppression of the faceless market? Perhaps capitalism is so successful because it appeals to our inherent materialism and greed.

The 20th century saw violence at an unprecedented level, eclipsing any previous century. World War I, World War II along with constant turmoil in Africa, the Middle East and Southeast Asia, the partitioning of India and Pakistan, (a partial list) and the multiple genocides which accompany all of them. Who knows what the 21st Century holds? No, we are not becoming more civilized.

The myth of progress is exposed. We have built a veneer of civilization around our animal nature, but the thin shell is cracking. At its center lies the conflict between our primal and individual animal natures and our rational realization that the only way to survive is in community.

The nexus of this overly simplified fundamental conflict is what we call tribalism. I can't survive as an individual so I must join a community of like-minded individuals. At the same time I channel my need for superiority and dominance into a hatred or fear of the "other". Let me know if you agree. I'll explore this further in my next blog.

So I continue to ask,

HOW CAN I BE SANE IN A MAD WORLD?
Samsa

Chapter 6

Preferring to work out of the house Michael had taken a job editing professional journals. He didn't miss office politics but found he longed for more human interaction. Amused by the paradox, he knew one couldn't exist without the other. There had been two editorial meetings today and appreciating even that limited contact he found himself in a more buoyant mood when Gabby got home.

"How was your day?" he greeted her.

"A mess, I'll tell you about it over dinner," Gabby called over her shoulder as she walked back to the bedroom to change into more comfortable clothes.

Ten minutes later they were sitting at the kitchen table eating a chicken Michael had roasted. He had also prepared a side of linguini, roasted vegetables, and a salad.

As Gabby sat down she remarked, "Well, you went to a lot of trouble. Did you have a good day?"

"Not too bad. I had two meetings today". The conversation continued on lighter topics including Samsa's latest post.

"Yeah, I read it, too. What did you think?"

"He's very angry but I don't disagree with a lot of what he says. I'm not sure what he's leading up to," Gabby said.

Rather than respond in kind Michael instead asked, "So what was the mess you told me about?"

Gabby recounted her meeting with Arthur Paulson and her subsequent encounter with Peter Keyes. She didn't share her ultimate concerns not wanting to unduly burden Michael with her paranoia, if that's what it was.

"Anyway, I guess I'll be home late tomorrow night. I don't know if this guy can help, but I figure it's worth a try."

"Where are you having dinner?" Michael asked absently. When Gabby told him, she sensed he had disengaged.

"Oh," he responded followed by, "Well, you need to get out more anyway."

"What's that supposed to mean?" she shot back. "Don't shut down. Tell me what you're thinking". Gabby understood his moods and had little tolerance for his passive aggressive behavior.

"Okay. We were going to talk about this anyway." Michael believed if he laid bare his feelings he would give life to his fears. But, despite his apprehension, he understood she needed to know what was on his mind. He understood it wasn't fair to her to keep his anxiety bottled up inside. He leaned back in his chair and began.

"I can tell I'm getting worse. It's not any one thing in particular. I'm having a harder time at the keyboard. I can't type as quickly, and my upper body strength isn't what it used to be. I know it's only a matter of time before I become a complete invalid. I had another MRI just a few weeks ago. Have you seen the results?"

Gabby found herself caught between her hopes and her fears. The MRI showed continued deterioration in Michael's parietal lobe indicating his motor control would continue to decline. The rate of deterioration was not clear, but the trajectory left no doubt. She didn't know when, perhaps in the next few months or years, Michael might lose all motor control. She found herself wanting to reveal the whole truth.

They had spoken about end of life situations, even before the accident. She didn't see him as a suicide risk, but, unsure, she wondered, how well do we really know each other? She couldn't bear to see him sink further into depression. She knew she was being selfish, but still held on to hope however tenuous. Michael had asked just that morning not to hold out false hope. She believed in her heart of hearts her hope wasn't false but knew the time was not yet right to expose him.

Unable to confront her deepest fears she instead responded, "There was no noticeable change".

"Well, I'm noticing a change and we need to talk about what to do next. I am imagining a future, not too distant, where I can't cook you dinner, where I can't sit at my computer working, where I lay in bed needing someone to take care of me 24/7. I don't want to be a burden."

Gabby started to protest but Michael cut her off. "I know you don't see me as a burden, but my continued deterioration will change who we are to each other. It already has."

§

Needing a job while in graduate school, Michael landed a real plum: evening administrator at the local teaching hospital. He worked three to four nights a week earning more than enough to pay for his room and board. And the experience would prepare him well for his chosen profession. While on duty, he would often roam the hospital making himself visible to the staff and trying to learn what made a hospital tick.

It was July, which meant the new interns had finally arrived. Michael knew their medical school classes hardly prepared the newly licensed physicians for the life and death decisions they

45

would be required to make on a daily basis. A common macabre joke passed around at this time of year suggested people should stay out of the hospital in July and August for just that reason.

One Monday evening as Michael made rounds on one of the medical floors he thought he saw a familiar face. The attractive young intern sat at the nurses' station reviewing a patient's chart.

"Excuse me, you look very familiar. I'm Michael Neumann. I'm the evening administrator. Have we met before?"

Gabby looked up from her chart. She almost blurted out 'that's a pretty lousy pick up line' but then hesitated. "Actually, you do look familiar."

"I know!" Michael said. "Did you go to Washington University? I think we were in organic chemistry together. Michael Neumann."

Gabby smiled in recognition. "You're right. I'm Gabriella Berry but my friends call me Gabby. You said you were the evening administrator?"

"Yeah, I'm finishing grad school in hospital administration this year and have been working as the evening administrator for almost a year. I assume you're one of the new interns. How's it going?"

Michael usually didn't feel like he had much in common with the physicians. Though their jobs were related, he found their priorities often in conflict. Michael was only now figuring out how to work with them. But seeing a familiar face among the enemy gave him an opportunity to connect.

Gabby smiled shyly, "I'm scared to death. While I have more experienced residents and attendings supervising me, I have responsibility for so many patients. I really don't know what I'm doing at this point."

Michael nodded in recognition. "Say, how would you like to go for a cup of coffee sometime? I imagine with your schedule you can use all the caffeine you can get."

Gabby, thankful for a friendly face, even one she barely recognized, said, "Sure, how about Thursday at," she paused, "6:30?"

It became readily apparent they would have trouble matching schedules. It took two weeks before they found time to get together.

They met on a Wednesday in a coffee shop not too far from where Michael took classes. Gabby arrived a few minutes after he sat down.

"Sorry I'm late. I'm still struggling to manage my schedule," Gabby confessed.

"No problem."

They both laughed as they placed their orders realizing neither drank coffee but nevertheless met in a coffee house. As they sat there nursing their drinks, they began by sharing their stories.

"So, now that you've completed two weeks of an internal medicine residency, have you thought about whether you want to specialize?" Michael asked, half-jokingly knowing most residents didn't decide until their third year.

"Actually, I know exactly what I want to do," responded Gabby. "After residency I want to complete a fellowship in neurology. From there I plan to join a medical school faculty and become a researcher."

"Why the interest in research, and neurology in particular?" Michael queried.

"It's personal".

Michael threw up his hands. "I don't want to pry; I'm just trying to make conversation."

Gabby smiled looking demurely down at her tea, "I didn't mean it's private. My father left when I was four and so, for a long time, it was just me and my mother. When I was in sixth grade she was diagnosed with Parkinson's disease. It was so hard as a teenager watching her deteriorate and not being able to do anything about it. She declined gradually, at first, but by the time I was in college she had difficulty taking care of herself. I got a full scholarship to Wash U and she insisted I go. I came home from school as often as I could. In the end, death was a relief for her but I still struggle."

Michael noticed Gabby chewed on her lower lip as she talked about her mother. "If I can contribute to finding a cure for the disease I'll feel I have done something meaningful to honor her memory. So what about you? Why hospital administration?"

"I had started out in premed but transferred to history. I figured out the physician's lifestyle wasn't for me but I was still interested in healthcare. Unlike you, I'm not entirely sure why. I don't know if it's the challenge in the complexity of the health care delivery system or the chance to have a good professional career while doing good for others. I like the classes so far, very different from my undergrad work, and I enjoy the challenge as an evening administrator."

"What do you do when you're not in class or working?" Gabby asked.

"I hang out with a few of the other students in my program when I can. I guess I would call some of them friends but between school and work I don't have much time for a social life. I feel like I'm on a different track. I don't have the same ambitions as many of my classmates who want to run huge hospitals or insurance companies someday. Plus, I feel like I'm in a fishbowl in either location where one misstep will be misinterpreted, how about you?"

"About the same, of course we're all pretty consumed at this point. But I don't feel I have a lot in common with most of the other residents. There's the group that wants to get through their residency destined for more lucrative specialization in cardiology or GI. There are others like me who are more interested in research, but many of them aren't very social and not very many women at that. I've made friends but I guess, like you, I'm not sure socializing with the people I work with every day is the way I want to spend my time."

Neither spoke for a few minutes nursing their drinks when Michael broke the silence. "This has been nice. We hardly knew each other back in college but I kinda feel like we made a connection here. Maybe we can get together from time to time? What do you think?"

"I'd like that."

They found it difficult making time for each other; both so consumed in their careers but it wasn't long before their coffees became more frequent and evolved into serious dating.

Michael was smitten and Gabby returned his affection. She enjoyed his humor and that he knew what was important to him while he admired her straightforward, driven manner. They often shared work stories. Michael enjoyed listening to Gabby relate her latest clinical adventure; while she found fascinating, the endless political challenges Michael faced, so out of the realm of her world. This was the first truly intimate relationship either had experienced. Eventually a deep friendship blossomed into love.

Upon graduation, the hospital offered Michael a job while Gabby was only a few months into the second year of her residency. At this point they found a way to get together practically every day no matter what was going on in their hectic schedules. On one rare occasion, when neither was on call, they arranged for a quiet evening at Michael's apartment. After having jointly fixed dinner, they sat at a small dinner table. It was the anniversary of their first date.

"Michael, I've never known anyone like you; someone I could say anything to and know you were listening and interested in what I had to say; and not only my ideas, but the feeling behind them. You know what's important to me. You've made this past year a real joy. I can't imagine what it would have been like without you."

Michael sat across from Gabby, his left index finger in a glass of water. He enjoyed cooking and had prepared veal parmesan. While sautéing the breaded veal on the gas stove he had accidentally spilled oil onto the burner and started a small fire which they easily extinguished, laughing the whole time. However, when he removed the burner to clean the oil underneath he absent-mindedly picked it up with his unprotected fingers which now sat in a glass of cold water.

"I have quite an imagination and I *can* imagine this past year without you. I don't want that to be a possibility any longer."

Michael removed his fingers from the water glass, stood, and walked around to Gabby's side of the table. Gabby gnawed at her lower lip and stared into Michael's eyes as he knelt before her.

"I don't want to spend another day without you. I want to spend the rest of my life with you. I want to grow old with you. I want a family. And I know you to want the same things." Michael withdrew a ring from the pocket of his jeans.

"Gabriella Berry, I will spend the rest of my life making you happy. Make me happy now. Marry me."

Gabby threw her arms around Michael's neck pressing her head into his shoulder laughing through her tears.

They were married soon after. Gabby had impressed the neurology faculty with her intellect and was chosen to remain on for a fellowship. She distinguished herself in research while Michael made significant progress at work instituting several innovations landing him a promotion to Vice-President. Upon completion of her fellowship, Gabby was appointed Assistant Professor of Neurology at the medical school. With their lives seemingly so well on track they decided to start a family.

It was a Thursday afternoon when Michael's cell phone rang. He was in the middle of a meeting but stepped out to take the call. Gabby rarely called him during the day unless it was important.

"Michael?"

"Yeah, what is it? Are you okay?"

"I'm on my way to the OB unit. Can you meet me there?"

"I'm on my way. What's going on?"

"I'm not sure."

"I'll be there in just a second."

Michael poked his head back into the conference room and announced he had to go. He practically ran the whole way to the OB floor and arrived to see Gabby in a wheel chair in front of the nurse's station.

She reached for him and Michael took her hand. "What's happening?" he asked. Gabby was three months into her pregnancy.

"I'm not sure. I'm cramping and there's some bleeding."

A nurse practitioner wheeled Gabby into an exam room and asked Michael to wait outside.

Ten minutes later the nurse stepped out of the room and asked Michael to come in. Gabby lay on the exam table dressed only in a gown. She looked at Michael with undisguised pain. Michael practically leapt to her side.

"I'm having a miscarriage."

Michael turned to the nurse practitioner, "Is there anything you can do?"

"I've paged the doctor, but I'm afraid not. I'm so sorry. He'll be here in a few minutes to talk about your options. I'll leave you alone 'til then."

Michael turned and held his wife. Gabby cried as he stared off into space. He released her and looked into her eyes.

"I wanted this baby so badly," she said

"Me too. We're going to be okay. You know that. We are in this together."

"I know. Just hold me for now."

The devastated couple took quite a while to recover. But as it is with all strong couples, this crisis brought them closer together. After about a year they decided to try starting a family again. Michael's accident intervened.

§

Michael had difficulty looking Gabby in the eye, but he continued, "I would appreciate it if you would hear me out. I want to explain what I'm thinking. I don't need you to react, in fact, if you would just listen, consider what I am saying, we'll talk further at another time. I've been giving this a lot of thought.

"As I get weaker the burden will fall on you. You have your career to think about and so I'll probably need someone to come in or even live here so you can continue to work and have some kind of life. Eventually you may have to put me in a nursing home. I don't want you to agonize about the decision."

Gabby started to protest and Michael held up his hand to stop her.

"Again, please, just listen. This has been very hard for me and I'm sure it is for you, too. I know you want to protest, but I need to let you know where I'm coming from.

"On many occasions we talked about how you ended up caring for your mother in her last years. You shouldn't have to go through that again. I haven't been much of a husband to you for quite a while. With my failing health we don't do many of the things we used to like go out dancing, see friends. We haven't made love in I don't know how long.

Michael shrugged, "I feel like I'm stifling you. You have a wonderful life ahead of you and I can't be the person to spoil it. I can't live with that."

Gabby wanted to object with every fiber of her being but out of respect for Michael and all they had built, she remained silent.

"I have started to research a number of fine facilities. We can go look at them and figure out what might work best. Or if you are insistent on keeping me here, I guess we can talk about it. Also, I want you to go out more. I don't want your life to revolve around me as I get worse.

"Finally", Gabby noticed a slight hesitation, "we may get to a point where it makes more sense if we separate. Divorce may make sense for both economic and personal reasons."

Michael sat back, finished or, at least, unable to say more. "Well, how was that for an uplifting presentation? Tomorrow let's talk about famine in Africa."

Gabby smiled indulgently. Neither had eaten much of their dinner and Gabby had lost her appetite. She knew how hard it was for Michael to say the things he did and she loved and admired him all the more for it.

"Michael, I know this has been difficult. And I will respect your wishes and carefully consider all you have said, but I think you can already imagine what my response will be. Now it's time for bed."

As they were getting ready Gabby knew she couldn't put off telling him much longer; about his prognosis or Ulysses. *Just hold on a little longer, darling. I will come through, I have to*, she thought, her desperation growing.

Again, that night they dreamed. But this dream was different. This time, as Gabby rounded the corner she saw the accident and Michael in the car. He was reaching for her. Michael, in his dream looked out from the wreckage and saw Gabby running frantically, reaching for him. Neither remembered their dream in the morning.

Chapter 7

Gabby spent the next day in a futile attempt to focus. Deeply shaken by her conversation with Michael she moved from task to task never really completing any of them. Instead she tried to think of ways to stall any further discussion until she could tell Michael with confidence she had a solution. At this point she wasn't sure how he would react; with guarded optimism or blatant skepticism. In fact, she wasn't even sure on which side of the fence she stood today. Frustrated she wasn't getting anywhere she spent most of her day gathering her thoughts for the meeting with Peter.

She found him waiting for her when she arrived at the restaurant. Nick Thai had been a favorite haunt of Gabby's and Michael's back when they both worked at the medical center. The restaurant held only twenty tables but the informal ambiance coupled with an extensive menu which included not only Thai but Japanese and Chinese specialties made it a popular location. She was greeted at the door by the proprietor who, though clearly of Asian ancestry, preferred his patrons call him Nick. She wasn't sure if that was his name or that he had a pathetic sense of humor. Nick recognized her immediately.

"Dr. Neumann, so good to see you. Will Mr. Neumann be joining you?" he asked with a slight Asian accent.

"Not this evening Nick. But I see my dinner partner over there. Thank you."

Gabby walked to the table and sat down across from Peter. They exchanged pleasantries while looking at the menu and began talking in earnest once their orders were taken.

Peter began. "Maybe the best place to start is for you to tell me about Project Achilles. Then we can try and figure out how I might help."

Gabby leaned forward, hands clasped in her lap. "I don't know how familiar you are with neuroanatomy but why don't I start with the basics and see where we go from there?"

Peter nodded.

"The cerebellum is a collection of neurons located at the back of the skull and the top of the neck right above the spinal cord." Gabby put her hand on the back of her neck to demonstrate.

"It is a very basic structure and found well-developed in all animals unlike the cerebrum", Gabby placed her hand on the top of her head, "which is responsible for higher levels of mental activity. In fact the cerebellum, which, by the way, is Latin for little brain, looks similar in all vertebrates including fish, birds, and mammals.

"In essence, it integrates sensory perception, coordination, and motor control. It coordinates the information in the neural pathways which connect the parietal lobe of the cerebrum", again, Gabby put her hand on the top of her head, "where motor control resides, to the spinal cerebral tract, which provides feedback on the position of the body in space. The cerebellum mediates nerve impulses to control and coordinate movement. Are you with me so far?"

Again, Peter nodded. He appeared to be listening intently.

"In fact, the latest research indicates the cerebellum is key to attention management, language processing, and other sensory stimuli.

"BioDigiTech initiated Project Achilles under a contract with the Department of Defense. I haven't been told everything and some of this is only speculation but, if we can advance cerebellum function, the theory goes; our soldiers will perform at a much higher level, physically. With faster reflexes and better coordinated movements they will be safer and more effective. I know it sounds silly but think of Kung Fu movies where the actors react and move in ways we currently consider impossible.

"This approach fits well with our current Defense strategy. It's well known the Pentagon wants to rely more on technology while at the same time creating a lean fighting force for surgical insertion. Smart bombs and drones are intended to keep our soldiers out of harm's way. However, there are times when only humans, with their judgment and intuition, are indispensable. And so the plan is to alter or improve physical coordination making our soldiers more effective at their job and safer in the field."

"You know, I thought I was being sarcastic with the Dr. Frankenstein remark yesterday", interrupted Peter. "Now I'm not so sure I was joking."

Gabby smiled. "No, you're not entirely off the mark, though I'm not harvesting parts from cadavers, at least not yet."

"You do have a sense of humor. How are you planning to alter these brains?" Peter quizzed. "I assume it's not by hoisting them up into a lightning filled sky."

"That's where it gets more complicated, but also more interesting," Gabby replied hoping to hook Peter.

"Most of the work done in this field revolves around tissue regeneration targeting the repair of spinal cord injuries. Under normal circumstances, once the spinal cord of an adult mammal is cut, the nerve tissue does not recover and paralysis results. Until recently repair was thought to be impossible but that's changing. Researchers at the University of Florida have grafted embryonic spinal cord cells in patients with a specific cord injury to regrow nerve tissue."

The waiter brought their dinners as Gabby continued.

"More interesting to me, though, has been the work done by investigators at the University of California, San Diego. They are using gene therapy to stimulate the growth of spinal cord tissue. Spinal cord cells can be stimulated to regrow when they are exposed to nerve growth proteins. In another case, taking a different approach, a chemist stimulated regrowth by using neurotransmitters to stimulate growth and reconnect nerve cells. If you remember any of your high school biology, a neurotransmitter is a chemical which carries information from one neuron to another. This technique integrated a neurotransmitter with a polymer, a plastic, and it generated significant new nerve development."

Gabby frowned. "I hope this isn't getting too abstract for you. Do you have any questions yet?"

"Not yet. I'll let you know."

Gabby continued, "My work takes the next step by increasing the number of connections within the cerebellum and not the spinal cord. I'm talking about nerve generation, not regeneration.

"How do you plan to do that?" Peter asked.

"First, do you know what a retrovirus is?"

"I've heard of them, but I don't know what they do."

"Okay, you've seen the BDT logo. Rising out of the computer monitor you see a double stranded DNA molecule. DNA is short for quite a mouthful, deoxyribonucleic acid. That'll be important in a minute. Think of DNA as the hard programming in your computer. It instructs the machine exactly how to do everything it does. DNA works the same way providing a code in each cell to tell it how to perform; an amazing piece of engineering far outperforming any computer."

"Now hold on," Peter objected defensively, "I know enough to know that sometimes there are DNA coding errors which result in diseases like cancer."

"Very true, but think of the billions of healthy people on earth, the healthy babies born each day versus how often computers lock up and have to be rebooted."

"Point taken," Peter replied.

Gabby smiled; pleased Peter appeared to be engaged in the discussion and not merely listening out of courtesy.

"Anyway, DNA uses a single-stranded complex protein called RNA, or ribonucleic acid (do you hear the similarity?) to communicate it's instructions to the cell. RNA acts as a messenger.

"Now you know viruses often cause disease; everything from the common cold to many types of cancer. One type of virus is the retrovirus. This is the type of virus which causes AIDS. In fact, most of what we know about retroviruses comes from studying the AIDS virus.

"A retrovirus is made up of a single strand of RNA and an enzyme called reverse transcriptase. The enzyme copies the RNA strand into the DNA in a cell thus changing the instructions of the original DNA. That's why it's called a retrovirus. It's the reverse of the normal process of DNA giving instructions to RNA."

"To carry your analogy a step further," Peter observed, "what you are saying is that computer viruses which change the programming in your computer can be considered retroviruses, as well, right?"

"Correct. I plan to use a retrovirus to introduce a new gene sequence targeted at increasing the neural connections in the cerebellum for greater speed and coordination of movement. I've been working successfully with lab rats but the problem I'm having is figuring out the right gene sequencing for a human being", and Gabby went on to explain how she was stuck.

When she finished she asked Peter, "Did that make any sense at all?"

Peter had been leaning in to the conversation for the past several minutes. He looked down at his plate, and then at hers realizing neither had eaten a bite. He didn't even remember the waiter bringing the food.

"Why don't you eat and I will repeat back what I think I heard," suggested Peter. He leaned back in his chair and articulated the principals Gabby had relayed as he understood them. She was pleased as Peter exhibited a solid grasp of the concepts missing little.

"Before I give you my thoughts on what I can bring to the table, I have a few questions," Peter began. "First and foremost, you are looking to manipulate human DNA. There are many who would question the ethics of such a manipulation. Second, how do you plan to conduct clinical trials on people when it's clear the treatment would carry considerable risk?

"I've thought a lot about it. We are very definitely in a gray area. Human DNA evolves slowly, but it does evolve. I think of this as helping evolution along; not very different from finding the genetic code for certain diseases, like diabetes or cystic fibrosis, using the same retrovirus approach to cure them."

To Peter, Gabby sounded as though she was trying to convince herself, but he let it pass.

She went on, "As to clinical trials; that is the part which worries me the most. If this were a cure for a terminal illness and we could deliver the treatment on a compassionate basis for patients who are dying and had no hope that would be one thing. I mentioned earlier about extrapolating what comes next. In my more paranoid moments I worry the Army plans to test the virus on willing recruits or military prisoners with or without consent: which is why it is so important we get this right the first time.

"I also suspect BioDigiTech plans other additional applications primarily in the realm of performance enhancement. Think about it. Normal people now take ADHD drugs to improve their focus and perform better at work or school. Is it so farfetched to think of athletes who now dope with steroids and other drugs to take the next step to DNA alteration? Anyway, that's how I justify it to myself."

Peter's thoughts swirled more quickly than he could articulate them. He needed to take a step back and think; to organize his thoughts. This was not at all what he expected. He had planned to half-heartedly help her and only because he had been pressured into meeting with her.

"Based on what you have told me so far, I think I can help. But, before we focus on your little problem", Peter smiled, "I would like to describe for you my areas of research. Bob knew what he was doing when he put us together because, in many ways, we are traveling down the same road."

§

Peter Keyes had been an only child, born into a close, loving family. Unfortunately, both of his parents were killed in a small airplane crash when Peter was only seven. Devastated by the loss Peter became withdrawn unconsciously avoiding close, personal relationships.

Raised by a wealthy uncle he rarely saw, Peter pored himself into his studies. His teachers found him particularly adept at math from an early age; so adept in fact that he entered MIT at the age of 16.

Peter found his real passion early in his college career. He noticed, during his freshman year in calculus, when faced with a particularly difficult homework problem, if he walked away and otherwise occupied himself for a while, his mind would continue working on the problem in the background and he would come back later and know the solution. Deciding to better understand how the brain works and indulging his passion for machines which think, Peter majored in computer sciences and neuropsychology graduating with a PhD at the age of 23. His particular area of interest: artificial intelligence.

Peter made the most of his time at MIT academically, but found it difficult to participate in the broader opportunities offered on campus. From the time he was in grade school and through his college career Peter didn't fit in. In his younger years his academic brilliance coupled with his social alienation made him an outcast. He was fine with that, preferring the world of ideas to the world of people with its inexact rules and seeming chaos. In college, handicapped by both his apparent lack of interest in social interaction and his young age he found a small circle of friends who didn't expect too much of him.

Upon leaving college Peter worked for a variety of companies and finally found himself at BioDigiTech where he could indulge his passion unfettered. His reputation grew in the computer sciences community as one of the leading experts in AI as did a reputation for being difficult; his long standing distrust of authority borne out of his social limitations were widely known.

Truth be told, he saw himself in a bubble. As long as he could manage what was inside his bubble, he could cope.

Peter eventually married and divorced, not too long after. His ex complained they never really had a marriage, just two people living together. She still cared for him but was convinced he had a hard time seeing anyone else existed outside of himself. He took the divorce hard owning up for his failure but not knowing how to change. Reflecting on the failure of his marriage he recognized the conflict in his soul arising out of his parent's death but felt powerless to do anything about it. It would take a radical opportunity to burst his bubble.

§

"As you probably know", Peter began, "I specialize in artificial intelligence with a particular interest in neural networks. I have found it helpful to understand how the human brain functions to see if I can create a parallel technology. Now, please tell me if I get any of this wrong. I studied neuropsych in college but that's a far cry from your training."

Peter went on, "The typical person's brain has about ten billion nerve cells. These neurons each have about ten thousand connections to each other. It's an incredibly massive computer-like network packed inside a very small area. But interestingly enough, there are parallels between the human brain and a computer. For example, each runs on about thirty watts of power, like a small light bulb. The basic processing units, whether neurons or transistors are about the same size: one millionth of a meter.

"On the other hand computers are about ten million times faster than the human brain. You would normally consider speed like that a real advantage but computers run in series meaning they can accomplish only one task at a time while the brain, which runs parallel functions, can complete many tasks at once because there are so many connections among the neurons giving the human brain the ultimate advantage over the computer.

"Is the parallel circuitry in the human brain really that much of an advantage?" Gabby asked.

"Do you remember a few years ago when IBM built a computer called Watson which competed against two guys on 'Jeopardy'? The computer won by a landslide. The most remarkable thing was the speed with which it deciphered human language and accessed its encyclopedic memory. But consider this: the Watson device was almost 400 cubic feet of integrated circuits, wires, memory, and the like while the typical brain weighs about three pounds and is the consistency of jelly. Not to mention the fact that Watson had to be cooled by a refrigeration unit housed in a whole separate room.

As Peter talked on Gabby found herself taken with the passion with which he described his work; quite different from the detachment and cynicism she had seen before. He was so consumed in his presentation he didn't seem to notice her.

"Let me give you another example: if a person's brain is partially damaged its function often degrades slowly or other portions of the brain may, in fact, assume the impaired portion's function as I'm sure you know from your medical studies. But, as you pointed out so accurately before, one small problem can shut a computer down.

"The human brain learns from experience, computers are moving down that road, but its slow going. Our brains process information so efficiently because of the multiple parallel connections. Complex visual patterns are usually recognized in less than a tenth of a second. No current computer can come close. And, of course, the human brain is capable of self-awareness and no one is quite sure, at all, what that's about."

Now it was Gabby's turn to be fascinated. "So how does all that fit with what you're working on?"

"The brain is a biological neural network," Peter continued. "Artificial neural networks, for the most part, attempt to mimic brain activity through programming. However, I am trying to tackle another, perhaps more difficult, problem. I am not convinced we will make enough progress with artificial neural networks on the programming side. I believe, instead, we need to upgrade the processor."

"Our fastest processors today duplicate the number of connections in the reptilian brain, pretty impressive, but they produce a lot of heat for all of the activity. Your home computer has a fan to keep the processor cool. Computers with these faster processors require water or even liquid helium cooling because they produce enough heat to boil a cup of coffee. By our current calculations a processor with the same number of connections as the human brain would produce as much heat as a small nuclear reactor. You can see the problem. I am working on technology to find processor configurations with significantly more connections in order to better imitate the human brain.

"To date progress has been limited. A team of researchers at the Ecole Polytechnic Federale in Lausanne Switzerland has modeled a portion of a rat brain about 1.5 millimeters by 0.5 millimeters that contains about ten thousand neurons. So, you can see there's a long way to go. I have a team of fifteen researchers at BDT working with me on this problem. Now, is this making sense and do you see how our work is related?"

Gabby smiled back. "So who's Dr. Frankenstein now?" she asked. "Are you thinking you can create a computer that performs, that thinks, that has the consciousness of a human being?"

Chapter 8

"I think it's too soon to speculate, but it's certainly possible," Peter observed.

"That's a little scary. I have visions of robots taking over the world," Gabby frowned, lost in thought.

Peter's attention took a different direction. Her science appeared sound but the ethical considerations gave him pause. She didn't seem like the kind of person to throw caution to the wind; and then there's that gnawing her lip thing. There was something she wasn't telling him.

But Peter knew enough to know a frontal assault would only force Gabby to put up her defenses. He may not have been good with relationships, but he did know how to avoid making people angry, that is, if he wanted to. And he found himself respecting, even liking her. He saw her as a fellow scientist with similar interests while appreciating her directness and no nonsense manner.

Instead, he asked her, "How did you get into this line of research?"

"My mother died of Parkinson's disease," she replied matter-of-factly, "so I felt like I owed it to her to try and find a cure, or at least a more effective treatment."

"That must have been hard for you."

Gabby nodded. "It was only the two of us. When I got a college scholarship away from home she insisted I go. But once I got there her decline accelerated. I don't know if it was the disease process or she finally felt she could let go, maybe both.

Each time I came home she was much worse. I took a semester off near the end, spending every day with her. But she wasn't who she had been." Gabby stopped, looking down in her lap.

"And where were you before you joined BDT?"

"I was an Assistant Professor of Neurology at the medical school".

Peter noticed Gabby appeared to be studying him.

He tried to look puzzled. "I don't understand. If you were working on a cure for Parkinson's at the medical school, why did you come to BDT?"

"There are several reasons. Apart from faculty politics, and a need to conduct my research as I see fit, I needed the money. My husband was paralyzed in an auto accident a few years ago, he couldn't work. I had to give up on my Parkinson's research to come here."

"Must be tough, first your mother and now your husband."

"It's so hard to see him every day, frustrated by the physical limitations produced by an otherwise healthy mind. And it's hard for us." Gabby looked away, seemingly lost in thought.

Peter sat back in his chair, looking down at his hands, thinking.

He looked up, leaned forward, put his forearms on the table and said, looking into her eyes, "Gabby, I don't mean to pry. I don't want to make you uncomfortable but this just doesn't add up.

"You admit you're no longer doing research in Parkinson's which had been your passion. I hear in your tone of voice you're not excited about Project Achilles. I sense you're not telling me everything."

Peter paused, "I see you get obsessive with those things you care about, and you need to care about what you do. What are you really working on?"

68

That was the question Gabby had been waiting for. Though she wasn't entirely sure yet if she could trust Peter; she knew she desperately needed his help. She found she liked this guy; and on top of that she had a gut feel she could confide in him.

Nevertheless she said, "Peter, I'm very uncomfortable talking about this. You seem like a good guy but you could be a company man for all I know. I could be risking my job."

"A company man? You've got to be kidding. I'm sure you checked me out and you know it couldn't be further from the truth," laughed Peter.

"Yes, I did hear something to that effect."

"So tell me," Peter asked, "I want to help."

"I was devastated by Michael's accident. He's doing OK, but it's been hard for us. And", she paused "the stress has also taken its toll on our marriage. Before I left the medical school I was trying to find a way to bring his function back. I was shifting my focus to find a way to regrow neurons, not in the spinal cord, but in the brain itself. My department chair was not supportive. She thought my methodology too risky and bad science.

"Coincidentally, at about the same time BDT came calling. They were aware of my work, rudimentary as it was, though not why I was conducting it. The fit seemed right with the new Project Achilles so they put me in charge of the lab. And they were supportive of whatever I did on the side so long as it didn't interfere with my other work. I'm sure they figured they would find some commercial use out of whatever I was doing."

"I agree. From that standpoint, BDT is a pretty good place to work. I have a few projects going on the side, too."

Peter noticed Gabby's demeanor suddenly change; her face took on a dark, determined cast.

"I assume you are familiar with Greek mythology. The first of Homer's two great works was the Iliad, which is the largely the story of Achilles. Part god, Achilles was the greatest of the Greek heroes in the war against Troy. The name for the project fits. We're trying to create superior warriors, gods in a sense.

"However, Homer's other great work, the Odyssey, is named for its lead character, Odysseus, Ulysses in the Latin; it's about his ten year struggle to return to his home following the war."

Her voice shook with emotion as tears welled in her eyes. "Project Ulysses is about bringing Michael home."

Gabby took a deep breath, regained her composure, and after a few moments continued, "The approach I developed for Project Achilles is actually based on the methodology I was developing for Project Ulysses using similar techniques. My goal is to increase the number of synapses or nerve connections in Michael's cerebrum thus enabling him to walk again, at least that's the idea. His injury was to the parietal lobe, the seat of motor control, among other functions. So far, my experiments with rats have shown promise."

"What does Michael say to all of this?"

"I haven't told him," Gabby replied sheepishly. "I've wanted to, many times, but I don't want to get his hopes up only to dash them if this doesn't work. We have to solve the immediate problem I spoke with you about before I can confidently share my plan with him."

"When do you plan on telling him? Surely he has a right to weigh in on this."

"Michael has a brain MRI regularly to assess the status of his condition. While he was fairly stable in the first few years, there are now perceptible changes pointing to a continued degradation. I haven't told him about the MRI results, or more accurately, I lied, telling him there's been no change.

"I don't think he believes me. He's noticed further deterioration and weakness in his upper body. What he doesn't know is that the process appears to be accelerating. At this point I'm not only worried about him losing the use of his upper body; his very life may be in jeopardy."

Gabby stopped and said, as if talking only for herself, "that's the first time I said it out loud, really admitted it to myself. I can't lose him, not when the cure is within my grasp. I can't fail him. I won't."

As Peter watched and listened he was struck by her determination and her zeal. Gabby's utter devotion to Michael and her marriage fascinated him having never experienced those emotions before. At the same time he was surprised to find himself empathizing with her situation.

What's going on, he thought. *I'm getting sucked into her problems and I don't understand why. In the past I would have blown this off; one more distraught person unable to deal with their own problems. Get a grip, I would have said.*

But Peter found himself caring, too. He was connecting with her plight, with her, at a visceral level. Inevitably, he wondered if he was falling for her. He knew she was married and he wasn't looking for a relationship. Here was someone he liked and respected who needed his help. A part of his mind told him he was taking a huge risk, professionally and personally.

Professionally, because if BDT got wind of what she was doing and found out he was involved, they would can him without a thought, his career ruined. He would never get a comparable lab again.

And personally, because her cause was becoming his, she was piercing his bubble. The scientific problem acted as a catalyst. Here was a challenge worthy of his intellect.

But there was more.

Somewhere below the surface of the problem perhaps below his conscious mind, Peter understood what they were attempting here would have implications far beyond what either could have imagined.

Here was an opportunity staring him in the face, a course of action he could commit himself to, a cause with meaning: he could save life. And at that moment he knew he had no choice.

Gabby recovered her composure and had been explaining the pressure from management to produce quickly. "I would appreciate it if you would help with both projects but I certainly understand if you don't want to get anywhere near Project Ulysses."

"I'm in."

She stopped talking and smiled. "You may regret this, you know. This is my fight," she cautioned him.

"No, not anymore. You made it my fight, too."

Gabby sat back and listened. She found herself more than a little surprised by his vehemence.

"I've been focusing my efforts on trying to find a way to get a computer to imitate human mental processes. You've opened my eyes to a whole new possibility. You've said you want to heal Michael's injury. I get it. I spend my time in my lab immersed in electronics. You've given me an opportunity I never expected and a chance to save someone's life. Have you thought about what might happen should your little treatment cause Michael's brain to produce more connections than the normal human brain?

"Apart from all of the consequences you have probably already thought about, if you look at the latest research," he offered, "the human brain differs structurally from the apes largely because of the number and stability of synaptic connections. I can't imagine what the implications or the effect would be; I'm dealing with images of aliens with oversized brains dancing through my head, like your robot dilemma."

Gabby found herself smiling. "Well, you can come into my animal lab and look at the rats I've been working with. They look pretty normal, although some of them have taken up reading my medical journals." Gabby's joke broke the tension so they could get on to the next order of business.

They talked first about what their next steps would be to find a way to resolve Gabby's current challenge. They decided to meet at the same time Mondays, Wednesdays, and Thursdays each week to go over results, deal with obstacles and plan next steps. They would still meet periodically during the day at BDT to keep up appearances, but much of the work would take place in a location where they wouldn't be overheard. At 11:30 they finally parted.

On the way home Gabby reflected on the evening's events; the meeting having gone much better than she expected. She believed Peter would be a productive colleague and trustworthy conspirator. As she thought about it, her confidence grew and she arrived home excited. Michael was already asleep and Gabby was so wired she didn't go to bed until after 1 am, pleased she didn't have to talk with him. It would be hard, in her current mood, to conceal her optimism. As she climbed into bed, she didn't notice Michael was awake.

When Gabby woke the next morning Michael was already out of bed. A good night's sleep had calmed her down. When she made it to the kitchen she found Michael already eating breakfast. "How did your meeting go last night?" he asked absently.

Without hesitation Gabby replied she was optimistic that Peter could help her. She told Michael the pressures would require her to meet with him three nights a week but that she wouldn't be making a habit of coming home so late.

"Whatever you need to do."

Unbiased Opinions of the Clearly Confused

Today's Message

I left off my last blog talking about the "other". Before we delve deeper, I want to clarify what I mean by tribalism: a group of individuals who identify with each other and that identity forms the basis for the membership requirements of the tribe.

It might be a geographic location such as where you grew up or where you live now. It could be the nation you were born in or the one you adopted or both. It might be what language(s) you speak. It can be your place of employment, your family. It is also your economic class, your sexual identity, or political party. And what about religion or favorite sports team? We belong to multiple tribes.

We belong to a tribe for a reason. We tell ourselves it's because we have something in common. But let's take a step back. Most people identify with their country because they were born there; same with their family or religion. Familiarity breeds content (contrary to the old saying).

It feels good to be included, at least for most people. It's quite likely the need for community evolved as a successful survival tool (more on that later). As human beings evolved, their ability to be successful in groups meant a greater likelihood of individual survival and reproduction.

But tribal affiliation is also the source of man's greatest destructiveness. Just as people acquire a sense of belonging from being a part of a tribe, they also often identify those not of their tribe as people to be feared and condemned.

Conflict between tribes can be fundamentally benign; take sports rivalries between schools or cities. While they do erupt in violence from time to time, they usually provide a relatively harmless outlet for us to work out our intertribal aggressions and rivalries. At the other extreme, identification of your tribe with an exclusive lock on the truth has been responsible for many of the worst atrocities in our history.

In the ancient Roman Empire religion was aligned with the State. That same attitude was adopted by the successors to the Empire in both Christian Europe and the Moslem world. That principal of unification became the source of terrible destruction prompting the Crusades, Muslim Jihad, the Holocaust, and the current problems between the West and the Islamic world.

But we also find conflict within tribes. Look at the Inquisition, thousands of Christians murdered, tortured and imprisoned for their beliefs or supposed transgressions. Or the intra-tribal wars among the Sunni and Shia Moslems.

There is a hierarchy of tribal affiliations. Let's take the average working person. They are going to have loyalties to themselves, their families, their neighborhood, their community, their place of employment, their church, their religion, their nation, and their favorite football team (mine is the Green Bay Packers).

How one values their tribal hierarchy has consequences. The man who works so he can enjoy his family is in a very different position from one who has a family as a support system and instead has as his primary loyalty, his employer. How many of us have found ourselves with conflicting loyalties between the two?

Conflict often arises because we have a need to exist in groups and yet we are individuals who don't necessarily fully fit in any one group. Do you ever feel like you don't belong anywhere? Jean-Paul Sartre in his drama, *No Exit*, asserts "hell is other people" ("L'enfer, c'est les Autres.").

Some people experience this conflict as loneliness or alienation. Others use the group to express their individuality such as the aggressive behavior one sees in middle and high school cliques. In the extreme we see this rejection as sociopathic behavior, a subset of which we might define as greed, the need to acquire power and accumulate material things to benefit one's own ends without regard for or at the expense of others.

This greed and lack of regard has brought down whole economies. Look at the global crash of 2008 or what we in America referred to as the Great Recession. The greed of the money lenders on Wall Street to the consumer on Main Street formed the foundation of the collapse of global markets when the hyper-inflated housing market collapsed. We will be paying the price for this utter disregard for our fellow man for decades, and most are oblivious they played a part in this debacle. I wonder if it's our society that makes us this way or is it something more basic, more fundamental.

So I continue to ask,

HOW CAN I BE SANE IN A MAD WORLD?
Samsa

Chapter 9

He would never admit to it and despite all his traveling, Arthur Paulson got a bit of a thrill every time he landed in Washington. The restricted flight path into Washington Reagan took fliers through a corridor such that if they were sitting on the correct side of the airplane they could see the Lincoln, Washington, and Jefferson Monuments and the Capitol Building.

Paulson fashioned himself a patriot. He believed in what America stood for, even if it often didn't live up to its ideals. He had particular contempt for the Congress. He believed the constant wrangling and evident corruption too often prevented his country from achieving the greatness of which it was capable.

Unlike most travelers to Washington, Arthur arrived in BioDigitech's corporate jet. He had brought no luggage anticipating a relatively brief meeting; expecting to be home in time for dinner. As the airplane taxied to the hanger, he wondered again why he was here. He had been called to Washington by his Pentagon handler, General James Scott. A man in Arthur's position was not accustomed to being summoned and he chaffed as he jumping to the General's whim. At the same time, he was a pragmatic man. If General Scott found it necessary to try and intimidate someone of Arthur's position and wealth to gratify his ego, Arthur was sufficiently secure that he wasn't going to take the bait. But he chaffed, nonetheless.

A black Town Car waited for him on the tarmac. As he exited the airplane a sharply dressed Sergeant stepped from the vehicle and opened the door for him.

"Hello, Sergeant," said Arthur. He had met the General's driver on previous trips to Washington. The man gave a barely noticeable nod and motioned for Arthur to get in. Arthur was struck by the fact that the man said little and smiled to himself as he considered whether the driver was, in fact, more than a driver.

The car left the airport and headed north on the George Washington Parkway but rather than stop at the Pentagon, they continued northwest along the Potomac. The drive gave Arthur a chance to get his thoughts in order. It was early autumn and the tree-lined drive calmed him. He hadn't been asked to bring any materials and to come alone. He assumed the meeting concerned Project Achilles. It had been almost 6 weeks since he had inserted Peter Keyes into the process and the reports he received told him the team was making significant progress. As usual, his ideas bore fruit.

§

For Arthur Paulson life began in a small town in Ohio, the only child of a factory worker and a stay-at-home mother. Neither of his parents was educated beyond high school and they instilled their son with the industriousness and seriousness necessary to meet the world's challenges. As with most first born, he demonstrated a strong need for their approval which the stoic couple found difficult to provide. Instead, he found satisfaction, though he couldn't articulate why, in manipulating his parents to get what he wanted, whether to stay up for another hour or make commitments in order to get a particular toy.

Arthur did find the approval he craved in school where his hard work and native intelligence paid off. He also found, from an early age, he could cajole others in order to get his way if he understood their needs, as well. He had a particular ability to find what other's wanted and used the skill to further his own ends. After a while, dominating those around him became a game, an end in itself. As a result, by the time he reached high school he had few friends and a reputation as a gifted loner to go along with it: someone who excelled at whatever he attempted while shunning the company of his peers.

Even before he entered college Arthur demonstrated a penchant for business, and sales in particular. While in high school he lied about his age and sold knives door to door becoming one of the top performers in his company. In fact, he did so well in high school that between his academics and work on the side, he could afford to attend an Ivy League College despite his father's desire he enter the military. His freshman roommate was an equally ambitious boy named Jules Allen.

Allen had come from a well-to-do family and as such held a different view of the world from Arthur. An out of the box thinker, Allen had a particular penchant for computer technology. And he liked to play with ideas almost as much as he liked tinkering with computers.

Though unalike in many ways, both possessed an ability to focus in the extreme fostering impressive academic performance. However, while Arthur often preferred spending hours at a time by himself, Jules made friends easily, finding the thoughts and ideas of his fellow students, professors, and even the random stranger stimulating.

As is the case with most college roommates, they would often talk long into the night about any one of a number of topics, jumping easily from economic theory to cosmology. Jules saw the potential in his reclusive roommate and spent time helping him understand he would never achieve his aspirations if he relied solely on his own efforts.

"Look, Arthur, you can never know everything, be everywhere at once. You're bright but that's not enough. If you are going to make the millions you keep talking about, how are you going to do it on your own?"

"You may be right. I'm not as smart as I would like," Arthur admitted, missing the point. "I left Ohio first in my class but here I'm one of the crowd. I see what you and others can do particularly in the sciences, and I'm envious. If I had some of your aptitudes coupled with my drive" . . . and Arthur trailed off, thinking. "You know, you and I could make a pretty formidable pair".

While in college, Arthur started several businesses many of which he was able to sell and begin quite a nest egg. By senior year, Arthur and Jules had hatched a plan for a software technology company with a unique proposition. It had been Jules' idea and Arthur understood how to capitalize on it. Even before graduation they formed their first joint venture and had worked together on and off until Arthur formed BioDigiTech with financial support (and not a few ideas) from Jules whose cultivated credibility in the business community helped solidify their position.

Over the next several years Arthur had shown an aptitude for building companies. His only real challenge, evident on multiple occasions and in multiple venues, proved to be his inability to understand the "people part". He didn't see this as a gap in himself, but instead, a weakness in others, an inability to

81

get beyond their need for validation. He became a master negotiator using his knowledge and preparation as a basis for his ever increasing success. When he believed in something he pursued his ends with single-minded dedication.

The lessons he learned in childhood, hard work and discipline, were paying huge dividends at this point. He knew no one would help him; in order to achieve the ends he sought he could rely only on himself. He tried dating and marriage. Women were attracted to his power, his money, and his good looks but the romance never lasted.

Over time his relationship with Jules Allen had become strained, too. He resented Jules' abilities with people. Arthur was the one who built BioDigiTech, not Jules Allen. But the world didn't see it the same way.

He knew back in college Jules was brighter and he believed if he had Jules Allen's intelligence, there would be no one on the planet who could stop him. He begrudged the fact that Jules forced him to recognize the importance of collaboration persuading him to champion causes which were good for the company. Jules could be hard to move once he set his mind on something which often came in conflict with Arthur's need for control.

In the final analysis, power and control motivated Arthur Paulson. Doing the deal was just one way for him to feel superior, to lord it over others, to demonstrate his prowess. Money was only valuable for the power it brought. And that power proved addictive. BioDigiTech was poised for greatness. He planned to use Project Achilles as a lever to even greater clout and influence ultimately supplanting his friend, Jules.

§

After driving nearly half an hour the car pulled off the highway and into the Turkey Run Recreation Area. They had driven half a mile into the park when the Sergeant pulled the car off the road into a secluded parking area.

General Scott stood outside his SUV dressed in khaki's, a print shirt, and a camel's hair sport coat. Even when he wasn't in uniform, Jim Scott cast an imposing presence. Despite his five foot six inch frame the broad-shouldered, square-jawed soldier exuded a commanding presence. Scott walked with a slight limp, the result of an injury early in career.

As Arthur stepped out of the car, the General came over to him and shook his hand. Arthur didn't believe he ever saw the man smile.

"Thanks for coming," his deep voice intoned. "Come, walk with me". The Sergeant remained with the cars.

Arthur soon found himself on a dirt path. "Do you know where we are?" the General asked.

Not knowing what the General was angling about, Arthur professed his ignorance, "No, not really".

"I like coming here. We're close to Washington and yet out of ear shot. I much prefer the company of nature to that of my fellows: too many complications, too much politics and bureaucracy."

"And," he paused and smiled pointing with his right thumb over his left shoulder without looking back, "back there about half a mile sits CIA headquarters. We're in Langley Virginia. I like to come here from time to time and thumb my nose at them."

"You don't think much of them," Arthur stated as they walked.

"Not especially."

Jim Scott was not much for small talk and to emphasize the point they continued walking in silence until they reached a small stream. Arthur considered the irony of Scott's comment given the obviously clandestine nature of their meeting. And he found himself wondering why they weren't meeting in a more public place or at the General's office.

They came to a small stream and Scott abruptly stopped and stared off into space.

Arthur asked, "Why did you ask me to come here General, and why the secrecy?"

"Straight to the point, good," General Scott began. "I want to know where we stand with Project Achilles. I have read your reports, but want to hear it from the horse's mouth, so to speak."

"There has been significant progress in the five and a half weeks since I assigned Keyes to the project. His simulation algorithms have helped Dr. Neumann shortcut months of development and research. Animal testing is going better than expected. What remains is largely a matter of quality control. Several more areas of investigation including verification of viral stability, the best means of introducing the virus, and scenario planning for unanticipated side effects have yet to be initiated. But you didn't bring me halfway across the country and out here for a status report, which you already have."

"When do you anticipate you will be ready for human testing?" the General queried looking off into the distance.

"That depends on what we find in the next stage. Our biggest concern at this point has been the loss of balance in roughly a quarter of the test animals. And in a slightly smaller percentage we observed hyper-aggressive behavior. But, best case, I would say we'd be ready to begin human testing in six to eight weeks, assuming we can work the bugs out."

Arthur had anticipated the question and so had no trouble coming up with an answer he believed he could easily defend and a result he could confidently achieve.

General Scott turned and looked Arthur in the eye. Without emotion as though speaking to a junior officer Scott said, "That will not be acceptable. Complete your verifications in the next three weeks. I expect to begin testing early next month."

§

James Scott's father, a West Point graduate, served with distinction in the European Theater during World War II. Following in his father's footsteps Scott enrolled in West Point, trained as a Ranger, and was sent to Vietnam as a Lieutenant in 1969. Command had learned of a major enemy troop movement and sent Scott's platoon, his first command, to participate in an ambush operation. Whether the trap was set from the beginning or North Vietnamese intelligence learned of the planned ambush and revised their strategy no one ever knew.

Staked out along the trail his platoon was easily outflanked when the enemy came upon them descending from the hills above his position. One third of his soldiers died in the subsequent firefight with another third wounded including Scott.

He took the defeat hard blaming himself for not anticipating the unforeseeable and leaving his men open and unprotected from the rear. The loss instilled in him a fierce, some would say pathological, distrust of the intelligence services and command in general and an all-consuming need to make up for his initial defeat.

Rather than dwell on the loss Scott poured himself into his duties distinguishing himself admirably and rising quickly attaining the rank of major before the war was over. His outstanding performance yielded an appointment to the Army War College where he learned strategy and continued to impress his superiors. Following the Gulf War, Scott served several roles in the Pentagon never quite fitting in with the entrenched bureaucracy.

His current assignment gave him responsibility for coordinating special ops with oversight for several black ops squads training in highly classified locations for overseas assignment in combat zones. When these units, under his command, demonstrated their overwhelming superiority in the field owing, at least in part, to the Achilles Project, that would indeed be his ticket to the role he truly coveted: Army Chief of Staff.

§

"General, with all due respect, we are not ready." Arthur had no difficulty looking Jim Scott in the eye and telling him the truth.

"For one thing, we will need more testing and review before trying this out on whomever you have chosen to test the virus. You know as well as I we might kill or seriously harm the test subjects. And I don't have to tell you what would result. If the general public is terrified of genetically engineered food, how are they going to react to a scandal of this proportion? Even you won't prevent word from leaking out. Your career would be over and the Pentagon's reputation will be seriously tarnished. There will a congressional inquiry. It could mean the end of BioDigiTech and, most importantly, I won't go to jail."

"You let me worry about my career." General Scott stared off into space again. "I'm in a tight place. I will only have my test subjects available for a few more weeks and I cannot afford to lose them. Once they are deployed it will set the project back, perhaps beyond recovery. I won't have it. I've worked too long and hard. This is my ticket.

"My superiors", he spat, "believe technology is the future. They have discounted the role of the foot soldier when it's always been the foot soldier who has won the war. Their skill, their judgment, their determination distinguishes America's military."

Understanding Scott now sat out on a limb from which he couldn't return, Arthur pondered his options. He now knew why they were meeting in secret. Scott's comments earlier concerning 'politics, bureaucracy, and complications' now came into focus. Scott's superiors were entirely unaware of Project Achilles which put Arthur and BioDigiTech out on that same limb.

He had to figure out how to turn this to his advantage. General Jim Scott didn't give a damn about accountability. An alternative path presented itself.

"I'm sorry General, I don't think we can move quickly enough," he began. "I can certainly try, but I will have to turn up the heat. I will need your help."

Jim Scott smiled to himself thinking Paulson was much too transparent. He would never survive in the Washington bureaucracy, could never deal with the life and death issues under General Scott's control. Scott would love to play poker with him someday.

He would really clean up.

"I can pay you another ten million dollars. Let's call it a timely completion bonus. Would that be satisfactory?"

"Yes, but", Arthur hedged, "you and I have talked about several other potential projects in the works." Arthur rattled off three of them. "I want a guarantee they will be awarded to BioDigiTech. I understand I will need to go through the bidding process but I am confident you can sway the committee in my favor." Nothing like a little ego stroking to ice the cake, he thought.

"Done. We have a deal." and General Scott reached out to shake Paulson's hand. But this time he held Arthur's hand in a crushing grip.

Looking straight up into Arthur's eyes, Scott's deep voice, barely audible, warned, "Don't disappoint me. This is our secret. It would not go well for you if you were to fail me in your commitments. Do I make myself clear?"

"Completely."

It was evident there was more on the line for the General than Arthur knew and he became convinced any failure, either in producing the virus when committed or exposing the secret, would be met with much more than a harangue and public embarrassment. He wouldn't put it behind this guy to put a bullet in his heart, or a knife in his back.

"Can you find your way back to the car?" General Scott asked. When Arthur nodded assent, Scott turned away.

"Very well."

Scott intended to remain by the stream communing with nature, Arthur thought, with a sense of irony.

On the flight home Arthur hatched his plan. He had no doubt that he could ready the project in three weeks. His briefings to the General had not been entirely accurate. He had been placing significant pressure on the team and was convinced they would be ready in only one to two months at the outside. There should be no problem in completing the project within the prescribed three weeks. They would have to cut corners, but it wouldn't be the first time. And if they went a little over the deadline, Arthur was sure he could stall. The only question was whether Dr. Neumann would get on board. If not, he had his contingency plan.

As the plane began its landing maneuvers, Arthur smiled to himself. It had been too easy: with information came power. He knew he could angle additional lucrative work from General Scott if he could find the right lever. Scott thought he was so clever, believing Arthur could be easily bought. But Arthur knew the real story and had manipulated Scott into a corner. Arthur would love to play poker with him someday.

He would really clean up.

Chapter 10

Gabby arrived at work eager with anticipation. Six weeks had passed since she and Peter began their collaboration. His contributions helped her leap over a number of problems she had encountered and a few she didn't even know she had. Though both projects had moved along rapidly she had unexpectedly made more progress with Ulysses than Achilles.

There were certain problems in connections between the cerebellar and cerebral tissue resulting in balance problems for a significant portion of the mice along with an, as yet, unexplained hyper-aggressiveness among a small minority. They hadn't quite worked out solutions but believed they were getting close.

She was starting to think about how to tell Michael. Her confidence in success had grown dramatically and not a day too soon. Michael's deterioration had continued to accelerate. On top of that she had noticed his depression was becoming more evident. He had lost his hostility and that worried her more; he appeared to be accepting the inevitable. He hadn't gone to his therapist in three weeks despite her encouragement. Gabby suspected she couldn't wait much longer.

It was mid-afternoon when Bob called and asked her to come to his office. Gabby guessed he was getting more pressure from above as his requests for status reports had been increasing in frequency.

As she headed down to his office she felt a growing sense of anxiety. She hadn't fully briefed him on the progress she had been making assuming they might run into a glitch. She needed him to have confidence in her ability to deliver. It wouldn't be too much longer.

As she stepped into Bob's office he motioned for her to take a seat. Bob was not his usual jovial self. His office had two guest seats arranged in front of his desk. He usually took one of them when he met with her. Today he sat behind his desk, leaning forward with forearms resting on the desk, hands clasped. Gabby knew something was up. Also, he usually opened with small talk and then would ask her for a general overview of her progress, not today.

"Gabby, it's evident you have been making progress far faster than any of us had anticipated but you need to turn up the heat. We are committed to delivering specimens for human testing in two and a half weeks. Do you see anything standing in the way?"

Unprepared for the question she had to think quickly; her hesitation obvious.

"Bob, I'm a little surprised," she confessed. "You know we still have issues with verification of viral stability, the best means of introducing the virus, and scenario planning not to mention the balance problem. I think I can be completed in six weeks at the outside, but not much sooner".

She had to buy time to thoroughly finish Ulysses. In fact, she thought she might be ready any day. Despite her optimism for Michael's cure, she didn't want to put him at any unnecessary risk. And, at this point she didn't give a damn about Achilles.

"Gabby, I really need you to step up here. I'm not asking *if*, but want to know what it will take to have the viruses ready for transport in two and a half weeks."

"Bob, I'm not used to telling you no, but I can't, with any confidence or integrity, commit to your new schedule."

Despite what she thought about project Achilles she would not release the virus before it was ready for human testing. She would not be associated with human experimentation which carried a high likelihood of failure. Based on years of experience working with Bob in difficult situations, Gabby knew he shared her need for methodological discipline and would back her with Arthur.

She couldn't have been more wrong.

"I'm sorry to hear that." Bob looked down as if thinking about what to say next. In fact, he had rehearsed his comments carefully before the meeting.

"I am well aware you've made more progress than you're letting on." He shook his head from side to side as he spoke. "I know you are close enough and the two and a half week timeframe is not out of the question".

Where was he getting his information, Gabby wondered. Her mind raced. Was it Edgar? She wouldn't put it past that ambitious little weasel. Then another thought struck her. *Oh my God, could it be Peter?* She rejected that betrayal with every fiber of her being. She knew he couldn't be responsible. Bob sat back, opened a desk drawer and withdrew a document.

As he handed the legal looking letter to her Bob intoned, as if well practiced, "Gabby, I have enjoyed working with you but your insubordination will not be tolerated. You have refused a direct request. And I happen to know you have continued to conduct other experiments which I specifically instructed you not to do."

He is laying the groundwork for my termination, Gabby realized.

"This severance agreement spells out the terms of your departure. You have one week to examine and sign it. If you so choose, you may review it with your attorney. In return for your signature you will be paid two weeks pay for each year of service along with your accrued vacation time. You are eligible for COBRA health coverage which you will have to pay out of your own pocket. Do you have any questions?"

"Bob, I know I made a mistake by not keeping you fully informed. You know I like to under-promise and over-deliver. It has made me", and she nodded to Bob, "and you very successful here. I might be able to complete Achilles in four to five weeks but no sooner."

Gabby hoped this compromise would work. Plus, who was he going to get on short notice to take over for her? There were few anywhere in the world who could step in.

"Gabby, this isn't open for negotiation."

Bob looked at her as if she was clueless. *Perhaps I am*, she thought. He *must have been planning this. He's been going around behind my back. He had the severance agreement and his speech prepared. He probably had someone ready to take her place, but whom?*

Bob interrupted her train of thought.

"And let me caution you. Under the terms of your employment contract you are prohibited from conducting similar research with another private corporation for two years. And in case you conscience prompts you to go to the press; Project Achilles has been classified as a Homeland Security project and as such you would feel the full weight of the Act should you choose to go public."

93

Gabby thought about her years working with Bob and realized she didn't know him at all. His jovial manner was only for show hiding a ruthless willingness to disregard ethics for expediency. He didn't care about the human subjects, only his own ambition.

Gabby found herself shaking her head in disbelief and disappointment. She now resigned herself to losing the job. In her time remaining she could still finish Ulysses. She knew she could go back to the faculty at the med school. She would make this work.

She calmly looked at Bob and asked, "So, when do you want me out of here?"

"Today, now," Bob replied. "Shirley from Human Resources is waiting for you outside the office to escort you to the lab. It's been a pleasure working with you Gabby, I'm sorry it had to end this way. Good luck."

He did not hold out his hand as he came around the desk to open the door for her.

The immediacy of her departure threw Gabby into shock as Shirley escorted her down the hall to her lab; Gabby's fear turning to panic. *How am I going to get the Ulysses viral specimens out?* she wondered. *Maybe there won't be anyone in the lab when I get there, maybe they'll wait outside while I get my things, but how will I keep the specimens at a cold temperature until I can find another Garden?*

Thoughts raced through her mind as she tried to figure out how she wouldn't lose years of work and, ultimately, save Michael.

When she arrived at the lab her worst fears were realized and then some. Edgar stood at his bench looking as though someone had smashed into his car and told him it was his fault.

The real shock came when she looked in her office and saw the security guard standing beside her desk while Karen went through her personal possessions, placing them in a cardboard box on her desk.

"What do you think you're doing?" she asked with undisguised anger throwing a sidelong glance at the security guard.

"This is my office now," Karen shot back. "I've put your things in the box. The rest stays here."

Gabby's eyebrows raised as a smile of incredulity broke across her face.

"They're putting you in charge of completing Achilles? I guess you must have been the one feeding Bob. What did he promise you? A bribe, give you my position if you were a good lap dog?"

Karen stood there, arms crossed, without responding. Gabby grabbed the box with pictures, her purse, car keys and the like, looked at the security guard and said, "Let's get the hell outta here."

Shirley and the guard escorted Gabby out of the building to her car, Gabby's anger tempered by the humiliation she felt under the sidelong glances from those who happened to see her. When they arrived at her car, Shirley took Gabby's name badge. Gabby placed the box in the back seat got in the driver's seat, turned the ignition, and left BioDigiTech for the last time.

At the end of the boulevard, before turning on to the main road, Gabby pulled onto the shoulder and stopped. The little control she had maintained since leaving Bob's office vanished as she slumped over the steering wheel and cried.

She had no idea where to turn. She had no income and they could only get by for a brief time with only Michael's editing work to pay the bills. It would take her a while to get another appointment at the medical school, if she could get one. She supposed she could work as a clinical physician but she would need to find a group with the capacity to hire her.

And then there was Karen's betrayal. *I must have been blind. I trusted her, supported her, and look what it got me*, Gabby thought. Was the world conspiring against her? Gabby rejected that paranoid delusion but reflected back on stories Michael had told her about politics in business. She realized, with complete clarity, that it was only her and Michael now.

As she pulled on to the main road, Gabby finally considered her real dilemma. The bigger problem, the real problem, the one she couldn't confront just yet: what to do about Michael and Project Ulysses. Gabby couldn't even think about alternatives, the problems were too daunting.

But she wasn't ready yet to give in to defeat. If she could find another job with a lab, maybe she could find a way recreate the virus. It might take six months or more, but she had to hope.

She hated not telling Michael. She wanted more than anything to confide in him. *I guess if I don't go into work in the morning he will know something is up*, she thought ruefully. At least now she could tell him the truth. At this point she very much needed to, but he would think she was deluded. *And maybe I am*, she admitted.

"I've been kidding myself all these years." Gabby spoke aloud to herself. "How could I believe I could cure Michael's paralysis? I'm only one person. I've been living in a dream world and I'm now waking up to my nightmare."

Gabby soon found herself in front Nick Thai's where she and Peter had been meeting three times a week for practically two months. It was Tuesday. Maybe he would show up even though he probably knew about her termination. She wanted to see him one last time. He was the one person she could open up to with all her fears.

Peter turned out to be a good listener, someone engaging to brainstorm with. Maybe he would have other ideas. She smiled to herself, thinking about their first dinner together, the promise she now saw dashed. *Yes*, she thought, *he could help me think through what to do next and perhaps help me figure out how to tell Michael.*

Sitting in the restaurant, entirely alone, her mind reflexively imagining her future without Michael, unemployed, adrift; she was interrupted by Peter's arrival at 5:30. He sat down at the table with a look of distress which Gabby figured was probably a small fraction of what she felt.

"I was hoping you'd be here. I heard what happened. How are you holding up?"

"About as well as can be expected", she replied with a shrug of her shoulders.

Gabby recounted the afternoon's events for him as they ordered and the waiter brought dinner. She shared her hopes and fears while Peter listened, not interrupting, nodding his head as she spoke. But Gabby sensed Peter was impatient and distracted. *Was he only listening out of sympathy?* When she had finished telling her story she asked, "So, what do you think?"

"Gabby, are you willing to do whatever it takes to complete the Ulysses retrovirus?"

Taken aback, Gabby replied, "Of course, why?"

Peter didn't respond immediately.

"Peter I don't know what you're trying to do. Whatever it is, I really appreciate it, but I don't think setting up a lab in my basement is a real alternative. I'm not the mad scientist you think I am."

"Yes you are and so am I. We have made phenomenal progress and we're too close. I'm not giving up now "

Gabby, struck by Peter's conviction wondered, *could there be a way out?*

Cautiously she asked, "Do you have a plan?"

"I'm working on it. Can you meet me back here tomorrow night?"

"I suppose so. Look, Peter, I don't want to get my hopes up . . ."

Before she could say more, Peter interrupted, "When we first talked six weeks ago you told me why you gave the project the name you did. You recall, Ulysses labored for ten years trying to get home following the Trojan War and along the way multiple barriers stood in his way. But he made it home despite every adversity the gods threw at him."

Gabby nodded.

"You need to trust me here. We'll talk more tomorrow". Peter motioned for the waiter. "I'll pick up the check, you're unemployed."

Gabby smiled not sure what to feel. She knew he wasn't making fun of her predicament; he was chiding her for her concerns. *He must know something I don't. There's much more here than meets the eye,* she realized.

She left the restaurant more confused than when she had come in.

What was Peter thinking? Sure he was bright and determined but what could he do?

Too many questions crossed through her mind. And the biggest one was what to tell Michael.

Gabby resolved not to say anything yet; not about her job or certainly about Ulysses. She had no idea what Peter's plan entailed, but she realized she needed to hear more, much more, before saying anything to Michael. *What was one more day?* she wondered as she pulled into her driveway.

Michael had spent the day working; editing three articles sent to him by his publisher and was halfway through the outline of another for which he was the principal author collaborating with a colleague at the local business school. The article dealt with alienation in the workplace and how to turn dissatisfaction into constructive energy. He enjoyed writing the article, in part, because it brought back his ambivalent feelings.

Michael had struggled to fit in at the hospital. While he found fulfillment in day to day problem solving and the art of strategy development; he felt like a duck out of water dealing with the self-serving politics necessary to survive. Oh, he could play the game well, but felt tainted by the gamesmanship.

Naïveté was not one of Michael's weaknesses. He recognized the difficulty making change happen in a sea of competing interests and personalities. He knew any organization from corporations to universities to the corner store; all were fraught with the difficulties posed when people worked together. He recognized he both craved and chaffed at human interaction.

Working at home as he did made him into something of a recluse. He used to go out and see friends but now found it too difficult. Instead he buried himself in online interaction. He had become adept at working on the internet. What he couldn't do physically, he made up for with his mind.

But while his cognitive function was undiminished, he found it increasingly difficult to do the tasks he had taken for granted only a few months before. He could still type at the computer but his fingers didn't move as smoothly or quickly across the keys. He lacked the strength which had come so easily in the past when maneuvering from his wheelchair into another chair or the bed using his arms and shoulders. Unsure of his reflexes and coordination he felt increasingly reluctant to drive even though the van had been specially outfitted for him. The upper body strength which had complemented his lower extremity weakness now waned.

Cut off and isolated, he worried he would eventually find himself a mind incarcerated in a body no longer of use to him; a prison from which there was no parole, no reprieve. While not wanting to admit the truth to himself much less to Gabby, Michael came to a decision concerning what to do as he arrived at the inevitable conclusion of what he considered to be the end of a very long journey.

Despite his growing depression, Michael couldn't help but smile as Gabby came in from the garage. As much as he struggled the one bright spot in every day had been spending time with her. But he knew how hard she worked, how he had restricted her life.

"How did your day go?" he asked with as much cheer as he could muster.

"Oh, you know, pretty typical," she lied. "How was yours?"

Michael recounted the activities of the day but didn't want to burden her further with his dark thoughts, fully knowing he had to unload his burden soon. He would have to be unmovable but wasn't sure how to maintain his resolve or if he even could when the time came.

"What did you do for dinner?"

"I made myself a peanut butter and jelly, can you believe it?" Michael told her about his plan for dinner the following night.

"Oh," Gabby added apologetically, "I've got a late meeting tomorrow night, too. You know we're getting so close. Is that OK with you?"

What am I supposed to say?, thought Michael. He wasn't surprised she was spending more and more time away and he really couldn't blame her.

He could only muster a, "no problem, I understand."

Gabby hated to see him like this. She knew he didn't want to put any more demands on her. It tore her apart, not being able to tell him.

With every fiber of her being she wanted to shout, "It's going to be OK, just stick with me a little longer." She wanted to believe it, too, but the events of the day left her more than discouraged. Now was clearly not the time to tell him she had been fired. She would find a way tomorrow. Maybe Peter will come up with solution she hadn't thought of.

Michael and Gabby found little comfort in the unconsciousness of sleep. Both dreamed and would have been surprised to learn, again, they both had the same dream, but neither remembered dreaming when they woke the next morning.

Unbiased Opinions of the Clearly Confused

Today's Message

You may remember last time I wrote about the conflict we often feel between wanting to be part of a group and yet feeling quite apart. We crave the security brought about by identification with the tribe while, at the same time, needing the freedom to be ourselves. Anyone (or at least anyone who has a modicum of self-awareness) who has tried to fit in at work or school recognizes you can't be completely yourself, quirks and all, because you won't be accepted.

There is a culture inherent to all tribes or groups which must be maintained for group stability. We can spend so much of ourselves trying to fit in that after a while our personalities change just enough that we may wake up one day not entirely sure who we are. This adaptation and the resulting unresolved conflict may cause us to cling too tightly to the group identity while producing the point of view that those outside our group are somehow unacceptable or even inferior.

How I define those not in my group ends up being how I define myself. "Those who don't believe as we do must certainly be in error." we hear. We live in fear of exclusion and so justify our inclusion in the tribe as verification we are better as a result of our affiliation. Groucho Marx, the great 20th Century philosopher, made the point perfectly, if in converse, when he said, "I don't care to belong to any club that will have me as a member."

The evidence indicates primate brain size dictates group size; the larger the brain the larger the group. But the human limit is 150 people. In other words, for groups beyond 150 people we cannot see ourselves as a part of the tribe and the hierarchical or status instinct comes through. Our brains have evolved to this capacity. We rebel in the larger, impersonal societies because we are programmed to do so. We struggle between the security of the tribe and personal freedom. We place our trust in others and are surprised when they betray us.

Our senses, our biology, reinforce our isolation. We aspire to community and yet rebel at its limitations on our freedoms. Those principles, those instincts which make tribes successful are the very same ones which alienate us from the tribes we want to be a part of.

I come back to the blog I wrote several weeks ago. Are we at a dead end? Are we, in fact, limited by our biology? Perhaps there is no resolution because we are wired that way.
So I continue to ask,

HOW CAN I BE SANE IN A MAD WORLD?

Samsa

Chapter 11

Gabby left the house early, before Michael woke up; worried the tension she was feeling might boil over and she might have to tell him what was actually going on. Maybe tonight would be the night. With all her might, she struggled, wanting to confess all.

Instead of driving to BioDigiTech she headed for the medical school. She wanted to look up colleagues she hadn't seen in a while and to see if she could get her old faculty appointment back. The sooner she was back in the lab, the sooner she could complete Ulysses. She was so close, only a few more steps. It was November 1st and she knew faculty appointments were only made in July. But, maybe they would give her access to a lab. She had to hope. *Hope,* she thought ruefully, *how delusional am I?*

Rain poured in sheets as she got out of the car. Opening her umbrella she pulled her coat close to keep out the wind. The smell of autumn filled her senses and despite the events of the last twenty four hours Gabby felt invigorated and found herself excited to be back on campus. The prospect of returning felt like coming back home.

One pictures college campuses as places where vintage buildings are set amidst pastoral surroundings; not so the modern medical school. These institutions, originally dedicated to training new physicians, had become the ultimate icon in the nexus between science and technology. And, as the science evolved so did the need for updated facilities. Gabby marveled at how the campus had morphed in the short time since she first attended class.

She walked through the motion-activated, transparent double doors of a glass and steel structure. Stepping into the cavernous atrium she encountered medical students, dressed like every other college student, walking deliberately to their next class unconscious of their surroundings. Gabby rode the elevator to the third floor, home to the Neurology department and its Chairman, Natalie Simms. She opened the door to the Department Chair's outer office and was greeted with a broad smile by Rachel Garber, Dr. Simms' executive assistant.

"Dr. Neumann, what a pleasant surprise," Rachel gushed.

"Haven't I always told you to call me Gabby?"

Rachel took on an officious tone, "Yes, you have and I will remind you again", she leaned forward, raised a finger, and admonished her, "some of the tight asses around here wouldn't understand."

Gabby laughed. "Is Dr. Simms available?"

"She's in a meeting with the Dean right now but should be back in . . .", Rachel looked at the clock on her computer, "oh about 15 minutes. Would you like to wait?"

"Thank you. I believe I will.", and Gabby sat in the waiting room chair closest to Rachel. She was about to make small talk when the phone rang and Rachel plunged into dealing with another crisis. It was almost half an hour before Natalie Simms arrived. *I'm back on University time*, Gabby thought.

"Well, look who's here", Natalie Simms said as she breezed into her office, "Come in."

Once behind closed doors Simms walked up to Gabby and hugged her.

"How have you been? It's great to see you. Come have a seat." While Simms office wasn't spacious or at all luxurious, she did have room for a couch and they both sat.

Natalie put on a serious face. "How's Michael?"

"Not well. His condition is deteriorating. I don't know what's coming next but I fear the worst."

"I wish I could offer some hope," she paused, "but you probably know more than I, perhaps more than anyone, what's going on. Nevertheless I wish there was something I could do", she said with genuine concern.

Changing the subject, Natalie asked, "How are you doing at BioDigiTech?"

Gabby wasn't the first faculty member to leave the medical school for the financial security of BDT. Natalie understood why Gabby had left the school but had never been very supportive. She hated to lose one of her most successful researchers (which meant grant money, in university parlance), and she saw a move to BDT as "selling out", choosing financial gain over public service.

"That's why I came to see you", Gabby answered. "I left BioDigiTech yesterday and wanted to talk with you about reinstating my faculty appointment. You told me when I left I was welcome back any time." As she spoke Gabby realized her statement sounded more like a question than a fact.

"Why did you leave?"

"I'm not in a position to say."

Natalie nodded thoughtfully. "I think I understand. You can't explain either due to your employment contract or because of the work you were doing. I'm not sure I care. When you were here you brought no small degree of recognition to the school and this department. And, you brought in more grant money than anyone other than me. Your research reputation in the neurology community was building to the point where you were developing a solid national status. We genuinely felt the loss when you left.

"At the same time, I appreciated your situation. You had to place your family first, but I wasn't sure you would fit in at BDT. Was I wrong?"

"Not entirely. But I had considerable freedom to pursue lines of investigation which would have been more difficult under the eyes of the NIH. I've made significant advances and would like to build on them back in my old lab. I am confident I could secure grant funding sufficient to generate significant profits."

"Listen to you," laughed Natalie, "you have gone over to the dark side: profits."

"Natalie, you might not call them profits here at the school but you know better than I grant money goes to paying all kinds of overhead around here from you to the Dean. We tag a hefty percentage on top of the actual cost of the study to cover other medical school costs. We may call it covering our overhead, but its profit all the same. So what do you say? Do you want me back?"

"Yes, of course." Natalie smiled. "I've forgotten how feisty you can be though I'm not sure I want to be considered overhead. I've missed our sparring. But you know this won't be easy. I have no way of funding your position, at this time. I can make the case to the Dean you will more than pay for yourself and bring recognition to the School and the Department, but there are some who will question the motivation behind your return and hold it over my head. In any event, I can't get you an appointment before July during the regular cycle."

Gabby didn't miss the politics or the bureaucratic rules intrinsic to the university setting but knew getting back into a lab was her best hope for Project Ulysses.

"I've already considered the problem and have a plan to deal with the July date and funding. I would like to meet with the grant people as soon as possible. If you can get me support from the Grants Office I will have a funding application to you for approval inside of three weeks. I can start on a provisional basis using those funds until faculty appointments this summer. With the money I can bring in I suspect the politics around my appointment will be just so much noise.

"As to my motivation for coming back; I am a research scientist first. I don't belong in private practice. There is no other opportunity in the private sector here and so this is the best place for me to be. Anyway, I have a non-compete which prevents me from conducting similar research at any other private facility."

"Good. You've thought this through. I will talk to the Dean. He likes you and so we might have a chance. Assuming I get the green light; I'll set you up with the grants people in the next few weeks. Rachel will contact you with a time."

Natalie stood. "I wish we could spend more time catching up but I'm already late for another meeting. I will let you know. Good to see you."

As Gabby left the office she knew coming back to her old position wouldn't be as easy as their conversation had been. Multiple roadblocks remained, any of which could derail her plans. The Dean may reject the idea for some reason Gabby or even Natalie might not be aware. Natalie's positive attitude encouraged Gabby but she knew Natalie was, at heart, a political animal and would only do this if she could play it to her advantage. She worried she might not get the grant or funding might be delayed. And ultimately she questioned whether she would complete Project Ulysses in time to save Michael. But this was her best hope.

As Gabby stepped out on the sidewalk she thought about what she could do to tide her over financially until her appointment came through. She knew many of the practicing internists in town having trained with or personally trained many of them. She decided to talk to a number of the larger groups to see if they had a short term opening for a neurologist; knowing full well it was a long shot. In fact, she pessimistically confided to herself all of her strategies would be long shots but determined if she tried enough paths one would turn into a real opportunity. Time was her only enemy.

The rain didn't let up as she walked to her car. Visiting the practices and taking a leisurely lunch would take most of the day. Then it would be time for her dinner with Peter. He had been of immense help, but there was nothing more he could do at this point, not realistically.

Gabby arrived at the restaurant about 20 minutes before the usual appointed time. The guarded optimism which began the day turned into a dark mood matched only by the worsening weather outside. Gabby was soaked by the time she entered the restaurant. The rain had grown into a hurricane-like torrent, winds rendering useless her umbrella and coat.

Her visits to each of the practices had not gone well. None had any positions for a neurologist, short term or otherwise. And while three of the groups had positions for general internists, she had been out of practice so long they were skeptical she could keep up the pace necessary to make a living in general practice.

As Gabby got into her car after the sixth and final visit of the day, her cell phone rang. It was Dr. Gandhi, the same radiologist who had diagnosed Michael's condition after the accident. Michael had an MRI the week before, but they hadn't yet learned the results.

"Gabby is this a bad time? I can talk with you later this evening, if that would be better."

"No, now is fine. What did you learn?"

"I apologize for taking so long to get back with you but I wanted to carefully review the previous images before I called."

Gabby's heart sank.

"It's clear. Michael's deterioration is accelerating. You probably know better than me what this means, but there can be no doubt. He may not have much time. Six months at the outside. I can go over the films with you if you like."

"No, not right now. I'll call you back later," was all she could manage as she hung up. Her well-conceived plans had been long shots at best; but now she saw all her hopes in vain, her worst fears realized.

Gabby sat in the restaurant in numbed silence. She was thinking about what to say to Michael when Peter came in.

"What a mess out there," Peter said as he shook the rain off of his faded brown leather jacket and sat down. He took one look at Gabby and said, "You look worse than yesterday. Are you OK?"

"Michael had an MRI last week and I just heard from the radiologist. He doesn't have much time." As if stating the fact out loud made the inevitable more immediate; tears welled in Gabby's eyes.

The waiter came over and Peter said, "Can you give us a minute?"

110

"All of this, my work, our work, all of this has been in vain. There's nothing left for me to do." Gabby couldn't look him in the eye and so stared down at the table devastated in her admission of defeat.

"You're wrong", Peter challenged. "Look at me."

Gabby looked up slowly. She did not want to deal with him right now.

"Peter, I want to thank you for all you've done. You've been a great colleague and a good friend when I truly needed both but this is the end of the line. I think I'd better leave."

Peter grabbed her arm as she tried to stand and forced her to sit down.

"What if I told you I had a lab ready to go, well, almost ready? That you could start up right where you left off?"

Gabby smiled indulgently. "Peter, how are you going to put together a genetics lab so quickly? It's just not possible, and it would cost a small fortune."

Peter pulled out several sheets of paper and slid them across the table to her. "Is there anything else you need?"

Gabby scanned what appeared to be a list of equipment and materials to outfit a genetics lab.

"Where did you get this?"

"It doesn't matter. Is it complete?"

The list affected Gabby's demeanor drawing her out of her despair into her comfortable analytic zone as if a switch were flipped.

"Largely; you're only missing a few items." Her heart beat faster.

"Write them down," he said as he handed her a pen. "Also we will need the equipment for a hospital room for Michael. Please add those to the list, too.

"OK, I'll play along." She handed the completed list back to him. "So, when will this lab be ready?"

Peter glanced at her additions adding absently, "Tuesday at the latest."

What's going on here? Gabby wondered. She leaned back in her chair looked directly at Peter and decided to take the bait despite her reservations.

"All right, I'll assume you've got it all figured out, you've somehow set up a working genetics lab. In any event, it doesn't matter. The viruses still sit in my Garden at BDT and without the cultures I won't have enough time."

Peter smiled and leaned forward. "I've thought of that, too. But, can we order dinner first? I'm famished. I've been very busy." With that he called the waiter over.

In these last few hours Gabby had given up on hope and was afraid to reawaken it. Now her curiosity collided head on with her disbelief.

"What's your plan; just walk into BDT and steal the cultures?"

"That's about it."

"Are you serious?"

"Yes, but now I have to know, are you? I've been listening to you go on about Ulysses for months now. We've hit a bump in the road, but that's no reason to give up. What are you willing to risk?"

"Do you mean am I willing to risk my career and go to jail? You've got to be kidding. This is nuts. I'm not going to spend the last few months Michael has on this earth locked in a jail cell."

"Again, if my plans work and you could repair the damage to Michael's brain; would it be worth it?"

"Of course," she replied with more force than she intended startling the diners around them.

With that a glimmer of hope rekindled deep inside struck by Peter's sincerity. It burned like a small flame melting the ice she had built around her heart to shield it, to protect her. *Is this really possible? Has he thought this through? Peter had a great mind . . .* her thoughts trailed off.

Peter could almost see her thinking. He had worked with her enough to know she would resist. Despite her bluster she played by the rules. He knew her need to play by those rules was not serving her now. She had to see her higher purpose.

He didn't ask if she wanted to go on, instead, he leaned in and in a conspiratorial tone asked, "Are you ready to hear the details?"

She nodded tentatively as the waiter brought dinner.

As Gabby drove home she went over and over the plan in her mind. It all made sense. Once they had the cultures, they would have to leave town. The lab was in another state. It became plain that Peter had resources far beyond what she could have imagined. He wouldn't tell her where the money came from or the lab's location offering only that anonymity was necessary at this point.

Caught between overflowing anticipation and the terror of losing hope again, Gabby cautioned herself not to be overly optimistic. At the same time, if Peter could do all he committed to: there was good reason for hope.

She knew it.

The storm raged as Gabby pulled into her driveway. She knew this was the night, here and now. She would confess everything to Michael.

All the years of secrecy were at an end.

Chapter 12

Elation, a strong sense of purpose, and relief accompanied Gabby into the house. She removed her raincoat and hung it in the hall closet. Not sure whether it was a result of finally having some real hope or finding relief at finally being able to confess all, Gabby felt positively buoyant but stopped short before she entered the living room.

She knew if she appeared too excited, too optimistic, Michael might not believe her or might think it all a lie. She realized if she didn't calm down and methodically walk him through what she had done and where they would go from here he might reject the plan. He had to be completely on board, willing and able to take the next steps to restore their marriage and save his life.

She found Michael sitting in an armchair, waiting for her. She calmed herself and began, "I'm sorry I'm so late but I'm glad you're awake. I've something we need to talk about."

"I can guess," Michael replied before she could say more. Gabby looked at him quizzically, wondering how much he knew. She sat down in the chair facing Michael and waited, confused, asking herself how it was possible. She had been so circumspect not sharing or even hinting at what she had been up to. And the latest, well, she only knew from her meeting with Peter this evening. *Had Peter called him?*

"Maybe it would be best if I laid it out for you. You can tell me if I'm missing the mark.

"Years ago, when you worked at the med school, you would come home and talk about how you had spent your day. Your stories might be about anything: the latest breakthrough in research, what your colleagues had been doing, an interesting patient in clinic, some medical student foolishness or the latest political nonsense. And you would ask me about my day.

"At times I didn't understand why you were telling me some of what you did. Some of your stories would seem inconsequential and I would wonder why you would bother to share them with me. But, over time, I came to understand this was your way of sharing your day with me and in a seemingly trivial way built intimacy, a real connection. The rational and male part of my brain finally understood.

"But, since joining BDT you've become increasingly distant. You don't talk about work."

Gabby started to protest but Michael cut her off.

"I know about security clearance and confidentiality but it's like you've become a stranger. You seem to be trying too hard, looking for things to talk about.

"For the last several months you have been completely preoccupied. You're out three nights a week often coming home after I've gone to bed. When I do see you, you don't want to talk about your work or your meetings with Peter. You always change the subject. You've closed me off from your life."

Gabby tried again to interrupt but Michael wouldn't allow her to get a word in. She knew she could stop all of this but he was right; they hadn't been communicating. And she had been the biggest part of the problem. She had her reasons, but couldn't share them until tonight.

Nevertheless as she became increasingly agitated, she rose from her chair and began pacing as Michael continued.

"I've been trying to talk with you about my future, our future, for weeks and weeks and you keep putting me off. It's as if you can't face the truth. I was going to force the issue anyway, but now it all starts to make sense.

"How was your meeting?" Michael asked.

Blinded by Michael's change of direction Gabby didn't hear the intonation.

"It went well, very well, indeed. That's what I want to talk to you about."

Michael didn't seem to hear her.

"And how was work or perhaps I should ask where you were today?"

Taken aback, Gabby was losing her composure. *Where was he going with this*, she wondered? *He must know something.*

Rain continued to lash the house, thunder booming overhead.

In a flat tone Michael recounted a call from early in the afternoon. "I took a message from a Human Resources person at BDT, someone named Shirley. Anyway, they found a few more of your things, put them in a box and wanted you to know they were couriering them to the house.

"I don't know why you couldn't have been honest with me."

Without giving her a chance to reply, to explain herself, he continued, "We've talked about this, well, I've talked about it. I'm getting worse and you need to move on. And it seems you have. Now you're no longer at BDT but you don't even tell me. I don't know if you have a job, if you resigned, or were fired. And then there's your evening meetings, if that's really what they are, with Peter, doing, I can only imagine what.

"As I said before, I'm stifling you. You have needs that I can no longer fill. It's OK you're getting on with your life, but I

117

wish you would've had the decency to tell me to my face."
Michael looked down into his lap.

"You can't even look at me now."

Gabby didn't realize she had turned her back to him.

"I'll move out, find a place. I imagine I'll probably have to be institutionalized before too much longer anyway. I've already moved my stuff into the spare bedroom though it was quite an effort. I'll need a hand with the heavier things.

"Look, I'm happy for you, that you found someone. I'll feel better knowing you have someone you can truly share your life with."

Michael paused, "I want you to know I'm disappointed, but I understand. With what you had to go through with your mother . . ." Michael trailed off.

That was it. She could contain herself no longer. A waterfall of emotions greater than Niagara itself burst within her, churning, pouring itself out; Gabby's self control shattered by Michael's accusations and subsequent resignation.

"You understand?" Gabby whirled around, livid. "You understand nothing!"

She shouted at him in anger; her arms gesturing wildly.

"My mother? This has nothing to do with my mother. And Peter? You think I'm having an affair with Peter?

"Do you want to know where I've been today?"

Michael, taken aback with the vehemence of her question, sat back wide-eyed having never seen her like this.

"Yes, I was fired from my job. You think I left the medical school to make more money, to support us? I knew with BDT I'd have the means and the opportunity to pursue lines of research which had meaning for me out from under the watchful eye of the school. For the last four years I've been working, spending most of my energy on one project, at times sacrificing my assigned duties, and do you want to know why?

"There's one reason and one reason only; one passion that's been driving me, one singular need."

Gabby was standing in front of Michael now. All the pain, the loss, the desperation built up over years cascading from her.

"I have been working on a cure for the hell that has trapped you in your failing body. For something that will keep you alive, make you walk again and," Gabby choked, "bring you back to me."

She dropped to her knees in front of Michael, took both his hands in hers and held on for dear life. As tears welling in her eyes, she softly confessed, "I have been secretive with you only because I didn't want to give you false hope. But you need to know this: Peter has been a good friend and confidant. He has helped me immeasurably and I am going to be able, God willing, to reverse your decline and even get you walking again."

Michael stared at her, uncomprehending.

"I know I've been distant, distracted. Partly because I was so focused on work, but also because I didn't want to discuss your concerns fearing I would say too much. I have always loved you and I'm afraid I always will. You are stuck. We have a bond, a connection, which will not, which cannot be broken."

With new insight, Michael now realized he had lost faith in her and in himself. As a child he had been a trusting soul and it wasn't until he became an adult he realized how harsh the world could be. Over time he had lost his trust in others, often for good reason.

Gabby looked into Michael's eyes, his tears now brimming over, matching hers.

"How could I have misread you?" he asked plaintively, barely able to talk through his pain. "We've been so close all these years, told each other everything. Lately I feel like you've been slipping away, but now I realize it's been me, too. I've been disconnecting, telling myself to hope for the best but expect the worst. But I'd lost hope. I saw no way out. Now you tell me you can cure me? How? Are you sure?"

Gabby began her story. Long in the telling she recounted every event, every turn. Michael listened, rapt, unable to take his attention away; staggered by her single-mindedness and devotion. From time to time he would ask questions for clarification and slowly, Michael began to find hope again.

He had saved the more difficult questions for last. "I think I understand, but what kind of risks am I facing?"

"You will only get worse if we remain on the present course. The experiments with lab animals have been very successful. The first few rounds presented problems but I refined techniques and in the last several weeks the animals have been very stable with no discernable side effects and their lesions were repaired."

"I know there's no alternative, but what if it doesn't work or there are unexpected side effects? What I am trying to say is: I don't want to be a vegetable or some kind of mutant freak. You have to promise me if this doesn't work or goes off course you will end it, you won't leave me that way. Can you promise me?"

"It's been so hard to see you suffer I couldn't prolong your pain. We may find it difficult to draw a bright line but we will do it together. And if we can't I will respect your wishes."

Michael remained thoughtful. "So, what's next?"

"It's now Wednesday. We will leave Monday evening, late. We're still working out the details. Peter wants you to be a part of finalizing the plans and so he will be coming here Friday night to make sure all three of us are on the same page. There's still a lot I don't know on but he assures me everything will be in place by Monday. I would really like to know where we're going but Peter is keeping it a secret for some reason."

"Do you trust him? We are taking quite a risk here."

"You'll have to decide for yourself, but yes, I trust him."

Michael nodded.

"I haven't told you the name of this little project of mine, now ours. I called it, 'Ulysses'."

"Well Penelope, it's been a hell of a night. Let's go to bed."

Gabby helped Michael into his wheelchair and as she wheeled him back to their bedroom, Michael suggested, "And tomorrow you can help me move my stuff back into our bedroom. You don't have anything else to do, do you?"

Gabby laughed a laugh of genuine happiness and relief. All the years of deception melting away; she knew it would take time for them to recover what they had, *if the Treatment worked as planned*, she thought grimly. But she didn't let Michael see her uncertainty.

"I think instead we ought to focus on packing. No need to move twice. I hope we'll be back in a couple of weeks, but let's see."

And outside, the storm had stopped. As they lay close in bed the gentle sound of rain on the roof lulled the lovers to sleep.

As they slept Michael relived his dream. Trapped in the car he saw Gabby running toward him and he reached for her. This time she made it to the car, they grasped hands and she pulled him from the wreckage. He wasn't injured and they walked hand in hand down the road back to their home.

They woke together without the alarm and found they were laying side by side holding hands. They smiled that knowing, wordless smile lovers share.

"How about if I make breakfast this morning?" Gabby offered.

Michael didn't object.

Gabby stood at the counter preparing cinnamon rolls while Michael sat at the kitchen table. The glow from the previous evening still enveloped them.

Casually, Michael began, "You know the recurring dream I've been having about the accident? In the last few weeks it's changed. I'm still trapped in the car and can't get out. But recently, you've been in the dream".

Michael didn't notice Gabby stopped what she was doing.

"I see you running toward me but the dream ends before you reach the car."

Gabby stood absolutely still.

"And then last night I dreamed you reached me, pulled me from the car and we walked away together, hand in hand. You know I'm not superstitious but I take it as a good sign."

Gabby had turned around to face him, nervously working her hands. She spoke deliberately, "For the past several weeks I've been having a similar dream. In it I run around a bend in the road and see you in the wreckage. I'm running toward you, reaching for you. Last night I reached you, pulled you out and we walked away together. What in hell's going on here?"

Michael could only stare back at her, mute.

Gabby continued, "It just doesn't make sense." Pacing back and forth, chewing her lip she continued as if lecturing, "On a psychological level dreams often reflect our inner struggles, what we're working through. To have them on the same night, well it's against the odds but I suppose it's possible."

Gabby paused to ask a question, afraid of the answer. "Can you describe anything, like what I was wearing?"

It's not easy to remember dreams in the bright morning light but Michael thought hard and described her clothing to a tee.

They stared at each other blankly, Gabby, wide-eyed, covering her mouth with her hand with no way to explain what they had separately experienced.

But in their minds each suspected that somehow in their connection they were touching on something, a capability, seemingly out of the realm of normal human experience. While such an event might have engendered fear in some; Gabby and Michael found comfort in the fact they were back together, whole again. And for a moment, they each thought, maybe there was more to being whole than either had realized before.

Chapter 13

Peter arrived on schedule Friday evening to go over the plan. Gabby and Michael arranged a simple dinner with Michael grilling steaks outside while Gabby concocted a big salad in the kitchen. Peter and Michael visited on the patio drinking beer while Michael kept an eye on the grill. Gabby knew they needed time to bond. The next few days and weeks would prove crucial to her plan and she wanted to surface and resolve any friction early. She couldn't have been more pleased when the two of them came back in the house smiling and laughing.

Without fanfare the back door opened and Michael rolled into the breakfast room from the patio as Peter carried the steaks and utensils in behind him. Gabby smelled the heavy mixture of smoke, garlic and cooked meat almost concealing the odor of beer.

"I knew you would understand," Michael said.

"Well, at least I don't have to live with her."

"Ok, guys, I don't like the sound of this," Gabby inserted, sarcastically.

"I was just saying you can be rather single-minded and demanding when you want to be. It's a compliment; especially under the circumstances," Michael replied innocently.

They sat down at the dinner table, switched to wine, and began discussing the arrangements as Peter laid out his plan for Monday evening. It was the second time Gabby heard it but she found it helpful to go over the details again. Michael asked a number of questions. They all recognized the risk but no one talked about the possibility of failure. Each had their role to play.

Towards the end of the dinner conversation Michael raised his wine glass and looked at the other two who, with a puzzled look, followed suit.

He looked lovingly at his wife, "To Gabby, the best friend I could have ever hoped for, the love of my life, who is willing to put her life on the line for what we have no matter how unlikely the outcome."

Gabby smiled back at him taking his free hand in hers.

"To Peter, whom I just met tonight; we are already becoming fast friends. A great fellow conspirator and without whose technical insight none of this would be possible. And, I hope, a very capable planner of dastardly deeds."

Michael tone shifted briefly becoming more serious. He stared straight ahead looking at no one.

"And to me, may I prove worthy of this gift. And, may it work." He looked lovingly at Gabby. "No offense intended, dear, for I so dearly don't want to leave this life."

Peter stood up, "On that uplifting note, I think I had better leave. It would be best if we didn't contact each other. I'll be back Sunday afternoon for a final run through."

Gabby walked Peter to the door. "Peter, I don't know how I will ever thank you."

"Don't worry about it. Let's just get through the next few days." And with that he walked out into the night.

Over the weekend Gabby and Michael didn't talk much about the conspiracy or what effect the Ulysses Treatment would have on him; instead relishing in each other's company and renewed intimacy. They stayed around the house, for the most part, identifying what they wanted to take with them. Peter had suggested they pack lightly with only a suitcase apiece. Not knowing when or even if they would return, in addition to important documents like their birth certificates and photographs recording better times, each selected a few items they truly valued.

Couples bring to a marriage their family traditions combining them to create new traditions. When they had first started dating, Gabby had made clear she liked receiving greeting cards and so Michael, while never having given them before, became quite creative buying cards which were at times sentimental and at others humorous. He would often write his thoughts inside bringing Gabby alternately to laughter or tears; though at times he would elicit a groan with a particularly silly pun. Gabby had kept all the cards Michael bought for her and several made it into her suitcase along with the movie ticket from their first date. She didn't own a lot of jewelry, but she packed a few sentimental pieces Michael had bought for her along with a rose-colored cameo broach her mother had given which had, in turn, been given to her by her mother.

Michael packed the first tie Gabby ever gave him. She had bought it for their first Valentine's Day. Covered with images of large pink candy hearts saying "Be my Valentine", Michael had been too embarrassed to wear it to work but had, in fact, worn it to bed that night. He packed his MP3 player. Michael used music as a spiritual escape listening to songs which invigorated him, calmed him, or produced fond memories of another time. And, of course, he brought the movie ticket stub from their first date. Finally he packed an old pair of running shoes. When Gabby saw them in the suitcase she asked why he wanted to bring them.

"I'm an optimist", he replied.

On Sunday they spent the day completing preparations. It proved a bittersweet exercise. Despite their struggles the life they began in that home held fond memories. Both Gabby and Michael had the sense they would never return, certainly not in the way they were living now. If the Ulysses Treatment didn't work, Gabby realized she may well be coming home alone; and she knew she couldn't bear to live there without Michael. If the cure was successful they could come back but what if Peter's plan got them into hot water with BDT, the police, or the federal government?

Peter returned for one final run through. It was still light when he left so Gabby packed Michael in the van without telling him where they were going. Before long they arrived at a park not too far from the house. Gabby helped Michael into his wheelchair and they began a stroll down the two mile paved hiking trail.

It was one of those crisp autumn days; a chill in the air augmented by an almost imperceptible breeze. The trees had lost most of their leaves; their naked branches reaching skyward sharply defined against a deep blue sky punctuated by only a few clouds. The sun, dropping toward the horizon, still shone brightly.

As Gabby wheeled Michael along the path she commented, "Isn't this a beautiful day? I thought you might like it here". Gabby and Michael used to come to the park often to picnic and had dreamed of one day bringing a family here.

"You know, people often equate autumn with death," Michael said. "The days get colder and shorter; the leaves fall leaving the trees looking so lifeless."

"Not another one of your puns," groaned Gabby.

"Please allow me some poetic license, it could get verse," he said with mock seriousness. "And you know Shakespeare loved puns. I'm in good company.

"Anyway, as I was saying, I've never seen autumn in that way. To me it's the most exhilarating season of the year. I'm not sure I can say why. I feel more energy, more alive. I sense promise in the air. Thank you for bringing me here."

They walked on, saying little until they got back to the car. The sun just beginning to set cast its rays imparting an orange-red hue on all they touched. The wind blew harder chilling the walkers. As Gabby began preparations to lift Michael into the car he grabbed her arm to stop her.

"One more minute, I want to take it all in."

Gabby's grimace prompted a stern look from Michael.

"No; not for the last time, but to steel myself for what is to come. I don't know, Gabby. I sense something. I should be afraid, but instead, I'm excited and full of energy. Perhaps I'm only convincing myself this will all turn out well but I don't believe that's it. Have you thought any more about our dream?"

Gabby stood shivering in the cold. "No," she shook her head and looked away.

Michael continued, "It's not your dream or my dream. It may have begun that way but now it's our dream. You know I don't believe in fairy tale endings and I know you don't either. You're a scientist first and yet you have been campaigning in the face of apparently insurmountable odds to cure me."

"For every new discovery, we uncover more questions," Gabby began. "Albert Einstein searched for a Theory of Everything to link quantum mechanics with relativity theory in an effort to come up with a unifying view of nature. Scientists have been pursuing that Holy Grail ever since Einstein posited it. String theory is just one example. I believe scientific discovery is largely incremental; scientists individually and in teams study complex systems to uncover one small explanation which helps us better understand our world.

"And yet, from time to time, there are revolutionary breakthroughs. Newton's and Einstein's contributions are but two examples. Do you know what benzene is?"

"I remember little from my organic chemistry days. That's why you're the doctor and I'm not," Michael admitted.

"For years scientists had been trying to explain how benzene could exist because its structure violated every known chemical law. Friedrich Kekulé, a German chemist, reported having a dream where snakes in a ring were going back and forth, grabbing each other's tails. That led to his discovery of the resonating carbon bond.

"When asked how he came up with the photoelectric effect, for which he won the Nobel Prize in 1905, Albert Einstein is reported to have said, 'I imagined I was an electron and watched what I did.' Some reject these stories as apocryphal, but I'm not so sure. I believe imagination and intuition can play a huge role in the scientific process. But I don't think we understand enough about how they work.

"You may be right, Michael. Maybe there is some intuition, some foresight working here we don't understand. But if I don't understand it, then there isn't much I can do with it. Now I'm freezing, are you ready to go?"

"Sure. Let' go home."

They spent the next day, Monday, completing mundane chores. Michael explained to his employer he was taking a few weeks off. Gabby adjusted the temperature in the house and turned off the water heater. She had already arranged for a neighbor to get their mail explaining they were going on vacation. A somber mood of anxious anticipation permeated the house.

Peter arrived on schedule around sundown with pizza for dinner. No one ate, too nervous in expectation of the evening's events and the unknown beyond. They reviewed the plan one more time.

"And you're still not going to tell us where we're going?" Michael asked.

"It's better if I don't divulge too much. I know I'm asking a lot. If I were in your shoes I'd want to know, too. But I can assure you I don't have some nefarious scheme up my sleeve. I want this to succeed, more than you know. Please trust me here."

"Peter, we do. It's . . , well, what if something goes wrong? How will we fix it? I'm thinking we'll be more prepared if we know everything," said Gabby with Michael nodding in agreement.

"You'll find I have it all well thought out, more than you might imagine. We'll be okay."

Peter looked at his watch. "It's 8:00. We'd better get going."

Peter and Gabby carried the suitcases and put them in Michael's van. He backed out of the driveway as Gabby and Peter left for BioDigiTech in Peter's car.

Chapter 14

Neither Peter nor Gabby talked during the twenty minute drive to BioDigiTech. Three miles away Peter pulled into a convenience store lot and parked on the side of the building. They both got out of the car. Gabby lay down on the floor in the back seat and Peter covered her with a blanket.

"Are you going to be okay down there?" Peter asked before he closed the car door.

"I'm fine," she replied in a muffled voice. "Let's get this done."

Though he sensed her unease Peter didn't ask Gabby if she was still willing to go forward knowing she had made her decision.

As she rode along on the floor of the car in the dark, Gabby struggled. She knew she was doing the right thing for Michael and for herself. But the certainty of her cause didn't stop her mind from rethinking all her alternatives. It jabbered at her like a monkey telling her she was making a big mistake, there were other solutions, and ultimately she was certain to end up in jail unable to help Michael or worse. Though uncertainty held her like a vise, she had learned many years before to separate her inner struggle from her resolve.

§

While in college Gabby had joined a sorority, one focused more on community service than social events. She had risen through the hierarchy to become one of the leaders in the group when they decided to go through a team building activity. Eleven of the members went out into the woods to go through a number of exercises intended to build mutual reliance. The ropes course, under the direction of an experienced guide, provided those eleven women with the opportunity to redefine their relationships through a number of physical tests requiring teamwork to complete.

However, the final test had been an individual one. The task involved climbing a telephone pole rising twenty-five feet above the field. The object was to climb the rungs hanging from the sides of the pole to ultimately stand on top and then jump to a trapeze about five feet away. There was little risk of injury as each person who attempted the 'pamper pole' was tethered to a safety harness.

Afraid of heights all of her life, Gabby didn't know if she could do it. She watched as two of her sorority sisters climbed before her and jumped with little difficulty. Screwing up her courage she volunteered to go next.

While she climbed with little difficulty, Gabby found herself six inches below the top clutching the wooden pole for dear life, her feet firmly anchored on the top rungs while her arms held on to the pole as if it were her long lost lover.

For ten minutes, ten long minutes, she didn't move. Shouted words of encouragement and support evidenced the success of the team building earlier in the day but they soon died down as her friends realized how deeply Gabby struggled.

All the while, she listened to her mind tell her there was no reason to go further. She could easily climb down and her friends wouldn't criticize her. She worked hard to calm herself but the mental chatter wouldn't stop. To distract herself she looked off into the distance and saw children playing soccer about a mile away.

And then she made a conscious effort to reject the noise in her head and slowly, by sheer force of will, climbed to the top. When she stood up, Gabby looked down at her feet and saw they barely covered the pole. Her knees shook so badly the shaft began to undulate back and forth. Resolved to beat her own limitations, Gabby stared straight ahead with grim determination and jumped for the trapeze. She reached it; her hands slipped, and her spotter slowly lowered her to the ground.

Back on her feet she could scarcely believe how wonderful she felt. The biochemistry major in her knew the adrenaline rushing through her veins fed her feeling of exaltation, but she also knew, deep down, she had conquered a demon using only her will. She held no illusions she would no longer be afraid of heights, but at least she knew how to rise above her fear.

§

Following the rules set down by society was inherent in Gabby's personality, not that she didn't rebel from time to time. But she still felt guilty every time she did, finding comfort in her boundaries. Now as she lay on the floor of the car approaching BDT, she forced herself to calm her nerves recognizing she served a higher purpose than her own needs.

Meanwhile, behind the wheel Peter remained focused on the task at hand replaying his strategy over and over. He pulled to the side of the road before entering the grounds and opened up the laptop sitting on the seat next to him. He punched in a series of codes transmitting instructions to the security system at BDT. Satisfied they were received; he closed the computer and turned onto the driveway heading for the security gate.

It was not unusual for Peter to work late so when they pulled up to the gatehouse, Tom, the evening guard was not surprised to see him. Peter tried to sound nonchalant.

"Hi Tom, how's it going this evening"?

"It's pretty quiet. What brings you back here?'

Peter didn't make a practice of lying; it made him nervous. So on those rare occasions when he found he couldn't tell the entire truth, he would offer a partial truth in hopes of calming his anxiety.

"I stepped out for dinner; just had to get away for a little while." The gate arm raised and Tom went back to watching TV while Peter drove to building E.

Multiple surveillance cameras surveyed the grounds leaving little hidden from security's watchful eye. Peter smiled to himself thinking back to Homer's Odyssey. Here they were, trying to rescue Ulysses under the watchful eye of Polyphemus, the Cyclops.

The security recordings were necessary given the highly secretive nature of many of BDT's projects; not to mention the potential for industrial espionage. The system digitally recorded and retained the images from all the cameras for a month. Several days before, Peter had hacked into the security system and found images he could cause the system to replay and record as new.

He had explained all of this to Gabby and Michael. But, he didn't tell them the security system was among the most sophisticated on the market and he would leave a trail anyone could find, if they were looking. In any event, he reasoned, they were, in all likelihood, safe for tonight.

Peter pulled into the parking space closest to the door with only a few other cars around. At this point they had to hope they didn't run into anyone who recognized Gabby or would wonder why Peter was in Building E.

"We're clear. You can get up now."

As Gabby came out from under the blanket and started to get out of the car, Peter went around to the trunk and removed two insulated canisters. These would be used to maintain the specimens during transport. Peter walked over to the side of the car where Gabby was standing, staring at the building. They were both running on adrenaline now.

"Let's go", he said.

They walked in through the front door and came to a second glass door with a slot for sliding a security badge in order to enter the building. There was no other way. BDT was very strict with its security policies. Employees were instructed to swipe their badges even if the door had been opened by another employee recording every coming and going. Peter had programmed the security system to permit him to enter Building E and to recognize this swipe as if entering his own building. That way, even if Tom were monitoring where he went, he would think Peter entered Building C.

They walked directly to the elevator bank. There was no one else around, the normally bustling halls vacant. As they rode up to the fourth floor, they stared straight ahead; focused only on the task at hand.

Exiting the elevator the two strode quickly down the hall to Gabby's old lab, each carrying a cylinder. As they entered the lab, Gabby felt disoriented, displaced, like she was in a Twilight Zone episode; the one where the hero returns to their town to find surroundings familiar, but no one recognizes them. The lab looked no different than when she left almost one week ago, but pulled up short when she saw Edgar working at his bench. He looked up from his task and stared at them. Gabby looked questioningly at Peter.

Seeming to read her thoughts, Peter said, "It's all right, he's with us."

Gabby stepped forward addressing Edgar. "Is that right?

"I imagine you're surprised," Edgar said. "I've known for a while you were working another project on the side but didn't say anything because I presumed if you wanted me to know, you would have said something. Some time ago you assigned me responsibility for maintaining the specimens. I regularly check the tanks and noticed there were specimens which weren't part of the Achilles project.

"Peter and I knew each other in college. He enlisted my help because, after you left, they put locks on the tanks. I think Bob," the note of condescension in Edgar's voice palpable, "knew you were working on another project and wanted to maintain those specimens for review at a later date."

Edgar walked over to the refrigerated storage tanks and opened them preparing to transfer Gabby's specimens to the transport containers.

As he worked he continued, "I asked Peter what you were working on and he said it was best if I didn't know."

"How is progress on Achilles going?" Gabby asked changing the subject. She couldn't stem her curiosity being more invested in the project than she knew only to have it ripped out of her hands.

Edgar smiled as he worked. "It's slowed way down. There're problems Karen can't seem to get her mind around, and I can't see myself helping the twit. She is getting a lot of pressure from Bob and I suspect she's not getting much sleep. Be careful what you wish for."

"Edgar, I misjudged you. We got off on the wrong foot from the start. I apologize."

Edgar looked back at Gabby. "It's my own fault. I'm not the easiest person to get along with. But you know that".

Gabby smiled to herself.

They transferred the specimens to her containers while Peter stood back and watched. Finished, Gabby and Peter walked toward the door carrying the specimens. Edgar offered a parting comment.

"I said Peter didn't tell me what you were working on, but I can guess. Gabby, I want to wish you good luck. You deserve it."

Looking over her shoulder, Gabby said, "Thank you Edgar, thank you for everything."

Riding down in the elevator, Gabby wanted to believe the worst was over, but she knew she wouldn't feel right until they were off the grounds. The elevator opened on the ground floor and they stepped out to the echoing slap of footsteps coming toward them. The consequences would not be pleasant for either of them to be seen here, but Gabby posed the greatest risk. Thinking quickly, Peter pushed Gabby behind a column and gave her his tank.

He then turned and walked toward the sound. Peering cautiously around the corner, Gabby saw Peter talking to a security guard. He maneuvered the guard so her back was facing Gabby. She caught snippets of the conversation.

"Peter, I'm surprised to see you here. What are you up to?" The guard didn't sound concerned. In fact, Gabby sensed from her tone of voice she was flirting with Peter.

"Do you know Edgar up on four? He knew I was going out to dinner and asked me to get him something to eat before I went back to my office. It's been a while. What've you been up to?"

Gabby saw her chance and quietly left the building, knelt down next to the car and waited. It was five minutes before Peter arrived. When he got there he motioned for her to stay hidden, but after a minute, opened the back door for her to slide in with the canisters. She lay back down on the floor holding them closely.

Before Peter started the engine Gabby heard him make a call on his cell phone asking Edgar to back him up on the meal story. Peter put the phone away, pulled out of the space and headed for Building C. Gabby pulled the blanket over her making sure she and the canisters were well covered.

Once he arrived at his building Peter entered and rode the elevator up to his lab. Having told the guard he was returning to his lab, Peter needed to validate his cover story. Gabby remained on the floor of the car patiently awaiting his return. She clutched the canisters closely to her as if they were her children.

After about 20 minutes, Gabby heard the car door open and Peter drove back toward the security gate. He lowered the window and Tom waved him through. Peter drove to the same convenience store and Gabby climbed out of the back seat and got in front leaving the canisters on the floor in the back.

As they pulled away Gabby asked, "Okay, what was that about?"

"What do you mean?" Peter asked innocently.

"I think you know: the security guard. It sounded to me like she was flirting with you."

"She's been coming on to me for a long time now. I've been friendly to her in the past but I didn't want to encourage her.

She works evenings here while going to school for her Master's in psychology."

"Why haven't you gone out with her? I've seen her before and she's pretty cute."

"I asked her for a date Friday night as a cover, but now I'm feeling badly since we won't be here."

"And just where will we be?"

"Remember no more questions, you will find out soon enough." Peter pulled into the parking lot of a nearby grocery story and parked next to Michael's idling van. They stepped out of Peter's car and transferred the canisters. After Gabby and Peter climbed in Peter instructed Michael to drive to the airport.

"If we fly away somewhere and they discover we left, won't they be able to track us, or do you also have fake ID?" Gabby asked sarcastically.

"Don't worry, I have everything arranged," Peter replied.

"How'd it go?" Michael asked.

"I don't think anyone saw us", Gabby replied.

Before they entered the highway, Michael pulled off on to the shoulder.

"Are you OK"? Gabby asked.

"I'd feel better if one of you drove."

They helped Michael into the passenger seat and Peter got in on the driver's side. Gabby looked Michael over, worried about him.

In response to her unspoken question Michael replied, "I'm fine, feeling a little weak. It's probably all this excitement. It'll pass."

Gabby reached forward and took Michael's wrist. His pulse felt strong enough but raced faster than she would have liked.

Peter pulled back on to the road and soon entered the highway. Ten minutes later they took the exit to the airport.

They bypassed the entrance to the parking lot, but Gabby wasn't surprised. She figured Peter would drop them off at the terminal with the luggage, park, and come back to join them. But Peter breezed past the terminal entrance. Michael looked back at Gabby but said nothing. After passing the main terminal Peter turned right on a side road and headed for the private air terminal.

Rather than pull up to the entrance, Peter drove around to a gate manned by a security guard. The guard didn't ask for ID and waved the van in. Peter drove on the tarmac directly to a waiting private jet. The non-descript white aircraft had its rear passenger stairs down and appeared to be waiting for them. Peter pulled up next to the stairs and began to unload the luggage.

As Peter carried their suitcases on to the airplane, Michael turned around and asked, "What do you think?"

"I'm not sure what to think. I assumed we were going to drive off to some secret location but I guess I shouldn't be surprised. If he has the kind of resources to equip a lab there's no reason he couldn't charter a jet. And, it makes sense. It'll be harder to track us."

While they sat waiting Gabby continued, "Now that I think about it I'm glad we won't have to sit in the van for a long, uncomfortable ride. You'll just get cranky. Are you feeling OK?"

"Yeah, the weakness passed."

Peter came over to the passenger side which he had pulled next to the stairway and opened the van door. Gabby got out on the opposite side while Peter helped Michael up the stairs and into the jet.

The evening felt unseasonably warm. Gabby stood on the tarmac looking at the sky; white fluffy clouds, illuminated by the airport lights, rushed quickly across a pitch black sky as if they had somewhere to go. *This is really happening,* she thought. *We're making a clean break; jumping off to God knows where. Well, I'm ready.* She turned to the plane as Peter called out her name.

"Gabby, come on, we have to go."

She walked deliberately to the waiting aircraft and up the stairs into the comfortably furnished cabin. Peter stood next to her raising the stairs as she heard the jet engines rev. The seats were arranged facing each other four across with an aisle in the middle. Michael was seated with his back to her in one of the blonde leather seats; standing near the open cockpit door stood Jules Allen.

"Dr. Neumann, it's good to see you again. You had better take a seat, we are about to take off."

Chapter 15

"No," Gabby was adamant, refusing to budge. "We have been going along with Peter, trusting him. But I need to know what's coming next. I don't mean to offend you, but how can I trust you? Your interests lie with Arthur Paulson and BioDigiTech."

"We've both been patient", Michael added, glancing back at Gabby. "We need to know what your intentions are or we're getting off right now"

Jules Allen looked directly at Gabby when he spoke, a slight smile creasing his face.

"No offense taken. And you both deserve to know where we're going and what I have planned. However, before you jump to conclusions, don't presume to know what motivates me or where my interests lie."

Peter walked forward from the rear of the plane and came face to face with her.

"Gabby, the secrecy was necessary 'cause I thought it would be better to explain in person. We can trust Jules."

Gabby, concerned she was being betrayed and knowing now this was her last hope, asked Peter accusingly, "How do you know?"

"Do you remember, I told you my parents died when I was young and how I was raised by my uncle? This is uncle Jules. He has his reasons for helping us and will explain everything shortly. But can we get in the air before we continue? I know I'll feel better the farther we are from BDT."

In response Gabby grudgingly sat down next to Michael and buckled in. Jules instructed the pilot to depart and sat down next to Peter as the plane taxied to the runway and took off.

Jules asked Peter to get everyone something to drink after they were airborne. Once Peter sat down Jules explained, "We are flying to northern Wisconsin. Have you ever been there?" Gabby and Michael shook their heads. "Magnificent country. The winters are harsh and the summers short."

"And the mosquitoes are so big they take a pint of blood in one gulp, but we don't have to worry about them this time of year", Peter interjected attempting to lighten the mood.

Jules continued, ignoring Peter's comment, "The area has been a haven for vacationers for over a hundred years. Dwight Eisenhower regularly traveled there to fish and play golf. Years ago I purchased a piece of lake front property and built a vacation home. It's secluded and private, a comfortable retreat and the perfect place for us."

"I wondered when we got in the plane, if we were leaving the country in the event we were followed. Do you think we'll be safe there?" Michael asked.

"Arthur will find us if he so chooses whether it's among the pine trees of the great Northwoods or the jungles of Borneo. I only want to put enough time and distance between us so by the time he does find us it's too late for him to do anything about it."

"Gabby and I are doing this because we have no choice", Michael explained. "I'm still trying to understand why Peter is taking the risk. I imagine a man with your money and power probably figures he can get away with almost anything. You may not see much risk to yourself or your nephew, but what *is* your interest here?"

"Peter came to me taken with your plight, Michael. We rarely talk about what happens at BDT; agreeing a long time ago to keep our professional and personal lives separate but this time we made an exception. I suspect he was moved both by the intellectual challenge and Gabby's persuasive manner."

Gabby interrupted. "I think you're mistaken, Jules. I never tried to persuade Peter. He came along of his own volition."

"You underestimate yourself, Gabby. I came along on my own, but you were very effective in making your case."

"Peter didn't tell me anything until you were let go last week," Jules continued. "He came to me and explained the whole situation. He wanted to know if I could do anything to get Gabby's job back. I told him I couldn't intervene but perhaps I could help in another way. He didn't give me much time but I think you will find we have a more than adequate lab set up for you."

"But you haven't told us why", Michael persisted, "why are you doing this? I find it hard to believe with what is at stake for you here, from a legal standpoint, and with everything else you must have going on, you would get involved."

"There are several reasons. First, like you, Gabby, Peter can be persuasive. And I have come to respect his intelligence and his insight."

Jules smiled fondly at Peter. Gabby and Michael found themselves liking this man despite their uneasiness and despite what they knew of his reputation.

"Second, I have a natural curiosity. The problem, as Peter described it, fascinates me." Jules looked at Michael, leaning forward in his seat, "Don't get me wrong, I'm not objectifying you. You aren't some inanimate object I want to experiment on. I can only imagine what you have been through," then looking at Gabby, "what you've both been through. At the same time you could, in truth, do some good here. Assuming you're successful, think of what this can mean for others suffering from brain damage.

"For both of your sakes, I hope the treatment works, but beyond your immediate problem, Gabby, this could provide hope for sufferers in every corner of the world. I have achieved financial success. But, this may be one way to give back, to make the world a better place.

"I don't know if you read Samsa's latest series," Michael and Gabby nodded, "but I refuse to accept his assertion that we're wired for our own destruction. I know he is immensely influential and popular, but I take exception to his negative view of humanity."

"You've been insulated by your wealth," Michael contested. "Look at history. Have we become any more civilized in the last five thousand years? I understand your idealism. Life is easier when you believe in a higher calling, a higher destiny, or even a higher power. But I think that same belief causes many to avoid dealing with the problems of today. We don't have to take responsibility for what we do in the here and now. Religion and politics reek with the hypocrisy of saying one thing but doing another."

Gabby shot Michael a withering look.

Jules, sensing Gabby's unease, continued, "I don't necessarily disagree with you Michael. We are a brutal species. But I can't help but hope we can achieve more noble aims. We have the capability for compassion. Perhaps there is a way to encourage or unleash it. There are wonderful acts of charity everyday which go unnoticed. I believe deep within us, sometimes very deep, burns the desire to do the right for ourselves and each other. I'd like to think Samsa will explore the potential for good in his next blog. Hope is a good thing."

Relieved Jules was trying to cut off the argument, Gabby was shocked when Michael continued but she was not at all prepared for what came next.

Michael looked Jules in the eye and smiled.

"You know Jules, you may be right. There may be other potentials within us. And given the events of the past few days, well, perhaps there is reason for hope. Maybe that's what I'll blog about next."

Politics bored Peter who was only half listening to the conversation. But he didn't miss that last statement. He looked at Michael and grinned.

Gabby turned violently in her seat gaping at Michael. All she could utter was a befuddled "What?"

As she regained her composure, Jules, leaned back and laughed. "Tell me Michael, why do you use a pseudonym?"

"I began posting as a diversion. There I was, stuck at home, with little outside contact. At least in this way I had the opportunity to put my ideas out there and get some reaction rather than just editing someone else's work. I figured no one would take a wheelchair bound journal editor seriously. I care deeply about what I write and didn't want to be sloughed off. Over time the anonymity added mystique and contributed to the reasons it's so widely read."

"It's amazing to me how people study and react to it," Peter said. "It's never been promoted except by word of mouth; but ever since the Magwe Incident even the newspapers and the cable news networks react to what you are saying, in effect elevating your influence. The more cynical have suggested you pick topics solely to get a rise out of people. But I think it is widely read because you're tapping into frustrations and anxieties most of us hold."

"But the name you chose, that was no accident," Jules observed.

"What do you mean?" asked Gabby.

Michael turned to her. "Gregor Samsa was the protagonist in Franz Kafka's *Metamorphosis*. I tried to get you to read it several times.

"Samsa wakes up one morning as an insect. His family is horrified but, more or less, puts up with him. Over time he becomes ill and eventually succumbs. At one point his sister explains that Gregor is no longer Gregor but truly an insect because if he were still himself, he would have left them out of love and lightened their burden. His family, relieved when he's finally gone, has learned to fend without him and is better off for it. Sound familiar?"

"Why didn't you tell me?"

"I wasn't trying to keep the truth from you but I needed an outlet that was my own. After the accident, I felt like I wasn't the same person I was before. I needed some way to define who I was beyond our marriage or work. I needed to create a new history, add another dimension for one which was taken away. Are you hurt?"

Gabby reached over, squeezed Michael's hand and smiled. "No, I'm fine, and more than a little impressed."

Jules jumped in, "Well, we've had a few revelations here tonight. Michael, it appears we have a real celebrity in our midst. And, Gabby, it looks like he's good at keeping secrets from you."

Everyone laughed, including Gabby who had been so good at keeping secrets from Michael.

"We have quite a little cabal, don't you think?" Jules observed. "Sitting right here we have someone who will prove to be one of the world's foremost medical researchers, a recognized up and coming computer scientist, and the voice of humanity."

"You've done pretty well for yourself, too," Michael added. Everyone but Jules laughed.

"We have a very real opportunity here," Jules continued, soberly. "It may seem inconsequential, the four of us sitting around, talking. But there is so much we can accomplish if we set our minds to it. Once we get through the next few weeks, I believe it will be worth our while to plan beyond our rehabilitation project for Michael."

Gabby found herself taken by Jules. She began to understand why he was so successful. Perhaps he was right. There were things the four of them could do together to make the world a better place. But what Jules said next brought her out of her reverie.

"It makes you wonder doesn't it? How the four of us came together? Doesn't it make you wonder about destiny, Michael, despite your cynicism?"

"I hate to sound like a broken record, but research has shown we're wired to see coincidences as more than random occurrences as if something was 'meant to be'. It's like the déjà vu experience. We want to ascribe a psychic cause to a neurological phenomenon. Neurosurgeons have stimulated nerve cells during surgery which, in fact, give the patient the same experience. It's a biological phenomenon."

"Maybe," Jules said thoughtfully, "but who's to say what our biology is capable of. I imagine you're familiar with research on the mind body relationship. For example, there is unambiguous scientific evidence of a connection between the brain and the immune system. We understand people who lack sleep or who are depressed have a less than adequate immune response."

Jules paused as if deciding what to say next.

"Which brings me back to your original question; there is another reason I am here. You may laugh at me especially in light of what we have been talking about. You may already think of me as an eccentric nut case.

"Last week I committed to Peter I would help because it was the right thing to do. You had run out of options. But something else happened, like icing on the cake. I didn't make much of it at the time but seeing you tonight has changed my mind.

"Last week, I believe it was Wednesday night, I had a dream."

Michael sat frozen, suspecting what was coming next.

"In the dream I was walking through a wooded area and came up to the side of a rural road. I could see a car accident."

Gabby found herself unable to shake a growing sense of foreboding.

"I didn't go to it; but instead hid behind a tree. I saw a woman. At first, I didn't know who it was, but then I recognized you, Gabby, running headlong to the wreck. I looked to the car and saw a man in the driver's seat, someone I'd never seen before, until tonight. It was you Michael."

Gabby looked at Michael and he nodded, almost imperceptibly. She turned to Jules and Peter. "For several years now, Michael's been having a vivid, recurring dream in which he relives the accident. A few months ago, I began having a dream where he calls out to me and I'm trying to find him. Michael had told me about his dream, but I'd said nothing

149

about mine. I assumed we were both working through our issues with the accident and our marriage."

Gabby paused as if trying to make sense of what she was saying.

"But Wednesday night, we not only had the same dream, the same one you described Jules, but we saw each other in the dream. And now you tell us you were there, too."

Before Jules could respond the pilot came on the loudspeaker and announced, "We are preparing to land. Please fasten your seatbelts."

"You know, I'm feeling a little left out here," Peter said with mock hurt.

Jules smiled but in a serious voice responded, "Peter, I find it hard to believe you will be left out. I don't think any of us is here by chance," as the airplane lightly touched down on the runway.

Chapter 16

After taxiing to the private field terminal, the jet parked and the copilot opened the door inviting a rush of cold air. They hurried to a waiting car which had been pulled up next to the jet. Peter again helped Michael down the stairs and into the car as best they could. Gabby noticed Michael couldn't assist very well. It was clear to her his condition was deteriorating. They had arrived none too soon.

Jules and Peter transferred the luggage to the trunk of the car while Gabby and Michael sat in the back seat out of the cold.

Peter offered to drive and Jules didn't object taking a seat on the passenger side. No one said much as they pulled out of the airport property and turned north on the highway. In no time they found themselves alone on a dark four-lane divided road cutting through the forest like a machete; dark ahead and behind with only the sound of the car's engine and the glare of its headlights disturbing the dead calm around them.

After about fifteen minutes they turned on to a two lane road and drove for another ten minutes and then turned right on narrow asphalt drive. A small sign near the entrance warned: Private Drive, Trespassers will be Prosecuted. Here the trees were so close to the road Gabby felt as if she could reach out and touch them. But that was all she could see, the darkness enveloping her.

They rode about a quarter of a mile and turned, as the road did, to the left and were almost blinded as a garage door opened, its beacon beckoning the car like a flame to a moth. After Peter pulled into the garage, Jules got out of the car, walked to the console on the wall and input a code disabling the security system.

A wheelchair sat waiting for Michael and they entered through the mudroom into the warm, well-lit house.

"I usually keep it cool when I'm not here but fortunately the house systems can be activated remotely," Jules explained to the unasked question. "I had the refrigerator stocked so we shouldn't need to go anywhere for a while if we don't need to. It's late and I imagine everyone should be ready to turn in."

"I'm tired but I need to get these specimens to the lab. Can you show me where it is?" Gabby asked. "I want to start early tomorrow."

"Peter, I'll show Gabby the lab. Would you please help Michael to their room?"

Peter, carrying Gabby and Michael's luggage guided Michael further into the house while Jules, carrying one of the specimen containers, took Gabby's elbow as she held the other container and led her to a stairway in the mudroom.

As they stepped down the finished wooden staircase to the basement Jules explained, "When I first built this place eleven years ago, I assembled a computer lab in the basement. I have cordoned a section off for your use."

The basement had space for a water heater, furnace, and limited storage but most of the floor space was taken up by a computer and electronics laboratory almost as large as the footprint of the house.

"This is remarkable," Gabby marveled. "It looks as well equipped as Peter's lab at BDT."

As Gabby surveyed her surroundings she saw several benches with electronic tools and equipment. On the tables sat multiple PC's and along one wall stood rows of servers protectively encased against water incursion.

"All you're missing is a clean room."

"I like to come down and putter from time to time and Peter, when he's here, can carry on his research. Here, let me take you back to your area."

Gabby wondered what "puttering" meant to Jules Allen. He led Gabby through the maze of workbenches and electronic equipment to an area in the back of the basement. Now in familiar territory, she recognized the setup.

"I hope you find all this acceptable to your needs. I understand Peter worked with one of your lab assistants to get it right."

Gabby walked over to a refrigerated storage tank and inserted the specimens. The tank was smaller than the one she used at BDT but adequate to the task. She looked around making mental notes for where to start in the morning.

"This should work out just fine and unless I'm mistaken and barring any unforeseen problems, we will be ready to go in about a week at the latest. Now I need to get some rest."

Carrying the luggage, Peter walked ahead with Michael in tow and led the way through a large, well-equipped kitchen and into the entry vestibule. From there they entered a hallway leading to the bedrooms. Michael caught a glimpse of the great room, its far wall held a picture window looking on to a wooden deck and then black nothingness.

"It's so dark out there, I feel like we're on spaceship in the midst of the void", Michael remarked.

Walking down the hall, Peter responded over his shoulder, "It's fairly secluded out here, but I think you'll like it when you see it in the light of day."

They entered one of the bedrooms; Peter put the suitcases down and showed Michael where the towels were located. The furnishings struck Michael, not as opulent, but as providing durable, high-quality comfort; and nicer than any hotel he had stayed in.

Gabby walked in as Peter was leaving. "Don't bother with a tip," Peter joked, "we'll settle up at the end of your stay."

"This is quite a place," Gabby said as she climbed into bed.

"How does the lab look?" Michael asked as he lay beside her.

"As good as I could have hoped. I'll have to rearrange a few things, but should be ready to go in the morning. Do you like this place?"

"It's nice", Michael responded distractedly.

"Are you feeling all right? Gabby got up on one elbow and looked down at her husband.

"I'm okay. I just don't feel like myself. I'm tired. It's probably just the travel and the excitement of the past several days."

Gabby continued gazing at him, looking for signs of distress but, seeing nothing obvious kissed him and then twisted to reach over and turn off the end table lamp.

She lay there for a long time, wondering. The day of reckoning would soon be upon her and Gabby didn't know if she was ready.

She would be prepared to administer the Ulysses Treatment. That wasn't the issue. But she couldn't help wondering if it would work as planned. *Am I trying to play God?* she thought. *Maybe I'm not being fair to him. What if there is some horrible side effect? It's not as though I haven't thought of these things before. The inevitable is becoming all too real.*

She lay there for what seemed like an eternity running through scenarios in her mind before she finally fell fast asleep.

Gabby woke, glanced at the clock and noticed it was after 8:30. She looked over at Michael, still asleep. He was breathing regularly but looked pale. She climbed out of bed and walked over to the dresser where she had unpacked her things and took a change of clothes into the bathroom where she showered and got dressed. When she came out, Michael was still asleep.

She went over to the bed and gently tried to rouse him.

"Good morning, how are you feeling?" Michael took a minute to take stock.

"Better than last night but I'm feeling weak. I think I'll stay right here for a while."

"I'll go to the kitchen and see if I can't find something for you. You need to eat."

Gabby left the bedroom and headed toward where she remembered the kitchen had been. She found Peter and Jules preparing breakfast.

"Good morning," Peter said.

"Good morning," Gabby replied with a half smile.

"I hope you slept well. How's Michael?" Jules asked.

"I slept very soundly once I got to sleep. Michael isn't feeling well so I thought I would try and find something for him to eat and then get started in the lab."

Jules said, "I'll fix breakfast for the two of you. Once you've eaten, I'll keep Michael company. It's a beautiful day. Maybe he'll want to go outside."

While Gabby worked in the lab with Peter assisting, Jules ventured down to Michael's room. He found him sitting up in bed and reading.

"Are you feeling better?" Jules inquired.

"Yes, thanks for asking and thanks for breakfast. I was hungrier than I thought. What's on the docket for today?"

"It's a beautiful morning. I thought you might like to go outside and see the grounds."

"That'd be a nice distraction. Let me get dressed and I'll call for you to help get me in my chair when I'm ready."

After a few minutes Michael called for Jules. He went into the room and helped Michael into his wheelchair.

"In addition to outfitting the lab I had a couple of ramps installed to help accommodate you but I'm afraid I can't do much about the ground."

"That's OK. It'll be nice to get outside."

Jules walked alongside Michael as he wheeled into the great room.

"What a magnificent view. We couldn't see much when we got here last night."

The floor to ceiling windows offered a striking vista. The house sat on a small bluff with a southern exposure overlooking a small lake; the shoreline dotted with boat houses and homes which would have been concealed among the trees in the summer.

"Would it be all right if I pushed?" Jules proposed. "The ground is hard and you might find it easier."

"No problem."

Jules Allen's property sat on ten acres of undeveloped woodland. Being much further north, the leaves had already fallen leaving only the green of the pine trees to punctuate the dormant forest. The moist, cool air smelled of rotting leaves and mushrooms. The sun shone uncommonly bright in a cloudless blue sky; the air cold enough they could see the moisture in their breaths. Jules pushed Michael's chair down a gradual incline to a boathouse along a dock on the lake.

"Do you have other properties like this?" Michael asked.

"A few; I have a cabin in the mountains in Montana and one in the Caribbean on a small island you've probably never heard of. I enjoy coming here for the fishing and golf. I used to travel here more often in the winter. The area is great for ice fishing, cross country skiing, and snowmobiling. But I don't enjoy the cold as much anymore."

"Why did you choose this one for our hideout?"

"It has the best facilities to support a lab. Would you have preferred somewhere else?"

They were headed up to the house now. Jules couldn't see Michael's smile when he responded, "a little beach time would have been nice."

Jules parked Michael's chair on the wooden deck surrounding the back side of the house and took a seat next to him. "Are you up to sitting out here a little longer? I know it's cold but it's such a beautiful day."

Michael nodded and Jules continued, "I hope I'm not speaking out of turn but I really admire what you're doing here. Your courage and faith inspire me."

With a furrowed brow, Michael asked, "I'm not sure I get what you mean. My greatest fear is to be trapped in this body unable to move and unable to be productive. I see the Ulysses treatment as my only alternative. If you're being pursued by a pack of wolves, it doesn't take much courage or faith to jump off a cliff."

"Oh, I disagree." Jules leaned toward Michael. "I believe most people, when confronted with either having to change their situation or accept the consequences and hope for the best usually choose the latter. I don't know if it's fear of the unknown or comfort with the predictable.

"Probably some of both, I imagine," Michael offered. "But I don't understand your comment about faith. Are you talking about religious faith, a faith in God?"

"I get the sense from your blogs you are not a religious man", Jules noted.

"That's fair. To tell you the truth, I would like to believe in God but not the one made in man's image; a human-like creature with likes and dislikes and not terribly different from the gods of the pagans.

"If he exists, I think it's a little more transcendent. We have incontrovertible evidence life on earth and man are far older than the scriptures tell us. And yet people continue to believe the earth is only a few thousand years old. We rely on ancient stories borrowed from even more ancient cultures.

"I believe mankind's idea of God has evolved as has mine over the course of my life. We began with cultures assigning personalities to the forces of nature, a way to assume some control over the uncontrollable. Over time those deities became consolidated into one. In fact, reading the early Hebrew Scriptures one comes away with a henotheistic concept where there are multiple gods, with one superior to all the others. It wasn't until the end of the Babylonian captivity when Judaism, the harbinger of both Christianity and Islam, became truly monotheistic.

"Later in the western tradition, whether in concert or on parallel paths both Greek philosophy through Plato and Plotinus and the new Christian religion further altered the concept of the one God. Although one could argue Christianity is henotheistic since many pray to saints and recognize angels and demons; not really gods but a more modern idea of other spirits involved in the world."

"I subscribe to a view popular during the Enlightenment, similar to one shared by many of our founding fathers, taking the position we see God's work in the forces of nature not in miracles or revelation.

"But that's neither here nor there. If you are talking about courage and faith, Gabby is your person. On this trip I feel like I'm along for the ride while Gabby steers the boat."

"Then how do you explain the Dream?" Jules asked.

"I have to confess, it's a real mystery to me. I want to believe it's merely coincidence, but my rational mind rejects that explanation. I had almost reconciled myself to the fact that Gabby and I are just very close, but with your revelation last night, well, I'm starting to wonder. The odd thing is: it's starting to give me hope and I can't put into words why. I don't believe in what some call 'signs' and yet there is a connection here we can't explain."

Chapter 17

At that moment, Peter opened the door, stepped on to the porch, and announced lunch was ready. Over sandwiches Gabby reported she was making real progress in the lab and had every expectation they would be ready to go as early as Friday. All of the specimens had transferred intact and she was preparing the retrovirus for infusion. Peter complained she was working him too hard, but received no sympathy.

After the four of them finished lunch Gabby led them back to one of the spare bedrooms. She opened the door to what now looked like a well-equipped hospital room.

"Things are going well downstairs and so when I am between tasks, I have been setting up Michael's treatment room."

A hospital bed occupied the center of the room but the equipment surrounding it drew everyone's attention.

"What's all of this for, Gabby?" Jules asked.

"I imagine Michael recognizes most of this from his hospital management days. A few of the items, like the ventilator and defibrillator sitting over there in the corner will only be necessary if Michael stops breathing or his heart stops beating. By the way Jules, I'm impressed you could get all of this together so quickly."

"Most of its borrowed from a local hospital," Jules replied. "I've given them a lot of support in the past. I told them I had a sick friend and his physician coming up and asked to borrow these things for a few days."

"What's with all this monitoring equipment?" Peter asked.

Pointing to the night stand next to the bed, Gabby responded, "That's a heart monitor and a pulse oximeter to measure how well Michael's blood will be carrying oxygen. It will also be used to take his blood pressure. Next to that on a separate table is an EEG machine to track his brain activity.

"Michael, we haven't talked about this yet, but I am going to put you in a coma for the treatment. I don't know what the immediate effect will be when I introduce the virus and so I want to minimize brain activity and then slowly pull you out."

Looking at Peter and Jules she continued, "We will have to monitor him 24 hours a day until he wakes up and then regularly thereafter. Consider yourselves my assistants. I will train you once Michael is unconscious so you can see how everything works. Do you think you can do that?"

Jules and Peter both nodded.

"How long do you think I will be unconscious?" Michael asked.

"It's hard to tell," Gabby began. "I have plenty of experience with mice but I want err on the side of caution for obvious reasons. I'll be watching your brain activity on the EEG and use the tracings to guide what I do next. It could be a couple of days or more, I just don't know."

They didn't talk about the possibility Michael might never wake up.

The rest of the day passed uneventfully. Michael, tired and weak, went to the bedroom to rest while Jules went to work in the study and Peter and Gabby went back to the lab. They ate dinner together at seven and Michael retired shortly thereafter.

Peter excused himself to go putter in the electronics lab leaving Gabby and Jules alone in the living room.

Gabby nursed a glass of wine while Jules sipped at a cup of decaffeinated coffee.

"You're not what I expected," Gabby began.

"What do you mean?"

"Well, to be honest, you have this reputation as a ruthless corporate mogul. Not the same as Arthur's but intimidating nonetheless. But that's not the Jules Allen I met last night."

"I would attribute my reputation to missteps early in my career. And, I suspect anyone with as much money and power as I've been able to accumulate finds themselves in the position where others may be harmed, even indirectly. And then there's the jealousy factor."

"Have you ever been married, Jules?" Gabby asked.

"Once, a long time ago. I dated Vicki in college and we were married shortly after graduation. I was the business and computer science nerd, she held a double major in psychology and political science.

"She wanted to change the world. It was the 70's and we were all tainted by the Vietnam War and Watergate. I was the outgoing type, she the policy nerd. There were some who didn't understand why we were together, but our close friends knew. We were soul mates. She was very challenging to live with; she had high standards for herself and everyone she came in contact with. But we were all the better for it. She saw the best in me and never let me get away with less.

"We had been married ten years and she was on track to be elected to the state legislature when she was diagnosed with ovarian cancer. There was nothing they could do for her and I lost her within a year.

"Until that point I had led a charmed life. As a child and teenager I never wanted for anything. I excelled in school and on the athletic field. On top of that I was popular. I had it all. Aware of my blessings I didn't think I took my good luck for granted until I lost Vicki. When I lost her, I lost my whole world."

"I'm so sorry," Gabby replied. "You never had children?"

"Initially we were so busy with our careers we thought we didn't have time and then she got sick and we never had time."

Jules paused and resumed speaking after a couple of minutes; Gabby reluctant to interrupt his reverie.

"At that point I had achieved considerable financial success. I realized, to honor her memory, I should get invested in interests beyond my work. I became active in causes which had been important to her: the environment, human rights among others. Her death changed my perspective on what is important in life.

"Anyway, Vicki had an older brother who was a small airplane enthusiast. Shortly after she died, he and his wife had gone out flying, the weather turned nasty and the plane was lost. I adopted Peter, and, well, you know the rest. I've tried to treat him like a son, but with all my distractions I'm afraid I wasn't the father I should have been."

"He turned out very well, Jules. You have nothing to apologize for."

"Thank you. I've been pleased with what he's accomplished. When he brought me your problem, it was evident you and Michael were very important to him. At first, I wondered whether this was some mad scientist scheme, but that's clearly not the case."

"I wouldn't be so sure," Gabby admitted. "I know the science is right, but I'm worried something will go horribly wrong."

"Then why are you doing this?" Jules challenged.

"Because it's my only hope."

Forcefully as if she had practiced this speech in the event she would be called before the state medical board Gabby said, "I was trained to be deliberate, to carefully test hypotheses, and to only go as fast as I was comfortable; and never to risk a human life. You know the provision in the Hippocratic Oath against doing harm? The problem is: I can't be objective. But I've convinced myself I'm not risking Michael's life. I know this is the only possible solution and in doing so I am keeping the good of my patient as the highest priority, as I am bound by my Oath to do."

"Do you know who Paul Ehrlich was?" Jules asked.

"I believe I've heard the name. Wasn't he the physician who discovered one of the early cures for syphilis, before we had conventional antibiotics?"

"You're right. In fact, he was one of the most prolific and successful medical researchers in the latter part of the 19th and early 20th century. He won the Nobel Prize in Medicine in 1908. In addition to a cure for syphilis he was the first to describe the blood-brain barrier.

"There's a story, it's probably a fabrication, but earlier in his career he developed a treatment for diphtheria and tested it without permission on a ward of dying children. He was roundly criticized and almost lost his appointment except for the fact the grandchild of the hospital's chief physician was a patient on the ward at the time.

"I believe it's passion for understanding our world and making it a better place which marks real scientific advancement. People confuse objectivity with a lack of passion. Any human endeavor whether in science, business, or politics should be guided by objective analysis in the service of passion. Vicki taught me that.

"Science has grown more through leaps of insight or intuition than plodding analysis. Look at Galileo, Newton, or Einstein. It's the mad scientists of the world who move us forward, or at least the ones called mad because they break with convention. It's your passion, and Peter's, which led me to believe in what you're doing here. I have never seen him so taken with a project that wasn't initially his own."

"You've given this a lot of consideration, haven't you?"

"In my leisure time, not that there's much of it, I have studied the history and philosophy of science; subjects I was barely exposed to in school. I guess you could call it a hobby."

"Well, I hope you're right. Now I need to get down to the lab one more time before I go to bed. See you in the morning."

"Before you go," Jules paused considering if he should ask his question, "Did you and Michael ever plan on having children?"

A wan smile crossed Gabby's face. "We really wanted them. I had a miscarriage shortly before Michael's accident. I haven't allowed myself to think of the possibility for years."

"You would make great parents. Have a good night."

It wasn't. Michael did not sleep well. His blood pressure was erratic but Gabby had brought medications with her which helped to stabilize him.

Wednesday and Thursday passed largely uneventfully with Gabby torn between moving as quickly as possible in the lab and keeping an eye on Michael. He maintained relatively good spirits but she could tell time was taking its toll. She wasn't sure how much longer he could hold out or whether she would be ready in time.

Initially, she felt her projection of a week to be optimistic, but working night and day, Gabby made progress faster than expected and by midday on Thursday announced she would be ready to go the next day. With that Jules proclaimed they would hold a celebratory dinner that evening.

Unfortunately, no one felt like having a good time. The stress of the past few days and weeks coupled with the uncertainty of what was to come showed on everyone.

The dinner hardly seemed like a celebration. Little was said during the meal; all four lost in their own thoughts. The somber mood improved when Jules brought out a bottle of Cognac and poured everyone a glass.

"This is very nice," Michael commented.

"I'm glad you appreciate it. It's a Courvoisier and close to two hundred years old. I've been keeping it for a special occasion and this is about as special as I can imagine.

"Now, you are all going to have to forgive me. I have some things I want to, no, need to say." Jules looked thoughtfully down into his snifter and continued,

"I apologize in advance if I offend anyone's sensibilities, but I learned a long time ago I need to make my feelings known or no one will know them. I appreciate being a part of this. Over the past several days I have grown close to Gabby and Michael and believe I am the better for it.

"I know everyone is very tense tonight, myself included, but I sincerely believe we are taking the first step into a realm of new possibilities. Gabby, this treatment you've devised could help so many and in ways I suspect we can't even imagine at this point. You may end up winning the Nobel Prize in Medicine yourself some day."

"Jules, I think you're getting way ahead of yourself here," Gabby replied with a smile. "I have to take this one step at a time. I'm sorry to say this Michael, but I won't be convinced until we see what happens tomorrow. I know we're all hoping for the best, but . . ."

Consumed with emotion Gabby said no more. Michael, reached across the table, took Gabby's balled fist in his hand and squeezed.

"On that upbeat note, I have a request," Michael said. A half smile crossed Gabby's face as she looked into Michael's eyes.

"Gabby and I have spoken briefly about this, but I need everyone's agreement. If things don't go well tomorrow, I need all three of you to agree you will pull the plug. If it's clear I won't regain consciousness or something worse happens, you won't hesitate to do what I ask." Michael looked at everyone and in turn each nodded their assent.

And then Michael looked into Gabby's eyes and smiled. And with that smile Gabby felt as though she had been struck by a thunderbolt. Instead of the exhausted, troubled person of the past few days, looking into his eyes she saw a man infused with energy and determination.

"Despite what I asked of each of you just now, I am convinced the Ulysses Treatment will work. Make no mistake, I am very nervous, my heart is beating like a trip hammer. But I don't know if it's due to fear of the unknown or uncertain knowledge of what's to come. Earlier, as I slept I had another dream."

No one said a word. A few days ago, no one present would have paid attention to what came next and now Gabby, Jules, and Peter sat riveted.

167

Michael continued. "Early in our marriage, I shared my dreams with Gabby. She thought they were pretty strange on most occasions and I can't say I blame her. And I came to enjoy telling her about them if only to get a reaction. This dream wasn't a dream of the accident. It was entirely different but vivid in the same fashion as our shared dream. I don't know that I should get into the details right now except to say I believe I saw a very interesting future here for all of us.

Peter, looking at Michael asked, "Is there a reason you're not telling us?"

"I'm not entirely sure what to think and since it appears no one else experienced it, I think it best to keep to myself for now."

"At least I'm not the only one left out of this one," Peter said.

"Peter, don't say that," Jules said. "In many ways, you were the one who set these events in motion. While this may have begun as a scientific adventure for you, you passed beyond that role months ago. You may be my nephew by relation, but are truly my son in fact and I couldn't be prouder of you."

"Thanks, Uncle Jules. I think you know how much it means to me. I'm usually the guy who plays fast and loose with authority and I hate to bring this up, but since Michael is so upbeat, can I change the subject for a moment?"

The other three looked at Peter wondering what was up.

"I am happy to have played a part, though I had no idea what I was signing on for when they asked me to help with Project Achilles or when I went to that first dinner with Gabby. But I'm very glad I'm here. What started as just another work project has become so much more for me. I don't know how I'll be able to go back to the same, mundane, day-to-day after this. But, I may have a different problem."

"If Arthur discovers the break-in and theft, and I assume there's better than a fifty percent chance of it; my digital fingerprints are all over this. He will come after you, Uncle Jules, through me bringing criminal or worse, national security, charges against me. I may not have been a part of the Dream because I won't be in the picture.

Jules' face took on a serious cast. "Assuming we are successful tomorrow, Arthur will be too busy considering profits to worry about our little conspiracy. He will use the break-in as leverage against me for a while but even that will pass with time. No, the real risk here is if the Ulysses Treatment fails. In that circumstance, Peter, I am ready to stand with you whatever it takes."

"As will I", said Gabby.

"Well, if the Treatment fails, I won't be standing", offered Michael, "but I'm with you all the way."

Gabby groaned. "Michael you've been spending too much time with Peter. Anyway, I need to get my patient to bed and all of us will have a long day tomorrow. I'm going into the lab bright and early. We should be ready to go by early afternoon."

And with that Gabby, Peter, and Jules rose and all went off to bed.

Chapter 18

It was Friday morning and Bob Arnold had been summoned to appear in the Chairman's office with no explanation. Bob didn't like last minute meetings preferring to prepare for any eventuality. As he walked to Building A he reviewed everything he was doing which could possibly grab Arthur's attention. He identified half a dozen projects the Chairman might want to talk about but he was pretty sure he knew what was behind the call.

When he arrived at Arthur's reception area, Arthur's assistant waved him directly into the inner sanctum, not a good sign. Bob was good on his feet but found himself uncomfortable nonetheless.

Arthur, sitting at his desk, was in the middle of a phone call and motioned for Bob to take a seat. Feigning a lack of interest Bob couldn't help but eavesdrop on the conversation listening for any tidbit which might be used to his advantage.

"Are you sure those were the times? Uh, huh. And he was the only one? Do you believe him? No, I don't either. Let me know if you find out anything else. Thank you and keep this quiet. You, too."

Arthur hung up the phone and turned to Bob.

"Bob, I've been reading your latest status report covering Project Achilles and I am not pleased. You had assured me you'd be able to meet the contract deadline without Dr.

Neumann. At this point, I don't see how we're going to get our performance bonus. Tell me I'm wrong."

Neither Arthur's accusation nor his attempt to lay the blame at his feet surprised Bob. Arthur had told him to fire Gabby. Bob had objected, weakly to be sure, to no avail. Now her untimely departure had come home to roost. It was "we" when things went well and "you" when they didn't. Such was life at BDT.

Arthur continued without giving Bob the opportunity to respond.

"You assured me you were far enough along, 'on autopilot' I believe you said, and the lab staff could complete the project. Now, I read in your report the staff has hit a 'snag', as you call it, and there will be another three week delay. Bob, this will cost us millions, how do you propose to get back on track?"

Bob knew he would get himself in deeper trouble if he tried to shade the truth

"Arthur, I've considered this from every angle. Karen is not the person to bring this over the goal line. She oversold her knowledge and her capabilities. The other lab specialist isn't suited. Short of getting another Gabby we may be dead in the water. And even if we could recruit another specialist of her caliber, it would take months to get up to speed. Our only solution will be to find a way to bring Dr. Neumann back."

"Do you know of any research she might have been conducting on the side?" Arthur inquired, changing course.

"Yes, I have no doubt she was pursuing something though she never confided in me. I know she was involved in research in Parkinson's disease at the Medical School and I assumed she'd continued in that vein."

Arthur nodded, and changed direction again.

171

"We had an intrusion in Building E, an unauthorized entry Monday night."

The admission shocked and confused Bob. Arthur's abrupt shifts in direction disoriented him. He wondered why Arthur kept changing the subject but was unwilling to challenge him, certain the connections in his train of thought would play out shortly. *Or is he only trying to keep me off balance*? Bob wondered.

"That was almost four days ago. How long have you known?" Bob asked trying to get Arthur to play his hand.

"I learned of it this morning. I was talking to security when you came in."

"Do you know who it was or what they were after?"

"I have an idea. During a routine review of the security data files the auditor determined that someone hacked into the system Monday night accessing the video surveillance files. He checked building entry but didn't find anything unusual other than an odd entry in your building. It took some digging but it appears a card was swiped in one building and recorded in another."

"How odd." Bob tried to figure out where Arthur was going with this. Arthur knew more than he was saying but Bob thought it best to listen, waiting for Arthur to reveal his agenda.

"The security director questioned the staff on duty and learned Peter Keyes was seen in your building at around 8:45 Monday evening."

Bob now understood Arthur's line of thinking. Peter had the technical knowhow to hack into the security system.

"The guard, who seemed reluctant to give him up, reported seeing Peter who said he had brought dinner to one of the techs in the Achilles lab. When questioned the tech said he was on break and I have no way to verify his story. Has your lead tech, Karen, is it, reported anything unusual or missing?"

"She hasn't come forward to report anything," Bob replied. "Any equipment would be next to impossible to remove. I suppose he may have gone into Gabby's computer looking for something, but I can't imagine what unless it's related to whatever she was doing on the side."

Bob now understood where Arthur was going with his line of questioning, the method in his seeming madness.

"He might well have taken a specimen for her use."

Arthur nodded. "I checked. Peter is on vacation. He scheduled it last week, said he would be out for a couple of weeks, but no one seems to know where he was going."

"What do you think they're up to?" Bob asked.

"I'm not sure. It's possible she found another job at another lab, but it's highly unlikely she has done so in only a few days. Could be she's keeping the specimens on ice for a few weeks until she finds another job but then why is Peter missing in action?"

And as he considered the facts Arthur had presented Bob realized how broadly the conspiracy might reach.

"You don't think Jules Allen is involved, do you?"

"I wouldn't put it past him, but I can't fathom why he would stick his neck out unless it's to get a leg up on me. At the same time this may put us back in the game with Achilles. I now have a lever to bring Dr. Neumann back into the fold. I'm going to figure out where they might be and take it from there. Don't say anything to anyone"

Bob left Arthur's office wondering how he would stay out of the middle on this one.

Chapter 19

They awoke to a light dusting of snow, the white powder cloaking the trees and the ground below. The irony didn't escape Michael. *It had snowed on the day this all began. And now it snowed on the day it would end*, he thought, but then caught himself. *No, this is the day it begins.*

Everyone, except Michael hustled about the house consumed in their assigned tasks. Gabby was already working down in the lab with Jules when Peter brought Michael into the makeshift hospital room. Gabby wanted Michael resting in the hospital bed. She told him she would come upstairs a little before noon to hook him up to the monitors. She had instructed him not to eat anything and, despite the butterflies rummaging around in his stomach, he found he was getting hungry.

True to her word, Gabby came upstairs at 11:30 and started Michael's IV. She hooked him up to the heart monitor, the pulse oximeter, and the electroencephalogram to monitor his brain activity. She then prepared a makeshift medical chart and made notes of the readings on the monitors.

Once satisfied there was nothing else she could do she left Michael alone with Peter promising to return in a few hours.

"Peter, I need to ask something of you"

"Anything."

"I know I got everyone's agreement last night, but I also know Gabby might find it impossible to pull the plug. I need to know you will take charge if needed."

Peter nodded. "I understand. Let's hope it doesn't come to that."

Michael smiled to himself.

"I don't believe it will. The dream I mentioned at dinner last night, I saw you in it."

Peter didn't want to show his curiosity, in part because he was skeptical and in part because he was afraid of what he might hear.

Until recently he thought psychic phenomena the province of the gullible or the psychotic. But the events of the past few days had him wondering whether he was in the middle of some bizarre ghost story or spiritualist convention. Uncle Jules had been a spiritual, if not, religious person, but Peter preferred things he could touch and ideas he could reason out. At the same time, he didn't believe Michael or Gabby to be taken in by sloppy thinking. In any event he couldn't help but ask,

"Really, and what great cosmic revelation did you have?"

Michael laughed.

"Actually, I'm baffled. This one was more abstract and yet still very vivid. I was walking along under my own power in some sort of city. People around me were working together on various projects. Some were building things, others helping to carry boxes and sacks. Everyone seemed to be caught up in what they were doing and I could tell they were calm, happy. They all looked the same and yet different at the same time.

"As I looked closely at them I found it hard to tell where one person's body stopped and the person's body next to them began. As I walked along, they all seemed to recognize me. And then abruptly the dream shifted and I was standing in front of a mirror and when I looked at myself, I saw myself, but I didn't. The boundaries were unclear or shifting out of focus. It's hard to describe.

"Anyway, I continued looking in the mirror and all of a sudden I was clearly divided down the middle. Half of me looked like how I see myself now, the other half was electronic and mechanical, but not like a robot or anything. This isn't making any sense, is it?"

Michael screwed up his face and continued, "It's more like I see cars, computers, flashing lights, and factories in the other half. And then you are standing next to me in the mirror telling me not to worry, this isn't anything new, it's always been this way.

"I turned around and noticed everyone I had been looking at before as I was walking now looked the same as I did. I turned back to the mirror and it was gone. A path lay ahead of me with multiple forks but there was one I knew I should take. You were still standing next to me and then Gabby and Jules were there with us and we started walking.

"I woke up with a feeling of contentment such as I haven't felt in a very long time. I don't know what any of it means, and maybe it was meaningless, maybe I'm just crazy."

At first, Peter didn't say anything, thinking. With a palpable sigh he said, "I'm not sure what to say and like you said before, speculation isn't going to help."

Peter looked at his watch. "I imagine Gabby will be up here soon. Are you ready?"

"As ready as I'll ever be."

They passed the time talking about nothing in particular until Gabby returned. She brought a tray of syringes with her. Michael felt as if he were sitting in the dentist's chair and the dentist was about to give him a good going over.

Gabby checked all the monitors and made notes in his chart.

"Are you ready?" she asked.

"Peter, can you give us a minute?" Michael asked.

Peter stood up awkwardly; feeling very out of place. "Call me when you're ready".

"In a minute," Gabby replied.

After Peter left, Gabby turned to Michael and asked, "How are you doing?"

"Nervous, tired, excited, terrified."

"You know, we don't have to do this. This isn't your only option. We could take our chances, see what happens."

Gabby stared at Michael, struggling.

Michael patted the bed next to him. Gabby sat down and he took her hand in his stroking the back of her hand with his thumb as he spoke.

"We've come too far. I don't want to live like this, each day feeling like the next will be worse. You've given me genuine hope, which is more than I've had for a very long time. I believe this is going to work. But if it doesn't," Michael paused, "I want you to know how lucky I have been".

"Don't," Gabby said emphatically. "I don't want to hear it."

"I know. Each morning I wake up happy to have you next to me. You taught me to see life in a different way. You've made me comfortable with myself and at the same time kept me on edge."

Gabby smiled recalling her conversation with Jules.

"That's all. I wanted you to know. The fewer words the better. I think you know how I feel. I'm convinced I will survive this, but, I'm equally convinced we will emerge from this altered somehow; not badly, but different."

Under different circumstances Michael would have said his first priority would be to start a family once the treatment was completed.

Looking Michael in the eye, Gabby said, "And you know you have been the love of my life. My only wish is for us to grow old together. That's all I need."

She stood. "I'll call the others back in here."

Michael nodded his approval marveling at her strength. He knew if the Ulysses Treatment didn't work he wouldn't know, but Gabby would be alone with her guilt and her grief.

Peter and Jules entered the room somberly. Gabby took her time pointing at the instruments, discussing their function and describing precisely what she was going to do.

"You see how all the monitors are hooked up. I'm keeping track of what they are telling me in this chart." She held up the medical record. "This way, if there are any changes we can see if there are any trends."

"I have given Michael an IV rich with nutrients for growing nerve tissue, proteins and fats along with carbohydrates to give him the energy he needs to regrow the cells."

Gabby looked at Michael.

"First I am going to induce a coma using pentobarbital. We use this when patients have suffered a brain injury to keep neurological activity suppressed during healing. It should also prevent you from having any seizures."

Turning to the others she said, "Once Michael is in a deep sleep I will introduce the retrovirus. Jules and Peter have agreed to take turns monitoring you."

Gabby walked over to the heart monitor and pushed a button. A loud noise shattered the tension.

"The monitors all have alarms which can be heard throughout the house. I'll wake you when I'm satisfied your vital signs are stable and your EEG shows no abnormal wave activity. Michael, do you have any questions?"

"Let's go."

Gabby walked to the side of the bed where the IV bag hung. She was about to inject the barbiturate, hesitated, and then leaned over and kissed Michael gently on the lips.

Michael smiled, "No wonder your patients get better".

"Good night my dear, sweet dreams", Gabby said as she injected the drug into his IV line.

She looked deeply into Michael's eyes and watched as they slowly closed. She stood there for a moment lost in thought. Then she checked the monitors making sure he was fully asleep and recorded the results.

When she was satisfied he was resting deeply she brought out the other syringe filled with a pale yellow fluid. She stared at it wondering for a moment if she held a loaded gun or the elixir of life.

Deliberately she injected the solution with the retrovirus into the line and watched. There was no change on the monitors, as she expected.

"There is nothing else we can do for now. We'll take turns sitting with him and check the monitors every hour. I'll take the first shift."

The rest of the day passed uneventfully but by late evening Michael showed signs of distress. His heart rate was elevated and the EEG patterns didn't look right. Peter, in the room with Gabby, watched as she fretted over the readings, unable to do anything. Finally a little before midnight she increased the pentobarbital dosage. Michael's heart rate dropped to the normal range and the EEG readings improved.

Saturday brought with it no real changes. There were periodic fluctuations in Michael's vital signs but they came further and further apart and Gabby satisfied herself she would avoid a catastrophe. By Saturday evening, Michael had fully stabilized.

Everyone busied themselves about the house taking short walks outside from time to time. The sunlight had melted the snow; the air crisp and invigorating. Despite the short breaks Peter, Gabby, and Jules felt immersed in the cocoon-like atmosphere which permeating the house.

In the wee hours of Sunday morning, Gabby noticed changes in Michael's EEG. Nothing dramatic, but she saw greater activity in the area which had been damaged giving her hope the repair was proceeding successfully.

But by sunrise, she wasn't so sure. The rhythms looked relatively normal except there were now tracings she couldn't explain. Jules and Peter were up and by her side.

"How's he doing? Peter asked.

"I thought he was doing fine but now his EEG tracings appear decidedly abnormal. There's a new wave form. They look like gamma waves which are normally associated with perception and consciousness but Michael is still unconscious. And they're of a much higher amplitude than I've seen before. It may not be a problem, I just don't know."

"How long did you think the repair would take?" Jules asked.

"I wasn't sure. Without a functional MRI we can't be certain whether the repair has occurred unless Michael is conscious."

"Did you have a clear idea of how you would know when you'd be ready to wake him up?" Peter asked.

"I am looking for normal vital signs and a normal EEG. Michael's heart rate and blood pressure are strong. But this EEG anomaly has me baffled."

"Do you remember our first dinner together?" Peter asked and Gabby nodded. "I asked you about the effect of increasing the number of synaptic connections. Could that be what you are seeing here?"

"It's certainly possible," Gabby responded lost in thought.

Interrupting her Jules asked "What do you see as the alternatives?"

She looked up. "I see two. One is to keep watching him and wait for a change. The other is to wake him and see how he responds."

"What are the risks?" Peter asked.

"The longer I keep Michael in a coma, the harder it'll be to wake him up. But if we wake him and he's not ready then we might do more harm than good."

"If you wake him up and he isn't ready yet, can you put him back to sleep?" Jules asked.

Gabby didn't respond lost in her own mental gymnastics.

Finally Jules broke the silence.

"Look Gabby, this isn't something we can vote about. Neither Peter nor I have the expertise or the connection to Michael you have. This is a decision you have to make. We'll support you either way."

Peter nodded in agreement.

Finally, in a firm voice, Gabby stated, "I want to wake him up but I also want to be prepared to put him back in a coma, if necessary. Once he's awake we should better understand his condition and know where to go from here. I'll go down to the lab and prepare the doses. Peter, can you help me and Jules, please stay here and watch him."

Chapter 20

Before long Gabby returned with Peter and the medications. Standing close to Michael, Gabby introduced the drug to bring him out of his unconscious state. All they could do now was watch and wait.

For the first few minutes nothing happened and then Michael's heart rate began to quicken as his EEG readings increased in amplitude.

He is dimly aware of his surroundings, unable to orient himself. Impenetrably dark. Numbingly cold. No frame of reference. Something is very wrong. He realizes he must have been unconscious as instinct takes over and he struggles to get his bearings. He is barely able to mentally voice the inevitable first questions: "Where am I, how did I get here"? He knows there is no one to answer.

Dimly he is aware he had an experience like this before, but this one is different.

How long have I been asleep? he wonders. He is aware of his body but unable to move or communicate as though he is in suspended animation, floating on a cloud. Before panic takes hold he experiences an indescribable feeling, like a gentle wind blowing through him. The pressure of the wind builds and grows filling him with a sensation like movement and yet, light and perfectly still. A rising sense of both anticipation and apprehension grips him. *Am I dying?*

And in response to the unheard question, memory floods back, and with it, Michael remembers where he is and slowly opens his eyes.

"Well, well, how are you feeling?" Gabby gently probed.

"I feel kinda fuzzy."

"You don't look fuzzy."

The other two pretended to ignore Peter's pun.

"My throat is dry. Can I have some water?"

Having anticipated the question Gabby raised the head of the bed slightly and handed Michael a cup of water with a straw for drinking. As he sipped from the cup, Michael noticed something seemed out of place but couldn't quite put his finger on it.

Gabby lowered the blanket covering his legs.

"Ow!" Michael felt a pin prick.

Gabby remained serious but he saw wide grins on both Jules and Peter causing Michael smile in return.

"Now I'm going to ask you whether what you feel is dull or sharp", and with that Gabby began poking both legs with either her finger or the needle. Michael responded appropriately each time.

"I have feeling back; it's a good sign, isn't it?"

"It's a very good sign. Can you wiggle your toes?"

Everyone in the room, including Gabby, laughed when they saw his toes move, if only slightly.

Gabby leaned close to Michael.

"It may be too soon to say with certainty, but it appears the Ulysses Treatment worked. I will want to get an MRI as soon as possible and you will need a fair amount of physical therapy, but . . ."

Gabby found herself at a loss for words. The objective clinician who had so meticulously cared for her patient dissolved in the realization of what her success meant. She recognized, despite all her optimism, a portion of her mind never expected to succeed. And with her skeptical reservations gone Gabby felt a torrent of emotion, built up over years of sacrifice and pain.

She could only muster a bare audible "Oh my" as tears filled her eyes and she bent to kiss Michael.

But before she could touch his lips Michael gasped.

Gabby pulled back. Wiping her eye's she asked, "What is it, are you all right?"

Reflex sent her eyes to the monitors but she saw nothing unusual except the same heightened gamma wave activity on the EEG and a slightly elevated pulse rate.

For a moment, Michael said nothing. Responding to Gabby's tears Michael, too, felt overwhelming emotion, but that surge of feeling triggered another, almost alien experience. While he saw Gabby's form with his eyes, a new impression intruded on his conscious mind, more subtle than the perception of light encountering his optic nerve. He experienced a sensation he never felt before; as though they were bonded together in some ethereal fashion.

Gabby looked at Peter and Jules and as she did, Michael looked at them as well. He sensed a similar bond with them. And he found he also perceived the bond between Peter and Jules. Probing further with his new sense he also saw that same bond among all four of them.

184

Feeling her unease, Michael turned back to face Gabby and smiled. "I'm okay."

"Michael, what is it?" Gabby demanded. "Every feeling, every nuance is important no matter how inconsequential you think it may be."

Michael looked at the three of them feeling their concern in a more direct and intimate fashion than he had ever felt before, as though they were a part of him, but not. He found this new sensation as tangible as the touch of hot water on skin or the smell of a rose.

"I'm not quite sure how to describe it," Michael began. "You may think I'm crazy but. . ."

Before he could finish he felt Gabby's panic rising. His head whipped around to her in response. Gently he said, "Gabby, there's no reason for panic."

"Michael, Gabby wasn't panicking," observed Peter.

Staring at Michael, Gabby said, "Yes I was. At least I was starting to. Michael, go ahead and tell us. I'll be all right."

Michael could sense Gabby controlling her emotions and the confusion Peter and Jules felt.

"Let me try and explain before anyone reacts too quickly. Earlier, right before you bent to kiss me, and I saw you overcome with emotion, it really got to me."

Gabby couldn't help but smile.

"It was as though I reflexively reached out to you with my mind. Like I wanted to touch you, but I didn't have to move. When I directed my mind to you I sensed a very real bond between us. And by sense I'm talking about something like sight or hearing, but more subtle.

"And I sensed the same thing with the two of you," Michael said looking at Peter and Jules. "I'm picking up on emotion or

185

state of mind; like I did a moment ago with you, dear." Michael paused, seemingly confused. "This is so hard to explain."

"Are you saying you were reading Gabby's mind?" questioned Jules.

"I don't think so, at least not in the way I might imagine it. It's like, when you look at a chair, you know it's a chair."

"What am I feeling?" Peter challenged

"Come on, Peter," Gabby objected.

"No, Michael said he can do this. I want to understand."

Michael looked confused. "I sense hostility but underneath it," Michael paused. "Hope."

Gabby and Jules looked to Peter who was nodding his head. "Cool".

"Can you send thoughts?" Jules asked.

"I don't think so. This appears to be a one-way perceptual thing."

"This is bizarre," Peter said, half to himself.

"Not as bizarre as you might think," Gabby offered thoughtfully. "As I said before, Michael's EEG is measuring abnormal amplitude in his gamma waves. I was watching when you tested him, Peter, and the gamma activity increased.

"Contemporary neuroscience is just starting to study gamma waves. Most of what you see published at this point you'll find in the fringe literature; the spiritualists and new agers claiming higher levels of gamma activity correspond with higher IQ's and greater compassion, whatever that means. Some have even tried to suggest they correlate with paranormal phenomenon.

"The medical community has rejected these claims as unproven but I've seen studies done by highly regarded universities funded from reputable sources which indicate gamma waves are correlated with perception and learning. I wasn't too surprised when I saw your EEG earlier because these waves are associated with greater brain activity, but what we are seeing here is out of the realm of my experience, and I'm not sure what to think.

"In any event," Gabby continued as she pulled up Michael's covers, "I don't need altered perceptions to know my patient is tired and needs to rest."

"You're right," said Michael as he yawned.

"I'm going to leave the monitors connected for a little while longer, okay?"

"That's fine," Michael said drowsily.

As Peter and Jules left the room, Michael asked Gabby to remain.

"What's happening to me?"

"I wish I could tell you."

"I wish you could, too. I feel okay but I can't make sense of this. This new perception seems real enough but how can it be?"

"I don't know. I feel like I'm flying blind here. It's as though your brain is encased in a black box I can't see into. Let's get that MRI and hopefully it will shed light on what's going on here."

"Sounds like a good idea. Maybe I'll wake up and this new feeling will be gone. I'm just glad I seem to be healed. As far as I'm concerned it couldn't have gone better. Let's take this one step at a time."

Gabby leaned down and completed the kiss.

"Well, that went better. Get some sleep," she said as she turned off the lights and left the room.

Outside in the hallway, the three visited briefly in hushed tones.

"He'll probably sleep for a while," Gabby offered. "A drug induced coma isn't the same as natural sleep and he's been through a lot."

"But it worked, didn't it?" Peter asked.

Gabby smiled a tired smile. "It appears so. But I'm worried. I don't know what to make of Michael's newfound perceptions."

"It's hard to believe Michael has developed psychic abilities despite the evidence to the contrary," Jules admitted. "It's too fantastic."

Gabby nodded. "I'm a skeptic when it comes to these things. I don't want to jump to any conclusions. I think the best approach will be to get an MRI and see what we can learn."

"I can get Michael in at the local hospital," suggested Jules. "I will try to schedule an appointment for him in the morning."

"I think we still need to take shifts and keep a close eye on him," said Gabby as she cast a worried glance toward the room where Michael lay.

Gabby's kiss brought deep contentment to Michael, contentment tinged with concern. As he thought about his recovery and newfound abilities wondering what they might mean, his mind shifted into overdrive seeing possibilities and pathways with new clarity and at a speed he had never experienced before. Along each path he saw the potential consequences of his possible choices.

He began to understand what his new abilities and perceptions might mean, not only for himself, but for those around him. And with keen insight he knew the change was just beginning as sleep took him.

Chapter 21

Michael slept through the rest of the day and woke Monday morning. He felt well enough so Gabby removed the monitoring leads and IV during the night. She was sitting in his room when he woke a little after seven.

"Good morning, how are you feeling?" she asked as she walked over to the bed.

"Very relaxed," Michael responded taking her hand.

"How would you like to come to the kitchen for breakfast?" Gabby had an ulterior motive using the seemingly innocent question to determine his drive and energy level.

"I'm famished and want to get out of this bed. I would also like to test my legs."

"Great! I want you to ride in the wheelchair for now. Let's work on walking after you eat, okay?"

"OK," Michael responded with a hint of impatience.

As she wheeled him to the kitchen Gabby explained, "I don't want you to overdo it, especially since you've been lying in bed for a few days and it's been years since you've walked."

"I understand."

Gabby suspected he thought he was ready to run a marathon by the tone of his voice.

"I'm glad you're feeling better but I don't want you to push too hard. We don't want to risk a relapse at this stage."

They found Jules and Peter preparing breakfast. The four sat at the kitchen table making small talk about the weather and the plan for the day; no one brought up the strange events from the previous day.

Following breakfast and while Jules and Peter cleaned up, Gabby wheeled Michael down the hall to a room where a set of parallel bars waited for him. Michael realized they must have been purchased in anticipation of his need for physical therapy.

As Gabby wheeled him up to the open end of the bars she cautioned, "I want to start working with you immediately. When we leave here, we'll get you into a more formal rehab program but I don't want to waste any time. I'm hopeful the therapy you've been receiving since the accident will help speed your recovery."

Michael reached for the bars to pull himself up and paused. The equipment required him to support himself with his arms and shoulders and knowing how much upper body strength he had previously lost, he didn't want to fall from the start. However, his eagerness got the better of him as Gabby tried to help him stand and he pulled himself into a standing position with little difficulty.

He found he could put weight on each leg and they responded well to his will. While he felt weakness from years of disuse he reached the far end of the bars with less difficulty than he expected.

"How did I do?"

Instead of answering, Gabby instructed, "Why don't you turn around and come back the other way."

Michael did as he was told walking clumsily back and forth for several repetitions, Gabby walking beside him, before she made him stop.

Back in his chair, Michael wanted to ask again how he did but knew Gabby would answer in her own good time when she was satisfied she knew enough to answer with a degree of certainty.

Gabby took his pulse and blood pressure studying his face. "Are you tired?" she asked.

"A little. I'm surprised I'm not having a harder time."

"I am, too. You're doing much better than I expected," Gabby marveled shaking her head. "I didn't think you would progress so quickly. You've achieved months of improvement in just one day. There are tests I want to run but we don't have the equipment here. Jules told me there is an MRI at the local hospital and he has the connections to get you in there this afternoon. I want a scan so we can see what's going on in there. Are you up for a drive?"

"Are you kidding?" Michael laughed. "I need to get out of here."

"Good, we'll go after lunch." Gabby continued strength training with Michael until Peter announced it was time to eat.

Jules drove Gabby and Michael the fifteen minutes to the local hospital and escorted them to the Administrator's office where they were met by the hospital CEO, Carol Young. Michael remained in his wheelchair, none of them willing to let on what had occurred.

On the way to the executive offices Jules explained how he had donated a fair amount of money to the hospital on several occasions and so was able to use his influence to get Michael in quickly.

"Mr. Allen, it's good to see you. It's been at least a year since you last visited." The administrator then turned to Gabby and Michael, "How do you do? I'm Carol Young."

"This is Dr. Gabriella Neumann and her husband, Michael."

"It's so nice to meet you", she said offering her hand to Gabby and Michael in turn. "You're lucky. The magnet isn't too busy today and we were able to work you in easily. My assistant Janet will escort you to Radiology."

She then turned to Jules and asked, "May I show you the new cardiac wing? We can meet your friends back in my office when they are finished. I want to show you what we've done with your generosity."

Gabby had warned Jules the test would take about an hour and he didn't relish spending the time pumped for additional contributions but knew they needed to keep a low profile.

"Sounds good. Let's go."

Young took Jules by the arm and headed for the elevator already talking his ear off.

Her assistant escorted Gabby and Michael to radiology where Michael put on a hospital gown and laid down on the table. Gabby waited in the control room watching the tech operate the control panel as the scan commenced.

While Gabby stood there, silently focused on the screen as the computer constructed the image, a radiologist walked in to observe and introduced himself. "Hello, I'm Tom Hill. I understand you are a physician and this is your husband?"

Gabby did her best to appear nonchalant. There was a chance the Ulysses Treatment did nothing but repair damaged tissue but the events of the past twenty-four hours didn't leave her confident the scan would appear normal. She didn't want attention but knew there was a risk either the tech or radiologist would see the scan and see something she didn't expect.

"It's nice to meet you. You have a nice facility here."

"Thank you. I understand you husband has a parietal lobe lesion. I haven't seen very many and so I wanted to see the scan and to meet you." Dr. Hill, a genial radiologist in his fifties, smiled broadly.

Gabby knew there was no way, in any event, to prevent him from looking at the image of Michael's brain. He would have to dictate the formal report. Gabby smiled back and shook his hand. She hoped any anomalies would be insignificant enough to pass off.

The two of them turned their attention to the monitor and Gabby practically gasped. The image before her differed markedly from any brain scan she had ever seen.

Michael's brain looked normal in every way but one. All the structures were where they should have been. In fact, Michael's parietal lobe looked normal, as if he had never been injured.

In the case of MRI brain scans the brighter the image, the greater the cellular density. The image on the computer display showed Michael's brain far brighter than Gabby had ever seen and she was certain Tom Hill had never seen anything like it either. Peter had been right. Michael's nerve cells in his cerebrum had multiplied well beyond her expectations creating almost twenty percent more brain mass.

Gabby had the advantage of expecting the unexpected. At first, Dr. Hill removed his reading glasses, leaned forward, and squinted at the screen, a look of confusion on his face. He asked the tech about the settings on her console but learned nothing to help him explain what he saw before him.

He turned to Gabby considering his words carefully, "I would like to visit with you. Could you come to my office?"

Gabby didn't want to speak with him but he had her in a corner. If she ignored his request he might share the scan with others and, invariably, word would spread.

"I'd like to stay until the scan is finished and then I'll bring Michael back with me." Gabby needed a chance to prep

Michael for the inquisition. She hoped having Michael, the patient, with her would limit Hill's questions.

Tom Hill nodded, stayed to watch the monitor for another minute, and then left.

Ten minutes later Gabby wheeled a clothed Michael down the hall to Hill's office. But with the radiology tech escorting them there was no chance to brief Michael ahead of time or to get his thoughts on what to say. She would have to wing it. She figured the only way to hold the radiologist at bay would be to come clean and ask for his discretion.

Once in his office Hill offered them water, coffee, or tea but both Gabby and Michael declined. The conversation began innocently enough.

"Mr. Neumann, how are you feeling?"

"Pretty good," Michael responded.

Dr. Hill nodded. "Dr. Neumann, the reason entered in the computer for your husband's exam was that you were evaluating the status of an old injury to your husband's parietal lobe. When did the injury occur?"

"Michael was injured in a car accident about four years ago."

Dr. Hill nodded again. "It's unfortunate I don't have the benefit of reviewing your previous scans for comparison, but that's not the issue. I don't see any evidence of a parietal lesion, do you?"

Dr. Hill swung his monitor around for Gabby to see the overhead and lateral images of Michael's cerebrum.

"No, I don't." Gabby thought it best not argue with him knowing any debate would prove fruitless. Michael sat relaxed and alert at her side. He didn't appear to be concerned.

"Now, I could guess there was some other reason for the scan; which would make sense given what I see here." Hill turned to Michael. "When I look at your scan Mr. Neumann, I see your brain tissue density is off the charts. I've never seen anything like it."

 Before Gabby could try and explain, Michael jumped in.

"I'm not surprised. I did have a parietal lobe injury but Gabby devised a treatment which cured me. It appears to have had additional side effects." Michael turned and smiled at his wife.

Gabby tried to contain her concern wondering what Michael was up to. She wished, more than ever, they had been able to coordinate their strategies before reaching the office.

Michael continued, "Gabby knew Jules Allen from work and asked him if he could find an MRI we could use which, well, let's just say, which wasn't located in an academic medical center. You can guess why. We weren't entirely sure what the collateral effects of the treatment would be."

Diverting Dr. Hill's additional questions before he could ask them, Michael continued, "So my wife wanted to get a baseline MRI thinking if it showed what we thought; we could conduct a functional MRI, as well. Would that be possible?"

Gabby now thought she understood where Michael was going and could guess at what Dr. Hill was thinking. Following Michael's lead she added, "The treatment is revolutionary enough that if I can establish there is greater cortical activity to correlate with the anatomical findings, we might be able to publish a case study in the New England Journal. What do you think?"

Hill shook his head back and forth, thinking.

"This is incredible. I can find a way to squeeze you in for another scan this afternoon Mr. Neumann and while we are doing it, you and I can talk. It's Gabriella, right? I want to learn more about this new treatment and we can discuss how we might approach writing the article."

"Could we come back in couple of days?" Michael asked. "I'm feeling a little tired and I have to confess I got a little claustrophobic in the magnet."

Hill smiled. "I understand. How would Thursday morning work?"

Gabby looked at Michael and he shrugged his agreement. "Thursday it is," she replied. "Oh, and since we're looking at publishing this, I think it best we keep this to ourselves before the piece is written, do you agree?"

"Of course. I will see to the schedule. I understand you are supposed to go back to Ms. Young's office when you're finished here. I'll be happy to escort you," he said as he came around from behind his desk.

As they walked down the hall making small talk, Gabby wondered how to get out of the corner Michael had put them in. They found Jules in Ms. Young's office drinking coffee.

"How'd it go?" Jules inquired.

"Everything's good," Gabby said. "I hate to rush but Michael's feeling tired. I think we should go."

They exchanged their goodbyes and Dr. Hill closed with, "I look forward to seeing you again on Thursday."

In the car Jules asked, "What's this about Thursday?"

Gabby recounted their discussion and Jules frowned. But before he could ask the obvious question, Michael explained his strategy.

"There was no way we were going to explain this away. While I lay on the table I sensed a change in Gabby's demeanor. Reaching out I sensed Hill's confusion. I couldn't know the reason for it, but he seems to have something of an inferiority complex and I thought to play off of it. I felt badly invading his consciousness without his knowledge but we need to keep this quiet until we decide whether to go public. It's one thing to connect with people who know what I am doing, but I don't like the idea of intruding on other's thoughts," Michael confessed.

"But now we're committed to going back," Gabby countered.

"We're not going back," said Michael. "The images are stored on a Picture Archiving and Communications System. By design the PACS connects to the internet so a physician can look at any image from anywhere in the hospital or even from home.

"When we get back to the house we'll ask our resident computer expert to hack into the hospital system and replace today's scan with one of the older ones you have on your laptop, Gabby. At least Hill won't have any evidence, only his word. He seems like a decent guy and I hate doing this to him, but it can't be helped."

Chapter 22

Once they arrived back at the house, Michael told Peter what needed to be done. Peter relished the challenge and immediately went down to the basement to get started. While Peter worked his magic Jules and Gabby busied themselves in the kitchen preparing dinner as Michael rested.

At dinner that evening Peter reported his success. "It wasn't too difficult. The hospital firewalls are not as sophisticated as the ones we have at BDT. I downloaded today's scan onto my computer and replaced it with one Gabby identified on her laptop."

"Well, that should cover us for now," said Gabby only somewhat relieved.

"It will for the time being," Jules observed. "But now we need to give thought to where we go from here. I'm not sure any of us has given much consideration to anything beyond Michael's recovery."

"What are you thinking, Uncle Jules?" Peter asked.

"Well, Gabby and Michael will need to figure out how their lives will have to adjust. Much will depend on how or even if we decide to take this public."

"What could we take public?" Gabby asked. "First of all, we really don't have a clue what we are dealing with here. We know Michael's injury appears to be healed, but we are seeing other effects we can't yet explain. Secondly, we still don't know what the long term effects on Michael will be. And then there is the risk of disclosure. We have a number of issues to consider before we can put together any kind of plan."

"What do you think we need to do before we announce this?" Jules asked.

"I want to continue with Michael's physical therapy and gauge how his recovery is progressing. I would like to conduct additional testing including the functional MRI Michael suggested earlier today. I don't know what the results of the MRI today mean. I've never seen anything even similar and I don't know that anyone else has either. The density of cerebral tissue implies a guess Peter made when we first started collaborating may have come true: Michael's nerve synapses appear to have dramatically multiplied resulting in a significant increase in neural connections."

"Michael, what are you noticing that's different from before?" Peter asked.

"Other than walking? I've noticed several changes in the last thirty-six hours. I already explained how my perceptions have altered. I can sense a connection with those around me and through that channel I can sense the mental state of that person. It's as though there is a conduit connecting me to each of you and through that conduit information flows. But there's more to it than that. It's not a one way connection. I get the sense it's two-way but since you aren't hooked in you can't perceive it yet." Michael paused, thinking.

"But maybe it's not in actuality a conduit at all, maybe . . . I'm having a hard time explaining the feeling without oversimplifying it, but it's as though we all share a piece of something. Does that make any sense?"

It was a few moments before anyone else spoke.

Peter spoke first. "Can you turn it off?"

"To a degree. It's like closing your eyes in a bright room. You can still sense light through your eyelids but can't make out any shapes or forms."

"I wonder if there's a limit to the number of people you can connect with or what the constraints on distance might be," Jules said.

"When I was laying there in the magnet, I was bored, so I reached out with my mind and perceived Gabby, the tech, and the radiologist easily. It felt like turning my head toward them to see them, but I didn't have to move and what I "saw" was not an image but, again, a sense of what they were feeling or thinking. I wonder what would happen if I tried to reach beyond the four of us?"

Michael quietly sat back, eyes closed. In the span of only a few minutes he opened them again, but as Gabby looked into his eyes she could tell something had changed. And as he spoke each word carried a sense of profound and crucial consequence.

"I'll do what I can to describe what I experienced but bear in mind, I'll do a poor job, at best, conveying what I found. What I felt before, it was superficial. This was wholly different as though focus and concentration took me to a new level.

"Imagine riding a fast moving current in an ocean. But keep in mind there's no up, there's no down, no sense of dimension. As you travel along there are bubbles. Some of the bubbles felt warm and light, in their own flow. There was a calmness to them which felt attractive. I wanted to stay near them. But those bubbles were few and far between.

"Most of the bubbles seemed stressed, the water around them choppy. I found myself uncomfortable as I'd approach them, the chop in the water feeling prickly: its touch cold and even painful, drawing at my essence. But the surf prevented me

200

from getting too close, the swells pushing me away though I could feel the same attractive need coming from the center of the bubble. And some were darker, or maybe even foggy around them. It's difficult to describe. Is this making sense?

"Go on, Michael", said Jules though his face and those of the other's betrayed their struggle to comprehend.

"There were other bubbles, dark as night, the sea around them rising in great swells, threatening to crush me. I could feel violence tearing at the air. It was terrifying."

He took a deep breath.

"What I'm describing is more like an analogy than what I actually experienced; like trying to describe a great song to someone who has never heard a sound. I've conveyed separateness where none exists." He stopped speaking, staring at no one in particular.

Michael spoke haltingly. "I'm not sure I understand. I'm still processing it all but there was so much pain. The space around the bubbles, where the wave like feeling came, it seemed so unnatural, contrived. I'm not sure I understand at all. I need more time to think."

"That's a lot to process. Have you noticed any other differences in your perceptions or thoughts?" Jules asked.

It took a moment for Michael to respond.

"As I was lying there in the magnet and sensed Dr. Hill's confusion, I started thinking about what to do if he figured out that all wasn't as it seemed. My mind quickly jumped to multiple possibilities with a speed I had never experienced before. I could think down multiple paths simultaneously." Michael paused again.

"I think I am better able to recognize patterns and, again, I'm having a hard time articulating this, it's like. . ." Michael seemed to be looking for the right words. "It's like I'm more intuitive, sensing what's to come."

"Are you saying you can see into the future?" Gabby asked incredulous.

"No, it's not like that at all. There are too many variables and too much randomness to predict with certainty. It seems I can do a faster and more complete job exploring alternative futures, considering the potential outcomes, and so arrive at a strategy which works best. Kinda like playing chess on steroids."

Jules noticed Peter appeared to be lost in thought. "Peter, what is it?"

"This actually makes some sense. Think about it this way. Studies on the evolution of the animal nervous system suggest mental activity becomes increasingly refined with greater brain complexity. The most basic thought, if you even want to call it a thought, is the reflex. It doesn't even engage higher brain function. Only the spinal cord is involved.

"As mental capacity increases in complexity, we move from reflexes to senses to instinct to emotion and then to thought. For example, amphibians and reptiles experience basic emotions. The more evolved brains of mammals experience higher levels of emotion: dogs have affection for their masters. Apes have demonstrated simple language skills. We may be seeing a new stage, generated by an even greater number of neural connections enhancing logic and intuition along with Michael's newfound sense perception. Gabby, what do you think?"

"I hadn't thought about it in that way before, but I can see how it makes sense. We know primate brains differ from the brains of lower mammals due to the number and complexity of neural connections. I think you're suggesting the Ulysses

Treatment causes a leap to a new, more evolved mental capacity."

Peter nodded.

Gabby continued, "But it still doesn't explain Michael's new perceptions or the connections he perceives."

"I think it might," Peter continued. "There's a theory I've come across in my research called quantum mind. Dendrites, the portion of nerve cells which receive messages from other nerve cells, can be connected in webs and their activity has been correlated to enhanced gamma waves on EEG. It's possible the Ulysses Treatment accentuated or further developed capabilities already present.

"You're saying there is a physical basis for the mind and thought," interjected Gabby. "I've read articles on the subject and I'm not convinced. We used to talk about mind and matter being two separate things. When you look at people with certain types of brain injuries, they suffer mental effects as well. Researchers have done experiments on monkeys which demonstrate a clear causal effect between mental state and brain function."

"Why does it have to be one or the other", Michael asked. Gabby noticed Michael seemed agitated.

"What do you mean?" asked Jules.

"We're talking about mind here. We think of our minds, the self-aware portion of us, as distinct from our bodies. You can find religious people and philosophers who believe the two are separate and when we die our mind or soul goes someplace, for better or worse. On the other hand many scientists think of mind as a result of the collection of neurons in a three pound mass of jelly we call a brain. Why does it have to be one or the other?

"We develop those theories based on what we observe. When our observations contradict what our theories tell us, we delve deeper to understand. There are events in physics where Einstein's general relativity and quantum mechanics conflict, and as a result, physicists are looking for principles which must underlie both. In the same way astronomers have hypothesized the existence of dark matter and dark energy to explain the observation that the expansion of the universe is accelerating. I think what you are proposing Peter, is a new understanding of how the mind works and it's link to the brain consistent with what I've told you about my new perception."

Peter nodded and continued, "There is a related proposition called quantum entanglement where matter is connected at a very subtle level irrespective of where it's located in the universe. Years ago when Einstein sat puzzling out certain theoretical subatomic particle interactions he came upon the idea of quantum entanglement and called it 'spooky interactions at a distance'. Since then experimental science has verified his theory.

"Our perceptions of separation are built upon the perceptions of our senses, but we know our senses can fool us. We think of space as an absolute. A mile is a mile, is a mile, right? That's not true when you are talking about the space around massive bodies.

"Isaac Newton described gravity as an attractive force like magnetism but instead of attracting iron, mass attracts other objects with mass. Einstein rethought Newton's construct saying instead of an attractive force, gravity bends space and time like a heavy iron ball forming a cone in a rubber sheet. No one had observed the phenomenon and at first it didn't make sense.

"Einstein hypothesized that gravity would bend light rays. Light isn't matter, how could it be bent by gravity? And yet later experimental observations proved just that. Think of a black hole. It's called a black hole because the mass is so great; the gravity so strong, even light doesn't escape. Quantum theory takes the whole concept a step further demonstrating particles can be connected irrespective of where they are located."

"Your explanation may be plausible," Gabby inserted "but there may be other, equally valid reasons. There's still so much we don't know. Perhaps we'll gain a better understanding with more testing."

"More testing?" Michael asked looking at Gabby. "Is your plan to sequester me in a lab somewhere until the pundits of medicine decide its safe for me to reenter society?"

"Michael! How could you think I would do that? We haven't gone through all of this so you would be put on display. And I can't believe you'd think I'd even consider it."

"You wouldn't do it intentionally; but how else you do think this could go? We dodged a bullet today with Dr. Hill. How long do you think we can keep my condition hidden once we get back home? Any additional testing you might conduct would certainly bring the interest of others. Word would get out and this will all be taken out of your hands. They'll put me under a microscope."

While Gabby shook her head in protest, Michael reached over and took her hand. "I understand. There are questions you want to answer. We all want to understand what's happening. But this isn't the way."

Michael paused, released Gabby's hand and looked at Jules, Peter, and Gabby in turn.

"I could die tomorrow or I could end up a guinea pig in a lab and no one would know anything about this breakthrough and all your hard work, Gabby, would be lost. There are interests that would not want your research to see the light of day for any one of a number of reasons.

"No, we have a much larger issue confronting us than speculating about the medical or scientific basis behind the effects of the Ulysses Treatment: how do we disseminate the Treatment to the rest of humanity?"

Chapter 23

The dining room erupted in a cacophony of questions and objections; Jules, Peter, and Gabby talking all at once. Michael waited patiently until the clamor subsided.

Jules began, "Before I can even have an intelligent opinion about the bomb you just dropped I need a better understanding of what you're proposing and what you think you'll achieve."

"Fair enough. In my latest series of blogs I wrote about the conflict we experience in needing to be a part of a community and yet believing we are alone. The human race is fractured by distrust and envy. Until recently I believed, fatalistically, we are wired for conflict. Now I see a way out, a way forward. We are, in fact, not alone. We simply can't see it.

"Peter, you're right. The Ulysses treatment is the way to go beyond the limitations of our biology and primitive natures. Our failures are only partially a question of character or moral strength. We've failed to realize our potential because we lacked the capacity. We can now take the next step in the evolution of our species."

"Michael, I appreciate your passion," said Gabby, "but we can't be sure the Treatment will have the same effect on anyone else."

"Gabby, let me ask you this. For the sake of argument, let's say it's possible to take one of my eyes and graft it to the back of my head so I could see forward and backward at the same time. If you did the same thing to someone else, would it be safe to assume they would have the same ability: to see backwards and forwards at the same time?"

"I see where you're going," Gabby replied. "But I'm still bothered by all the unknowns."

"I wish to disagree with Gabby's comment," Peter interjected. "If you had an eye in the back of your head, I don't think you would know whether you *were* coming or going."

A collective groan erupted from the other three causing Peter to smile. But then he asked the question on everyone's mind.

"Michael, are you telling us you want us to take the Treatment?"

"I can't tell anyone else to do this. It has to be your decision because you believe it's the right thing to do."

"Michael, we've all read your blogs and I think I understand where you're coming from but this is starting to sound like your personal agenda," observed Jules.

"When I reached out a few minutes ago and touched all those lives I learned there are larger issues here, greater than any one of us.

"Each of us lives in our own world unaware we are part of something greater. If everyone knew that one fact with every fiber of their being, we could create a more just, a more compassionate society. As silly as it may sound, especially coming from a cynic like me, I now believe this is our destiny.

"A week ago when we were all flying here Jules, you hit on it. You talked about our potential for good. The Treatment can take us beyond mere high aspirations. We now have a concrete means to realize our potential; to create a society which before has only existed in dreams.

"Michael, I can see you're changing, but I don't know if I'm ready for that," Gabby answered.

"I don't think this is a decision anyone can or should reach lightly. But I will tell you, I have seen enough to know we stand on a knife's edge. The events of the next few days will determine our fate. I don't have a choice. I can't be who I thought I was."

Jules smiled knowingly. "You know, that reminds me of a short story I read a long time ago. I believe it was titled 'The Traveler', but I don't recall who wrote it. The tale took place in some distant future. Man had traveled beyond Earth colonizing multiple worlds. The main character, Adam, I believe, had grown up on Earth as an only child. His mother died when he was young and his father made his living as an itinerant geologist. Out of necessity, young Adam traveled with him, learning at his knee. Adam's father took great pains to expose him to all the academic disciplines but naturally, instructed him more deeply in his own areas of expertise.

"Adam developed an appreciation for the wonders of the Earth. He sailed its deep blue seas and climbed many of its tall mountains. He visited the sites of ancient ruins. He also met many people in their travels who had been to the stars. Their exotic tales of other worlds fired his imagination. When he reached adulthood, Adam's curiosity drove him to take a job on an interstellar supply ship.

"Supply ships would occasionally transport people but more often they moved scarce supplies, materials, and equipment from planet to planet. They served as the only connection among the human inhabitants of the settled worlds. Traveling at faster than light speeds it might only take a few months for those on board to reach a destination; but due to the great distance between habitable planets many years would pass for those on the ground due to Einstein's time dilation.

"Adam and his father said their heartfelt goodbye's as he prepared to leave; both knowing they would never see each other again. But his father well understood Adam's wanderlust and need to grow into his own man guided by his own aspirations.

"Adam easily took to the challenges of space commerce and rose rapidly through the ranks to captain his own vessel. He traveled from world to world marveling at the uniqueness of each. Most of the people he met had never been to Earth, the home world of the species.

"He enjoyed the sheer variety of the planets he visited; whether it was the unique plant and animal life or the different geologic and geographic formations unique to each world. He maintained a catalogue of all he found.

"Of course Adam and the crew would bring news of what transpired on all the colonized planets. But over time, Adam relished, more than anything, sharing tales of Earth with those hungry to understand their origins. He developed into a more than capable storyteller and would find himself regaling interested adults and children alike long into the night.

"On the worlds which were largely dry land he would tell sea stories. On the ocean covered worlds he would talk of mountains and deserts. On the whole, many of the stories seemed fanciful to his listeners but they enjoyed them nonetheless.

"He would describe the origins of the human species in the plains of Africa and the great empires which arose from those humble beginnings. Earth had become a mythical place to the uncounted human multitude flung across the stars and Adam's stories built upon his listener's hunger to understand their origins. The only ones who didn't care to listen to his stories were those on the Dark Worlds.

"The Dark Worlds were old, lifeless planets whose suns had ceased to generate the tremendous radiation necessary to sustain life on their orbiting planets. Some of these suns had gone cold in the natural course of their life cycle while others were small dwarfs unable to generate enough heat to melt a passing comet. Without solar radiation all plant and animal life died. There was no weather or climate to speak of without solar heat to spur the winds. And without that same heat, each planet degenerated into a lifeless deep freeze. But the Dark Worlds often held great mineral wealth and so were a vital stop on Adam's circuit.

"It was virtually impossible for those on the Dark Worlds to appreciate Adam's stories. With no sunlight to illuminate the terrain and no liquid water the planets were left as a dark barren landscape.

"Adam didn't care for the Dark Worlds. Apart from the lifeless terrain it was next to impossible for the ones who lived on those worlds to appreciate Adam's tales of Earth; their hard life reflected in their faces and their attitudes. Parents attempted to prevent their children from listening to Adam's stories as they saw them as a fanciful waste of time.

"During his shore time on one particular Dark World he had found a willing listener. While telling a story the listener interrupted and asked, 'If Earth is so wonderful, why did you leave?' Adam tried to explain his wanderlust but once back on his ship confessed to himself he missed his home planet more than he thought. In fact, as he reflected he realized that someday, when he was tired of traveling, he wanted more than anything to return to the world of his birth.

"As his longing to return home grew, Adam's stories of Earth became more fanciful. With deep insight he understood he had spent his entire life torn between his curiosity for other people and places and the love of his home. Finally, when the time for his retirement arrived, he informed his superiors that he wanted to return to Earth for his final voyage.

"Cruising through space, another, younger captain at the helm, Adam could barely conceal his anticipation. Standing on the bridge of the supply vessel as he neared the planet, unable to contain his excitement, he looked at the image of Earth in the video.

"Something didn't look right. He asked the captain if they were off course. The captain, confused as well, checked his instruments and compared them with the star charts. 'No,' he replied. 'This should be Earth.'

"Instructing one of the crew to conduct a broader sweep of the solar system, Adam saw the problem on the view screen. The Sun had gone dark. Uncounted years in relativistic time had passed since he left leaving a Dark World in their wake. The truth proved too much for Adam and he spent his last days in madness on the Dark World which once had been Earth."

"Well, that made me feel better," said Peter.

Indulgently, Jules replied, "I told the story to make a point. Michael's right. We tend to idealize the past but we can't go back there both because it never existed as we remember it and because the passage of time changes much we do remember."

"I think there is another point here," added Michael. "Adam spent his entire life conflicted between his ambitions and his love of home, of comfort. For many of us, this inner tension simultaneously provides the source of our achievements and our pain. Is there a middle path, one which isn't black and white that we can choose to rise above the natural tension? I wonder."

Later, as Michael and Gabby lay in bed she said, "I was listening to you tonight and thinking how different things are now; how different you are. I'm not talking about these new abilities. You're more direct, more sure of yourself, driven. Aren't you worried about where this might lead?"

Michael rolled on his side to face her. "Of course. It's all happening so quickly. I feel like I'm the same person, but different. For years I felt like an invalid, and now I'm starting to walk again. It's like that. I feel as though blinders have been removed and I see in a whole new way."

"What about the rest of us? Do you see us the same way? Am I the same or different?"

"I feel like I can see you so much more clearly than before."

Gabby didn't say anything for a few moments and then asked, "Why do you believe we should offer the Ulysses Treatment to everyone?"

Michael rolled onto his back, staring at the ceiling. "I could offer you a thousand good reasons, all of them logical. What I didn't want to say tonight . . . I see this as the only possible alternative. I said earlier we stand on a knife's edge. Logically, this could go a number of ways, but my intuition tells me we are only seeing the tip of the iceberg here and in the next few days the game will change dramatically. We've set events in motion from which there can be no return. It's something on the edge of my consciousness. I think it's related to my other dream."

"The one you mentioned the other night?" Gabby asked, half afraid of the answer.

"I didn't tell you because I had it right before the Treatment and we've been too caught up ever since. I told Peter because he was in the dream."

Gabby said nothing after hearing his story. Instead she moved close to Michael.

"Michael, I'm afraid. This is all happening so fast and I worry I'm going to lose you again."

In response Michael pulled her close and kissed her.

"I promise we will get through this together. I told you before. You're stuck with me."

Despite the darkness Gabby looked into his eyes.

She didn't know if she believed him because she trusted his newfound prescience or for the simple reason she needed to. At this moment it didn't matter. She took comfort in knowing with all her heart and mind, after all they had been through, no matter what happened, at least they would have each other. And that was quite a lot.

Michael reached up touching Gabby's face. She could feel his warm breath; see his smile, even in the dark.

"Guess what."

"What?" Gabby responded confused by the question.

"It's not only my legs that are working again. I believe I can rise to the occasion."

"Michael!" Gabby giggled like a teenager.

"It's been a long time."

"Too long."

The lovers embraced rekindling an intimacy they had missed for so long.

Chapter 24

Activity the next day, Tuesday, began bright and early. It was mid-morning and Gabby had just finished putting Michael through his paces. Though he now used a walker he looked as though he hardly needed it. As the two of them trudged into the living room, Peter and Jules marveled at the progress he was making when the phone rang.

After a brief conversation Jules said, "Thanks, Alice," and hung up the phone. "That was the airport. Arthur landed a few minutes ago. I'm sure he's on his way here."

"What do you think he wants?" Gabby asked.

"I've known him for over thirty-five years and I should be able predict what he'll do. I suspect he learned of the break-in. He'll come in, act very cordial, and get to the point quickly. I suspect he's having trouble completing Project Achilles and needs Gabby to finish it. In all likelihood he will threaten you, Gabby. Don't rise to the bait. He will be using this as a lever to get to me. Stay calm and let me handle it. Everything is a negotiation to him and he has to win."

"Do you think we should all be here?" Peter suggested. "Maybe we should just stay out of sight."

"He'll have a pretty good idea who's here. I don't want him thinking he has us on the defensive. Just stay put."

Before long the doorbell rang and Jules went to answer it.

"Hello Arthur, welcome."

"Good morning Jules, nice to see you, may I come in?"

"Certainly", as Jules led Arthur into the living room he introduced the others. "I believe you know Dr. Neumann." Arthur nodded his head in recognition. And that's her husband Michael seated next to her."

Arthur walked over and shook first Gabby's and then Michael's hand. "I believe we met once before, Mr. Neumann. Hello, Peter," he said as he turned to recognize Jules' nephew.

"Won't you have a seat? Can I get you something to drink?" Jules offered.

"No, thank you," said Arthur as he sat. Jules and Peter followed suit. Arthur spoke before Jules had the chance.

"I'll come right to the point. I'm here to see you, Gabby. I believe Bob acted rashly in terminating your employment. I was putting quite a bit of pressure on him and he buckled. I didn't find out you were gone until it was too late. I came to offer you your job back."

Arthur's conciliatory tone surprised her; but returning to BDT held little interest. Project Achilles was only a means to an end. Now that Michael was well, her old job held little interest.

"Arthur, I want to thank you for your offer. But after what happened last week I wouldn't be comfortable coming back."

Gabby thought she saw a malicious smile briefly cross Arthur's face.

"I'm sorry to hear it," he said. "Your comfort is of little concern to me. I need you to come back and complete Project Achilles. You will be free to leave once you deliver the completed retroviruses.

"Free to leave?" Gabby said. She knew this moment might come; they had talked about it. But now that the threat was out in the open it struck her like a baseball bat causing her heart to race. She could sense Michael's growing agitation as he sat next to her; but she was too preoccupied to wonder what he might do.

"What is it you think you can do Arthur?" Jules asked.

"I know Peter broke into Gabby's lab on the Monday following her termination and now I find the four of you here. I don't know what you're up to. I don't care."

Arthur pulled his cell phone out of his pocket.

"I have General Scott on speed dial. All I have to do is push one button and I can have a Pentagon forensics team here before the day is out."

Arthur addressed his threats to Jules now.

"I have no doubt I can make the case you've violated national security. At a minimum I can assure you your nephew and Dr. Neumann will spend time in a federal prison. You will be disgraced, Jules, and I will be in control of the company. I don't believe that's what you want. I don't want it to come to that but I will make the call if you force my hand."

Turning back to Gabby, Arthur asked, "So Dr. Neumann, what is your decision?"

Gabby noticed Arthur was watching Michael. She moved her head slightly to see what he was looking at and saw Michael tapping his foot nervously. She was certain Paulson knew about Michael's injury.

Before she could respond to Arthur's question Michael turned to Gabby and said with real conviction "You don't have to go back there if you don't want to."

"Its okay, Michael, as distasteful as this is, it doesn't seem I have a choice".

Arthur smiled to himself but before Jules could protest or threaten him, Michael leaped from his chair.

"You're not going to get away with this," he roared, anger seething from every pore. "I won't let you bully my wife."

Arthur smirked while Jules, Peter, and Gabby sat frozen in shock.

Has Michael completely lost his mind? Gabby wondered.

"Well, well, well. The truth comes out."

Arthur addressed Gabby again.

"I had my suspicions. While I thought it a possibility you might have tried to complete Project Achilles on your own; that didn't make sense. Bob told me you had another project on the side. It appears you were successful; my congratulations to you and your husband. Now I must determine what to do with this new information. But first, tell me, what is this new treatment you've devised?"

Not knowing what else to do, Gabby recounted the story behind the Ulysses treatment. In an attempt to garner his sympathy and understanding Gabby described Michael's worsening condition. She detailed the method used and how she introduced the retrovirus. "Finally, when Michael awoke . . ."

But before Gabby could continue, Michael turned to Gabby. "Please, let me tell the rest."

Surprised, Gabby nodded in agreement. And then she realized Michael had orchestrated the discussion to get to this point. He had a plan. Looking at Peter and Jules she suspected they had come to the same conclusion and waited for Michael's next move. Gabby marveled at how much he had changed in the past 48 hours and how he was now taking control of their destinies. Perhaps this was the knife edge he mentioned the previous evening.

"So I was lying there in bed; Gabby testing my sensations and movement. I couldn't believe it. I could feel it when she touched my legs and I could move my toes."

"How long had you been paralyzed?" Arthur asked.

"It'd been about four years," Michael replied.

"And you received the treatment last Friday? That's truly remarkable progress."

"That isn't the half of it. There have been collateral benefits: primarily a significant boost to my intelligence. I can think more quickly and see patterns in ways I never had before."

Hearing that last statement Arthur could not maintain his detached demeanor, his excitement readily apparent to all.

"And there have been no negative side effects?"

"None."

"Dr. Neumann, what would happen if the treatment were given to an otherwise normal person?" Arthur asked.

"This is still so new there's no way to predict with complete certainty what would happen. I suspect they would experience the same effects Michael has," Gabby speculated glancing over at Michael and doing her best to play along in his high stakes game.

"Mr. Paulson, are you considering the Treatment?" Michael probed.

Gabby couldn't believe what she heard. *Was he so desperate to extend the Treatment he would recruit anyone*?

In all he attempted Arthur struggled to prove himself seeing rivalry whether competing against himself or anyone else. Though he would be loath to admit it; in college he envied those whose minds worked more quickly or were more creative though he felt himself superior in every other way. Here he saw an opportunity to achieve what he always dreamed of; capabilities he had come to believe would be forever out of reach, his pathological need for dominance overcoming any common sense.

Trying to avoid telegraphing his growing excitement Arthur asked, "I'm intrigued. What's the likelihood of success?"

"My experiments with mice yielded no adverse side effects unlike the Achilles tests. I had to test it on Michael. We had no other option. However, I think you're way out on a limb here. There's too much we don't know. Much more testing is needed."

"It seems to me you've already had significant success with no hint of trouble. Am I correct?"

"Yes. But . . "

Arthur interrupted shaking his head. "I've seen and heard enough. More testing could take years if the FDA approves this at all. And it sounds to me as though this is no more risky than my last acquisition which, by the way, has beaten all expectations. I'm willing to sign a document absolving the four of you of any and all liability if that's what you're worried about. And I'll throw in an additional accommodation."

Worried for multiple reasons but seeing no real way out Jules asked, "Arthur, are you sure you want to do this?"

"In return, I won't pursue charges against any of you. In fact, I can let the Achilles project go. This is going to be so much bigger. When can I start?"

Gabby looked at Michael and then at Arthur. "I can be ready in a couple of hours. Peter, would you please take Mr. Paulson into the treatment room and get him ready?"

Peter nodded, rose, and motioned for Arthur to follow him.

After they left Gabby turned to Michael accusingly asking, "What are you thinking?"

"I echo that," Jules added. "Why Arthur? Are you trying to buy him off?" Jules shook his head. "If it's successful, and that's a big if, he will pervert the Ulysses Treatment to achieve his own ends."

"We need him, but not for the reasons you suspect," Michael replied. "BDT will provide the platform for dissemination of the Ulysses Treatment. We need Arthur to mobilize the complete capacity of the company."

"What reason would he have to work with us?" Jules countered. "Michael, with all due respect, and despite your newfound perceptions, I've known him for his entire adult life and I can't trust his motives."

"But Jules, that's just what you're missing. I'm not counting on my perceptions; I'm counting on his. I told him about only one of the side effects. We haven't said anything about my change in perception. When he starts to connect with those around him, he won't be able to cut himself off any longer. He'll understand the effects of his actions and act accordingly."

"Michael, even if you're right, do you think we should do this to him without fully informing him of the effects?" Gabby asked.

"We'll talk to him in a few minutes. We can't do this unless he understands what he's in for."

Gabby nodded. "Okay, I'll go down to the lab and prepare. I'll let you know when I'm ready. Oh, and by the way Michael, I did like the way you stood up for me, even if you only did it for effect." Gabby turned and headed down to the basement.

"That was quite an act you put on there," Jules commented once Gabby had left. "But there's something still bothering me. Why did he accept so quickly? Arthur's a risk taker but this is pretty extreme, even for him. I can't figure why he jumped."

Michael pursed his lips.

"Something I said when I confronted him hit hard. I don't know what it was but it's buried deep in his mind. And the memory catalyzed a whole range of emotions. Arthur possesses a deep hunger for domination. It was matter of channeling his need for control. We didn't do anything but lay out the facts. He made his own decision."

"I'm beginning to think you are right and I ought to take the Treatment, too. But why do you think BDT is so vital to this effort?"

"To tell you the truth, I'm not sure. There's something else going on. It's on the edge of my awareness. Whatever it is it will involve Peter and, I suspect, BDT, as well."

Chapter 25

Before long, Gabby announced she was ready to proceed. Peter had gone to the basement to help her in the lab after getting Arthur set up in the Treatment room. She had come up from time to time to start his IV and monitor his vital signs. For the past several minutes Gabby and Peter busied themselves in the treatment room while Arthur Paulson lay in the bed. Gabby had connected all of the monitors, explained the procedure and began taking baseline readings. She then called for Jules and Michael to join her.

They had agreed Jules would be the one to explain the full effect of the treatment.

"Arthur, we need to talk. We haven't told you everything. There are additional effects."

Arthur said nothing, waiting to be enlightened.

"We're still in the process of figuring all of this out, but in addition to increased intelligence, Michael has also seen an improvement in his intuition and seemingly can use his new intelligence coupled with his intuition to better predict the future; not as if he's looking into a crystal ball but instead able to see multiple potential outcomes of any one action to arrive at the surest alternative."

"If you're trying to convince me not to do this, that's not the way to go."

Jules nodded. "I expected as much. Michael is also experiencing a new perception. He sees links among people and connects with them on a fundamental level none of the rest of us do and it's caused him to see a bigger picture. I think you know what I mean. I tell you this because it may alter your priorities."

"Jules, I've been listening to you spout this crap my entire adult life; how we all need to rely on each other. But I've achieved what I have under my own power. With this treatment, I will have the intellect to complement my ambition. No one will be able to stop me. And I won't have to listen to your quasi-spiritual BS any longer.

"Arthur," Michael stepped forward steady on his feet looking deeply into Paulson's eyes, "you will change. You have been a loner your entire life, pushing away anyone who tried to get close. Once you've undergone the treatment you will embrace your fellow man and *you* will make the choice."

Before Arthur could protest Michael added, "I'm not here to convince you, only to prepare you."

Gabby stepped forward. "Are you sure you want to do this?"

"Absolutely." Arthur said smiling as he spoke, glaring at Michael with sheer contempt. *Who in the hell did he think he was?*

Gabby injected the drugs to induce a coma. While Arthur lay there, waiting for the medication to take effect Michael smiled. And with a foreknowledge he didn't know he possessed Arthur realized Michael might be right. Now, comprehending he was no longer in control he felt a fear such as he had never experienced.

Following dinner that evening Gabby visited Arthur's room to check on his condition. While she was monitoring his EEG Michael walked in. He moved well now under his own power each hour increasing his strength and mobility.

"How's he doing?"

"So far, so good."

"How would you like to go for a walk outside? I won't take you away too long."

Gabby looked up at Michael and smiled. "Nothing would make me happier. It's been a long time since you and I went for a real walk together. Are you sure you're up for it?"

"I'm tired but I'll be fine for a little while. It's pretty cold, in the teens. You'll want your heavy coat. Let's go without a flashlight. I want to look at the stars."

Gabby and Michael walked arm in arm under a cloudless sky. The moon hadn't yet risen and their eyes adjusted slowly to the complete darkness. They were amply rewarded for their patience.

"I don't think I've ever seen so many stars," Gabby observed. Tiny points of light filled the sky blotting out the darkness.

"Do you see that band of stars?" Michael asked. "It runs across the entire arc of the sky. That's the Milky Way galaxy."

"Oh look," Gabby exclaimed pointing north. There, not far above the horizon Michael saw what looked like faint, undulating waves like curtains.

"It's the aurora borealis," Gabby declared.

"I've never seen it," marveled Michael.

"Neither have I, except in photographs."

"You know, in the city you look up, see a few stars and think most of the night sky is black totally missing out on this beauty. Out here you realize the sky is full of light.

"Poor Arthur, I hope he finds his light," Michael added.

Gabby couldn't remember being more content. Here they were, just the two of them out in the middle of nowhere, their breath forming clouds in the air with nothing around but primeval forest and the night sky; the pain and stress of the past few years gone leaving only the two of them.

"Are you happy, Michael?" Gabby asked.

Pulling her close he looked down at her and replied softly, "very".

"Look, a shooting star," she cried as she pointed.

"Do you ever wonder if there is life out there?" he asked.

"I figure there must be. The chance life only exists here on Earth, with all the billions of planets out there; it's so unlikely we're the only ones."

They stood there for a few minutes staring at the sky when Gabby noticed Michael wasn't moving. She looked into his face. His features had gone slack.

"Michael?" she shook him. "Michael," she called and shook him harder. He still didn't respond.

Jules and Peter heard her scream and were upon them in moments.

"What happened?" Peter asked.

"I don't know," Gabby replied through her panic, "One minute we were talking and the next he was like this."

"Let's get him back inside," suggested Jules.

They walked Michael into the house under his own power but his catatonic state didn't change. Peter and Jules laid him on the couch while Gabby retrieved her medical instruments from the treatment room. She returned shortly with her bag.

"His pulse, blood pressure, and respirations are normal and his pupils are reactive," Gabby reported. "I don't think it's a stroke."

"Do you have any idea what's going on?" Peter asked.

Sitting on the edge of the couch and continuing to observe Michael, Gabby conjectured, "It could be any one of a number of things from exhaustion to some other side effect. He's been

226

pushing himself mentally and physically the past few days," she said shaking her head.

"If we don't see any change in the next few minutes, I'm going to get the EEG machine from the treatment room and see if we can learn what's happening here."

Looking up at Peter and Jules she said, "I never should have let Arthur take the Treatment."

Neither said a word. Gabby continued to observe Michael. After about five minutes she rose to her feet and announced, "I'm going to go and unhook the EEG from Arthur. I'll be back in a minute. Please keep an eye on him."

Before Gabby made it to the treatment room though Peter shouted, "Gabby, come back here."

"What is it?" she asked as she dashed back into the living room.

"Michael closed his eyes," Peter responded.

And while Gabby looked at him, trying to discern what was going on, Michael's eyes began to flutter and then open.

Seeing Gabby standing over him, Michael smiled and said "Hey." He looked tired and then a quizzical look crossed his face. He sat up and asked, "How did I get here?"

"We were outside looking at the stars, do you remember?" Gabby probed.

Michael tilted his head to one side, "Yeah, we were standing there . . ."

A look of recognition crossed Michael's face

"Peter, get me paper and something to write with," he commanded.

Michael practically tore the legal pad and pen out of Peter's hand and began to write furiously, like a man possessed.

"Michael, what's going on?" Gabby demanded.

"Hold on, just give me a minute."

In no time Michael filled five pages with notes, equations and drawings. When finished, he handed the pad back to Peter.

"What do you think?" he asked.

"I'm not sure," Peter stated absentmindedly as he studied the papers. He took the pad over to a table, sat down, and began poring over Michael's scribbles.

"Michael, what happened?" Gabby demanded.

"We were standing there, talking about whether there was life elsewhere. Almost as a lark, I wondered what would happen if I reached out, tried to find consciousness out there, beyond Earth. I sent my perception out toward the stars. I don't know what I expected to find but I encountered intelligence.

"It understood me and communicated with me. It's hard to articulate how." Michael seemed to be struggling again for words.

"It spoke to me in images and concepts rather than words infusing understanding directly into me. And then it took over."

"It took over? What do you mean?" Jules asked.

Michael sat staring for over a minute and then responded, "Jules, I'm sorry but I'm feeling very tired and disoriented. I really need to lie down. Would it be all right if I go to bed and we talk about this in the morning?"

"Certainly," Gabby replied as she helped him to his feet her features making no secret of her concern.

"Are you sure you're all right?" she asked as she led him to their room.

"I think so. I feel as if I haven't slept for a while and my mind's too jumbled to put any coherent thoughts together. I just need to sleep. I'll be okay in the morning."

Ten minutes later Gabby returned to the living room after having helped her husband into bed.

Jules stood as he asked, "Is he all right?"

"I don't know. If we were in a hospital with all its diagnostic capabilities I might know more. It might help to talk with other physicians. But what we're dealing with here is so new, I'm not sure that would help anyway. To tell you the truth, I'm feeling very alone and isolated.

"I want to believe Michael will be all right, but ever since he demonstrated these new abilities and I saw the MRI I've been feeling as though I'm a ship at sea with no anchor, at the mercy of whatever wave comes next. I'm worried and I'm not even sure what to worry about first."

Plaintively she looked at him, "Did I do the right thing? I can't help wondering if I'm losing him."

"What do you mean?" Jules asked.

"He's the same but he isn't. He's filled with a purpose I don't understand. I only wanted him to get better. I guess I assumed we would go back to life as it was. It never occurred to me we could never go back."

Jules looked into Gabby's eyes and saw a lost, frightened woman. "You know Heraclitus said 'You can never step in the same river twice"?

Gabby nodded.

"Change is inevitable. They say over the term of a life-long marriage you are, in truth, married to three different people, we change so much.

"You're not alone. I see the way he looks at you. And that look hasn't changed one bit in the short time I've known you. But he's going to need you more than ever now. You've emerged from four dark years. While Michael's change has been nothing short of miraculous and revolutionary; you have to figure out what the change means for you and how you're going to make it work.

Gabby's rueful smile told Jules he got through.

"Thanks, you're right," she said. "It doesn't make it easier but we'll work it out. Frankly, I worry as much about his sanity in the midst of all this change. Now he's talking to aliens? Come on."

"Maybe you'll accept this," Peter said as he walked over to where they were sitting.

"I didn't know you were listening," Gabby said.

"Only half listening, and you have no reason to be ashamed. I'm surprised you've held it together as well as you have. I feel like I've been on a rollercoaster ever since this whole thing started. And this latest," he said nodding at the pad he held in his hand "well, I don't know where to begin. This looks too good to be true."

"What is it?" Jules asked.

"You both know I've been trying to find a way to develop a computer processor which more closely corresponds to the human brain. Gabby and I've been working on parallel paths for some time; she's been coming at the problem from the biological standpoint while I have been approaching it from the electronic side. Until now I've been facing hurdles I haven't a clue how to approach. The notes Michael gave me provide the blueprint to build a processor with more connections than the typical person's brain, perhaps on a par with what happened to Michael.

"Beyond the processing speed and the capability to deal with higher order problems, I think there may be much more here. Michael's neurological changes have enabled him to connect with us and we theorized this occurs on a quantum level. These notes support the theory and make me wonder whether this will allow us to communicate mentally through and with the processor."

"Peter, I hate to interrupt but I want to go and check on Michael. I'll be right back."

Gabby left the room.

"Peter, this is very exciting."

"I'm a little overwhelmed but I think there's enough here I can get started on a prototype. This may be connected to what Michael saw in his latest dream. I don't know if he told you but he saw himself and those around him as both human beings and machines. With this discovery we could alter the entire course of automation on a par with the development of the steam engine and the internet."

Gabby returned.

"How's Michael?" Peter queried.

"He looks fine. His vital signs are normal. I think we let him sleep for now. I checked on Arthur, too, and everything looks good. What did you figure out in my absence?"

"I've got a lot of work to do and I'm chomping at the bit to get started," said Peter. "I think I'll go down to the lab and see what I can cook up. I believe I have most of what I need here."

"Do you need any help?" Jules asked reluctantly.

"Not really. I can accomplish more on my own at this point. You two need to go to bed."

"I'll take the first shift with Arthur," Jules volunteered. I'll wake you in about four hours."

"OK, that way I can keep an eye on Michael. It doesn't look like any of us will get much sleep tonight."

Chapter 26

They got a late start the next day. Jules had let Gabby sleep for six hours. Then he went to bed while she alternately watched Arthur and checked on Michael.

When Jules saw Peter, bleary-eyed and unkempt, entering the living room at noon, he asked, "How's it coming?"

"Not too badly. I worked all night and I'm making good progress. I'm having to jury rig the thing so what you'll see here isn't very elegant. The device should work better once I have the resources back in my lab. I hope when Arthur recovers he will be open to working with us."

Gabby entered.

"How's Arthur?" Jules asked.

"He's doing well," she replied. "He stabilized more quickly than Michael probably because there was no damage to repair. I think we will be able to bring him out of his coma this afternoon. And he's exhibiting the same increase in gamma activity that we saw with Michael"

"And how is Michael?" Peter asked.

"He slept well last night. I checked in on him a few minutes ago and he's beginning to stir."

They began talking about what to do next and before long Michael entered the room.

As if compelled, they stood in unison, Gabby walking over to him.

"How are you feeling?"

Instead of responding directly Michael first looked to Peter and inquired, "How did the notes work out?"

"They're not too hard to follow. But you should see the contraption. I was up most of the night working. It looks like something out of a 1950's science fiction film with wires and circuit boards everywhere. It seems to function as a highly complex feedback loop simulating the parallel circuitry of the brain. I still have a few connections to puzzle out and so may need your help deciphering these instructions."

"I'm not sure I can."

And then as if confused asked, "Why is everyone standing?"

The other three grinned sheepishly as they all sat, Gabby next to Michael.

"I'm sorry I didn't answer your first question Gabby but I needed to understand something before I could even tell you. I wasn't sure if what happened last night was a dream or some form of psychotic break. There's been so much happening to me of late I'm having a hard time discerning what's real and what I seem to perceive. In any event the answer to your question isn't simple but I'm okay.

"You don't sound fine," Gabby replied. "If you are having a hard time distinguishing between your dreams and reality there may be a problem."

Michael smiled and took her hand. "Do you remember the time Megan was staying with us for a few weeks?" Gabby nodded and Michael continued, "I don't remember how it came up but she told the story about how she had accidentally overdosed."

"I remember."

Michael turned to Peter and Jules, "My sister was something of a wild child as a teenager and she once took a handful of pills. I don't think she was trying to harm herself but she was very depressed and looking for relief. Fortunately when she realized what she'd done she had sufficient presence of mind to call our father and he rushed over to where she was partying and took her to the hospital. They spent a few hours in the emergency room and then came home. Megan went directly to bed.

"The next morning we were sitting in the kitchen when she came downstairs. She was in her pajamas and looking fine like she just had a good night's sleep. When she was in the emergency room they took her blood gasses."

Gabby jumped in, "Usually they take blood from a vein in your arm but if they need to test your oxygen, carbon dioxide, and pH they need to stick an artery instead. It's more painful and they have to wrap the site when they're done. Typically they draw from the wrist."

Michael continued, "Anyway, as she walked into the room, she looked at her wrist and saw the bandage. Her eyes went wide as she collapsed in tears realizing the events of the previous evening had been real.

"Before I said any more about last night, I wanted to make sure it actually happened. Oh, and Megan never did drugs again."

"Does that mean you won't be contacting any aliens after this?" Gabby asked tentatively.

"No, I won't. I wouldn't want to do it again; it was foolish of me, and won't be necessary anyway."

Peter interrupted. "Could we continue this conversation in the lab? I want to keep working on the BRIDG."

"The bridge?" everyone asked at once.

"That's what I've named it," Peter said as they walked down the stairs to the basement. "It stands for Brainwave Receiving Integrated Digital Gateway or BRIDG without the 'e'."

Once they got to the lab everyone crowded around Peter's workbench.

"What is all this stuff?" Michael asked.

"Surrounding my work area here I have a digital voltmeter to test the circuits as I build them. This over here is a wave generator. It creates sine waves, square waves; it's used for amplitude and frequency modulation."

Peter could see Michael and Gabby's eyes glazing over.

"Anyway what I have here is a breadboard, it's like a circuit board but it's used to put together prototype circuits without using a soldering iron. I can't put it all in one chip at this point so I'm rigging several components together that I already had down here in the lab to approximate what Michael's notes instructed me to do. I never would have thought of this configuration."

"Speaking of instructions, Michael, you were saying it wouldn't be necessary to communicate with the alien intelligence again?" Jules asked.

"Keep in mind; I'm only relaying what I learned during my blackout. And Peter, please jump in if you think I miss anything. In addition to processing data and information in a much more complex fashion there is an additional capability which will prove even more revolutionary. For the first time people will be able to communicate directly through and with a computer. This will open up possibilities which, until now, were confined to the imagination. Also because this technology is not spatially dependent, we can use it to communicate without the use of wires.

"That makes sense," Peter said not taking his eyes from his work. "But I'm still reeling with the confirmation there is life on other worlds."

"It began simply enough. I felt a light touch, an unarticulated question. Very seamlessly I felt another presence, not unlike when I reached out to each of you. It was very odd; I couldn't say if it was one individual or many. But I could feel it probing. The interchange began like a history lesson."

"There are a couple of ways this can go. The Ulysses capabilities can evolve over tens of millennia or humanoid species can reach a tipping point where they uncover a way to improve mental performance much the way the Ulysses Treatment does. In those cases where one incident, a sentinel event, occurs which forces the evolutionary process; those situations have to be handled very deliberately and with great care 'cause they can destabilize whole civilizations when this newly capable group comes in contact with groups unprepared for the implications. Perhaps you could draw a parallel with the contact between Homo sapiens and Neanderthals, no offense intended."

"None taken", said Jules rolling his eyes as they all smiled.

"But that's at the heart of what I've been worrying about and one reason why I'm pushing to offer the Treatment more broadly. I was on the right track."

"Did they recommend a path to get through all this safely?" Peter asked in jest.

Michael paused, careful in framing his response.

"I'm still trying to absorb what happened. I believe my contact with them thrust me forward; augmenting my perceptions and capabilities as though I've been stretched to a new level. It's like when you play a video game or learn any new skill. You start out limping along but with practice you become a pro and you never go back to your old skill level. I see what we need to do with even greater clarity now. I want to figure out our next steps but I would like to wait until Arthur is awake before we talk further. When do you think you can wake him Gabby?"

"I'll check on him again in a little while."

Michael kept to himself the other reason he now understood for the need to offer the Treatment more broadly. There would be time enough for that later.

Following lunch Gabby checked Arthur's EEG again and saw the same distinctive wave pattern Michael exhibited a few days earlier and determined the time was right to begin the process to bring him out of the coma. She injected the drugs with Jules and Michael standing in the room while Peter labored over his newfound obsession in the basement.

He is dimly aware of his surroundings, unable to orient himself. No frame of reference. He realizes he must have been unconscious as instinct takes over and he struggles to get his bearings. He is barely able to mentally voice the inevitable first questions: "Where am I, how did I get here"?

Dimly he is aware he expected this.

How long have I been asleep? he wonders. He is aware of his body but unable to move or communicate as though he is in suspended animation, floating on a cloud. Before panic takes hold he senses something is different. He notices an indescribable feeling, like a gentle wind blowing through him. The pressure of the wind builds and grows filling him with a sensation like movement and yet, light and perfectly still. A rising sense of both anticipation and apprehension grip him. Am I dying? And in answer to the unheard question, memory floods back, and with it, Arthur remembers where he is and slowly opens his eyes.

Chapter 27

He saw a woman standing next to him, Gabby Neumann; and standing next to her, her husband, Michael. Arthur turned his head and saw Jules on the other side of his bed.

"Well, Jules, it's like old times. Have you come in to wake me up for class?"

"No, my friend, you are waking from a different sleep," Jules gently replied.

"How long have I been out?"

"Less than twenty-four hours," Gabby replied.

Arthur now recalled his choice. Like an athlete whose cast has been removed Arthur wanted to flex his new found mental capacity but before he could do so he heard another voice.

"Arthur." He turned his head toward Michael. "Tell me what you feel."

"What do you mean? I . . ." Arthur felt another awareness touching his, gently, like a breeze just strong enough to raise the hair on his arms. The sensation confused and mystified him. Michael's gentle probing acted as a catalyst causing Paulson to perceive his connections to those in the room for the first time.

He looked from person to person, consternation written across his features. "This is odd."

The other three remained silent. Gabby, looking at the monitors, saw a spike in his gamma wave amplitude and a significant increase in his pulse rate.

"What's happening to me? My heart, beating so fast. Can't catch my breath."

"You're having an anxiety attack," said Gabby looking from Arthur to the monitors and back again.

"What do you mean? I've never had an anxiety attack before! What did you do to me?"

Gabby glanced at Michael hoping he had a solution while Arthur looked around him as though trying to figure out how to get out of a trap.

"Arthur, stop, remember," Michael commanded.

Taken aback by the force of Michael's authority Arthur sat back and looked curiously at Michael. As he plunged into memory a look of recognition crossed his face.

§

Arthur Paulson sat at his desk, nervously fidgeting with his pencil, worried the teacher would call on him. Third grade had presented more of a challenge to the young boy than he had experienced in earlier grades, especially in math. The teacher had been grilling her students on multiplication and was preparing to call one to the board.

Arthur enjoyed demonstrating his mastery and so usually got a thrill when the teacher called on him. But even though he had studied the evening before he still had trouble grasping the basics in the latest assignment. He had asked his father for help but had been told to figure it out for himself.

"Arthur, please come up to the board", said the teacher.

Arthur nervously rose from his seat and approached the green slate monster taking the chalk in his hand and looking up at Mrs. Moore. A map of the world had been lowered to cover the problems.

"There are ten multiplication problems on the board. Let's see how many you can do in the next sixty seconds."

Mrs. Moore looked at the large white faced clock over the classroom door while her hand looped through the wire hand hold at the bottom of the map. As the second hand swept past the twelve she pulled down releasing the map.

"Go!"

Arthur's adrenaline crashed into his heart increasing his pulse by a factor of two. He completed the first problem easily. The second problem proved more difficult. But the adrenaline which had such a stimulating effect on his heart confused his thinking. Arthur froze on problem three and had made it only to problem four when time ran out.

Now deflated by his utter failure and the after affects of the hormone rush, Arthur turned to Mrs. Moore at a loss. A dark cloud seemed to have descended on the room. The other kids stared at him thankful that it hadn't been them.

Torn by the hormonal imbalance and his humiliation Arthur felt his bile rise and knew in an instant what was to come. Unable to avoid the inevitable Arthur's breakfast disgorged violently striking the floor and spraying Mrs. Moore's feet.

Staring in horror Arthur uttered an apologetic, "I'm sorry Mommy" loud enough for everyone to hear.

The class erupted in uncontrolled laughter.

"Bobby, please take Arthur to the boy's room so he can clean up and then take him to the nurse's office. Class, I will be back in five minutes. I expect everyone to behave."

Arthur wanted more than anything to go home but the nurse told him he was fine and sent him back to class. As he walked back into the room, shoulders slumped and looking only at the floor, he could feel the other students' eyes boring into him.

He took his seat and finished the day as best he could. When the final bell rang Arthur hurried out of the school yearning for the refuge of home.

He walked quickly in the cold winter air. After turning onto a quiet side street they caught up with him.

John Mauer stood taller than the other boys in the class. He had been left behind after first grade. He had two other boys and one girl with him.

"Where do ya think you're goin', Momma's Boy?"

Arthur pretended not to hear and kept walking head down, his heart beating hard.

Mauer ran in front of Arthur, turned to face him and held out his hand to stop Arthur's progress.

"You really screwed up today little boy. You puked on your 'Mommy'." Arthur tried to walk around the bully but the others blocked him.

"What're ya gonna do tough guy, puke on me, too?"

Arthur continued looking down not willing to confront the much larger and more aggressive child.

"Look at me." Arthur reluctantly raised his chin and saw Mauer's threatening eyes staring back at him. "Whatta ya say?"

"No" came out as a mumble.

Mauer pushed Arthur hard enough for him to fall back landing on his rear end in a puddle of melted snow where he remained not wanting to escalate the confrontation.

"Get up and fight."

"No." Arthur shook his head and stared at his feet.

"Then stay there 'til ya can't see us."

The girl in the pack reached into a snow bank, and, while pulling Arthur's jacket and shirt back, stuffed a handful of the melting snow down his back. The four walked away laughing, periodically looking over their shoulders at him to make sure he didn't move.

Arthur stayed in that position for what seemed like an eternity; the icy snow trickling down his back. Dimly sensing the passing cars Arthur felt utterly isolated; the drivers oblivious to his disgrace.

When he got home he went straight to his room. His multiple humiliations weighed on him blotting out all feeling. After changing his wet clothes, he stared out his bedroom window in despair watching a crow perched on the tree limb outside his room. In his imagination the crow appeared to be looking at him. And then, in a flash the bird left its post diving to catch a passing insect.

In that moment with the power of deep determination Arthur Paulson resolved never to put himself in a position to face such humiliation again. They would never find him unprepared; they would never be able to take advantage of him.

And he reached one more decision, one he barely understood with his conscious mind: he couldn't rely on anyone. There had been no one to speak out for him. The class had laughed at his pain. His teacher and the nurse dismissed his shame. He didn't dare tell his parents what transpired. They would see his admission as a sign of weakness and think him less for it.

No, he was on his own.

And so effective was his resolve that over the years he forgot the experience of that February day, its aftermath guiding his every action.

§

Arthur Paulson took a deep breath. The memory so long held in the clutching shadows of his unconscious now occupied his waking awareness as if it were yesterday.

But it wasn't yesterday. Arthur now had the benefit of a mature mind honed by experience and coupled with the power of the Ulysses Treatment. Instinctively his newfound awareness understood and simultaneously accepted and rejected his defensive reaction, his self-awareness growing at an exponential rate.

"This is incredible. I believe I understand what's happening to me. When my anxiety kicked in I felt as though I had been backed into a corner and I was flailing away trying to get out. Michael, you got my attention forcing me to confront what I had avoided for so long. I've never experienced anything like this, well almost.

"Jules, remember when we took Psych 101 together freshman year? We studied Maslow. He wrote about transpersonal states and peak experience as the source of religious and mystical insight. This fits with his concept of self-actualization."

Arthur looked at Gabby and Michael, "You'll have to forgive me for this. Jules and I, well, it was the 70's and we experimented. There was a lot of talk about drugs causing peak experience. We knew it was false and unsustainable but felt we were touching on a world beyond ourselves. Over time I came to the understanding I was engaged in self-delusion and abandoned that counterfeit experience."

"You denied that stage of your life, however brief, for so long. It's good to hear you recognize your past," said Jules.

"You tricked me," said Arthur.

Gabby turned to Jules and Michael. "I was afraid of this."

Michael only smiled.

Jules moved to correct Arthur but before he could get a word out Arthur, a look of wonder on his face, said, "it's okay. There's no way I could've prepared for this. It's fascinating and I'm at a loss for words. I can sense each of you, what you're feeling."

Arthur paused as if considering what to say next.

"Jules, I'm so sorry. All these years. I didn't know."

"What do you mean?" Jules asked.

"You genuinely care for me. I've never felt anything like this before, with anyone."

"We've been through a lot together; I always wanted your friendship but ever since we left school, I felt it was one-sided. You wanted me as a friend for what you could get out of it, not for the sheer value of camaraderie. I hope that can change now."

"Dr. Neumann," Arthur appeared to be considering what to say next. "I sense a wall. You don't trust me. I can't say I blame you. I've given you sufficient reason to question my motives. I've awakened in a world I recognize only poorly. It's as though someone turned on a light and I now see in clear relief features which I perceived only indistinctly before, if at all. At this point I'm more than a little disoriented. There is so much which isn't as it appeared, at least to me."

Arthur looked at Michael.

"You're different," he observed.

"What do you mean?" Gabby asked.

"It's not that you've had the Treatment, too," Arthur said still looking at Michael. "There's more to you. I can't explain it."

"We have a lot to talk about. Are you ready to get up?" Michael asked.

"Michael, be patient," Gabby interrupted.

Arthur lay there uncomplaining while Gabby checked his vital signs.

"How are you feeling?" she asked. "Any headache, other discomfort?"

"No complaints. I feel fine and would like to get out of this bed." he stated.

Gabby stood there considering his request.

"All right, but let's not push it."

Jules left to grab Peter and all five convened in the living room fifteen minutes later after Arthur had dressed. Surprisingly Arthur was the first to speak.

"I want to apologize to all of you, especially to Jules and Gabby, for the way I behaved yesterday. I came out here thinking I was the spider but instead got caught in your web. A whole new world has opened up to me. Thank you."

He looked down into his lap, when he looked up his eyes glistened. "I had no idea. I've missed so much, blinded by my self-centered arrogance. How could I have missed it with the evidence all around me?"

"You didn't," Michael replied. "At a subconscious level you felt the connection but the reptilian portion of your brain saw control as your means to connect to those around you. The problem was compounded as you tried to dominate others; you distanced yourself and got caught in an endless loop. The more you pushed others away the more you craved the connection. But that's behind you now."

Arthur nodded in recognition.

"But we need to determine where we go from here and we don't have much time to deliberate," Michael cautioned.

Chapter 28

Michael began by recounting for Arthur his own experiences of the past 24 hours. The others listened in rapt attention gaining new perspective.

"So you're saying Peter's developing a chip, a processor with which we will be able to communicate directly with computers?

"Not only computers," Peter corrected, "any machine which uses this processor chip. If you have one in your car you can tap into it, too."

"Which means we can type into any computer without even using a keyboard?" asked Gabby.

"A simple example, but you're right," said Peter. "This will open up whole new avenues of software development. And the very nature of software will change.

"Take the internet. Started as a means to communicate and share computer resources it now serves as the very backbone of day-to-day business and culture. Its capabilities and functions evolve as we come up with new and better uses. The leisure time which has been the unfulfilled promise of machines since the dawn of the industrial age will finally come to pass."

"It's starting to sound like we're creating some brave new world here," Jules interjected. "Do you think mankind is ready for this? What's to stop a computer as smart as a person from taking over? I've read too much science fiction to feel comfortable with this."

"Uncle Jules, you're missing the point," Peter jumped in. "For our entire history we have been on a convergent evolutionary path; our simplest tools evolving as our needs change culminating in the twentieth century when we began to create tools which think. We often don't foresee the potential of new technologies, but they develop in spite of us. The internet's a good example; here's another."

"The internal combustion engine was developed in the early part of the nineteenth century. Back then factories ran with the help of steam engines. But steam engines are bulky and require considerable space. The internal combustion engine was invented to provide mechanical power to factories too small to utilize a steam power. Do you think the inventors envisioned an entire industry to support motorized vehicles rather than horse drawn ones; or the interstate highway system which grew out of it for that matter?"

"And that's my fear," said Jules. "Do we really know what we're getting ourselves into here? How do we avoid making the same mistakes we've made with other innovations? The internet has made many slaves to their computers. And for those of us who grew up with the Cold War; we know how the revolution in atomic energy could lead to our mutually assured destruction."

"Jules, I think your concern would be supportable but for two objections", began Arthur. "Keep in mind I'm still trying to sort much of this out, but your misanthropic view of human nature, while valid from a historical perspective, must be reevaluated in light of the Ulysses Treatment. I now believe perceptions I've gained would make it extremely difficult to act in a manner which would be detrimental in the long run. First because, I believe I'll be better able to anticipate and predict the outcomes of my actions and second, I believe the connection I now experience comes from an intrinsic connection which has always existed in some fashion below conscious perception.

"I also believe," Arthur continued, "it's impossible to stand in the way of technological progress, at least in the long term. Peter's right. I know our capacity to design better, faster tools has exceeded our ability to use them wisely at times; but we've adapted. Technology has always been an integral part of our lives whether you're talking about the spear, the printing press, or the integrated circuit. And we have always been inextricably linked. Do you think it random chance that both the Ulysses Treatment and this new BRIDG technology arose at the same time?"

"Jules, the problem with your extrapolations," Michael explained, "is that they assume a static human nature. We are now talking about a leap forward in our evolution. We've been well aware of our limitations as a species for millennia. Religions have created codes and dogma; societies have created laws to control our more primitive natures. While we have chaffed against the yoke of control, we knew it was necessary. Now knowing what is possible we're looking at whole new levels of social consciousness and material progress."

"Do you sincerely believe those with the Treatment will behave differently?" Gabby asked.

"I know it's hard to believe with so much history of misbehavior," said Michael. "Imagine you live in a place covered in thick mud. It's usually up to the middle of your thighs. Each step requires a major effort. Occasionally your legs are only covered up to your knees. When that happens you're elated. Life is easier, walking doesn't require as much effort and you can get where you're going much faster. There are also times when the muck is almost up to your waist. In those situations moving becomes such a chore you stop walking altogether, depressed because there is no escape. One day you find yourself on dry land. Not only can you walk but you can jump and run: activities you could have never conceived. Imagine how your perspective would change."

"It's hard to believe it's that different," Jules stated.

"It's revolutionary," Michael explained. "Here's a very practical example; something I learned during my contact last night. Jules, you brought up the mind/body connection when we were on the airplane last week. And Gabby, you and I have talked before about the linkage between the brain and the immune system."

Gabby nodded as she said, "Some of my colleagues have published in the area. It's called psycho-neuro-immunology. They're finding hormones released by nerve cells can influence the behavior of the immune system. And researchers have also tracked nerve fibers which connect the brain with the thymus, spleen, lymph nodes, and bone marrow, all parts of the immune system."

"Exactly; Arthur and I can now mentally control how our bodies react to disease in the same fashion my mind tells my arm to raise or my head to nod. Many, if not most, illnesses including heart disease, cancer, and arthritis have strong ties to the immune system. Think of the potential here."

"So much for BioDigiTech," Peter observed.

"On the contrary," Arthur offered. "I see a new role for BDT. Rather than an engine for generating wealth I can see using BDT as a platform to develop Peter's BRIDG processor and its applications. In addition, we refine the Ulysses Treatment making it available to the general population. And we can train people to integrate the Treatment with the BRIDG processor."

Arthur stopped talking staring into space contemplating retooling his company; becoming the vehicle for transformation.

"Gentlemen, I agree the Ulysses treatment can be a boon to mankind but I'm surprised none of you see a much bigger problem confronting us here," Gabby said. "Michael, I'm most surprised at you, Mr. Samsa."

"That's you?" interjected Arthur.

Michael nodded as Gabby continued.

"There will be fierce opposition. I'll be surprised if all of us don't end up in prison or worse. When this gets out they'll take away my medical license and that's trivial compared to what's to come. I don't need your foresight to know we'll be fought at each turn. Organized religion will see this as an affront to God. Governments will see a threat to their sovereignty and move swiftly to make the Treatment and the BRIDG illegal.

Michael sensing her very real concern said, "Your fears are well-founded. And all which you envision can and may happen."

Gabby frowned. "You're not helping."

"Do you think I like what's going on here, what's happening to me? You know me well, Gabby. I've never been a revolutionary. Oh sure, I offer my armchair observations in my blog and wait for the fallout. But I've never been on the front lines; never truly put myself out there fighting for what I believe. I couldn't live with myself if I squandering this gift.

"I know I don't show it but I'm struggling. I don't want to be a lightning rod for what's to come. But what am I supposed to do? There is so much anguish in the world. You've seen the response to my blogs. Now I can actually feel other's pain. And for the first time we can do something about it. How can I look the other way?

251

"No, the revolution will begin with Samsa's voice offering hope. What do you think the established power structures can do to stop the tide? Oh, in the short term they will make our task very difficult but in the long run we must prevail."

"You talk as though the end result is predetermined," said Jules.

"This could end badly for any one of us," Michael observed, his candor sobering. "We may fail but I genuinely believe if we proceed together we will succeed: the more people who've had the treatment the better our chances for success. And with Peter's BRIDG we'll have a tool, a lever to bring others along."

No one spoke for what seemed like an eternity. And then Gabby broke the silence.

"I don't know where all of this will lead. The path forward is still dark to me but I'm ready. I want to take the Treatment."

Jules nodded. "I'm ready."

Peter shrugged. "I guess I assumed it was a foregone conclusion."

Gabby looked at Arthur and could see exhaustion in his eyes. "My patient needs rest, let's have a quick dinner and call it an evening. We can make our plans tomorrow for who goes next."

They gathered in the kitchen a few minutes later for a quick meal: omelets á la Jules. Peter was joking about how one of the big benefits of the new processor will be that people won't feel the need to text when driving their cars or sitting in the movie theaters when Arthur entered the room.

"Change of plans," he announced. "I was checking my messages. I hadn't called in since yesterday and there was a message from General Scott. He's on the warpath. He's heading for BDT tomorrow to take possession of the Achilles virus and he expects my cooperation."

"We can't let that happen," Gabby warned.

"I understand now," said Arthur. "If he gets his hands on the virus he will induce his troops with disastrous consequences. And as a result he will do untold damage to our cause and create a real nightmare. Ulysses will be tainted by the Achilles scandal perhaps beyond recovery. We need to get back to BDT."

"We won't be able to get a flight out tonight but I can have a jet waiting for us first thing in the morning. I'll make the arrangements." Jules left the room.

"I'm going to put security at the company on notice and make sure they alert us if they see Scott or his minions although I don't think our BDT employees can handle a frontal assault if that's what the General has in mind", said Arthur.

He left to call BDT.

"Michael, I need to go. You understand, don't you?" Gabby asked.

"Of course, but we're all going."

Gabby didn't question Michael's decision. She was beginning to understand she could trust his instincts. She would have to put off her own transformation until they resolved the current crisis.

Chapter 29

They rose before sunrise and finished packing begun the night before. They had decided to take only what was necessary but Peter insisted on bringing the BRIDG, too. As he entered the living room carrying a box with the components he saw the other travelers busying themselves in preparation for departure. Looking out the window he noticed it was darker outside than it should have been at that hour.

The outside lights were on and gazing out the window he saw snow swirling in the wind.

Jules entered the room and announced, "I just checked the weather and there's a blizzard warning. We'd better get going if we're going to make it."

They loaded their luggage into Arthur's rental car and began the drive back to the airport. The snow had only just started falling and so they made it off the property with minimal difficulty. Before long, though, they had to slow to only 35 miles an hour, the snow blowing hard, reducing visibility. Arthur tried his high beams but quickly lowered them again when it only made visibility worse.

Gabby stared out the window at the passing countryside wishing they could have stayed back at Jules' and sit quietly around the fire. She suspected there would be little chance of that for some time to come.

It took an hour to reach the terminal. They unloaded their bags and Arthur drove the short distance to the rental car return. They gathered together in the small terminal while Jules consulted with the pilot about the weather and flight plan.

Arthur walked into the building stomping the snow off his shoes as Jules came over to join their party. "Visibility isn't good but the pilot informed me we can still go but we should hurry."

As they gathered up their bags Michael, sensing Gabby's unease, pulled her off to the side.

"Are you okay?" he inquired.

"I'm feeling very nervous and on edge. I don't know if I'm more worried about flying in this weather or what we will find when we land."

Michael took Gabby by her shoulders looking deeply into her eyes. "It's going to be okay. We'll stop Scott."

Gabby smiled back at him. "That'd be good but is this roller coaster ever going to end? When do we get to rest, get time for us?"

"You've been through a lot," Michael responded. "I can't imagine how you've carried your burden all these years. And it's not going to get easier, I'm afraid. There's so much more for us to do. But what we're doing here is important, not only for us, but for our children, too."

Gabby looked up at Michael and smiled. She hadn't seriously considered having children for so long. And yet, the desire never left her. But how could they start a family, she wondered, with what there was ahead of them, the trials they would face in the coming months and years.

And then, gazing into Michael's eyes, seeing his warm smile, she knew, she knew with every fiber of her being.

"Oh, my God. Really?"

Michael's smile grew into a grin such as she had never seen in all their years together. She didn't have to ask him how he knew, not anymore. He pulled her close, wrapped his arms around her and they kissed.

Jules, Peter, and Arthur standing nearby witnessed their public display of affection.

"What are you two up to?" Peter asked.

Without letting go of each other, tears in their eyes, they turned their heads and Gabby announced, "We're going to have a baby!"

The three stood there dumbstruck for a moment and then Peter rushed over and hugged Gabby.

"I'm so happy for you," he said with genuine affection.

Each shook hands and hugged in turn, including Arthur.

Intruding on their good news, the pilot reentered the terminal and warned, "We'd better get going."

Hurriedly they gathered up their luggage and headed for the door. The wind driven snow swirled in eddies about them as they trudged to the waiting jet. The white powder already crested over the tops of their shoes.

Looking across the runways Gabby noticed small drifts forming on the far side of the airport. Carefully they climbed the few steps into the cabin. As Peter, the last to board, came through the door, the co-pilot stepped over, raised the stairway, closing the cabin door, sealing them off from the storm.

Once settled in their seats the pilot started the engines and began taxiing for takeoff. He pulled up short a few feet before the runway and announced, "The tower has asked us to wait. I'll let you know when we get clearance."

Looking out the window Gabby noticed the runway hadn't been plowed. Ten minutes passed before the pilot got back on the loudspeaker and told his passengers they had been cleared.

The jet taxied into position; the roar of the engines announcing their departure. Outside the shelter of the cabin the snow continued to blow and with their gathering speed the passengers couldn't see more than a few feet in any direction.

The jet bumped along the snow covered runway as though driving a dune buggy over rough terrain but before long they were airborne, climbing through the buffeting currents. Jules and Arthur, the most seasoned fliers showed little anxiety but the others clutched at their seats in obvious distress.

But, in no time at all they were surrounded by clouds until finally the airplane broke through into the sunny sky above. The plane leveled off and everyone relaxed.

"Is there any way we can find out what General Scott is up to at this point?" Jules asked.

Arthur had the pilot connect him with BDT security where he learned all was quiet.

"Why don't you reach out and see if you can get a sense of what he's up to," Michael suggested. "You know him best and so can probably find him quicker than I can."

Arthur sat back, concentrated, and after a few minutes informed the group he could sense Scott was on the move but could determine little more.

"Arthur, do you think we can reason with him?" Gabby inquired.

"We can try but I'm not optimistic. Reasoning with a person requires they share the same view of the world. He operates in a whole different sphere. He bases his decisions on entirely different assumptions from the rest of us as to how people behave. He sees deception and one-upsmanship around every corner." Arthur smiled. "I used to share the same perspective.

"He believes the Achilles Treatments will provide the Army with an unassailable strategic advantage and is blind to the risks. Having reached out to him I sensed grim determination.

He's set on a path and is prepared to do anything to get what he wants. He believes he is in the right and that little stands in his way. I don't know why he feels the time pressure he does. I doubt we can deter him with reason."

"What do you think he'll do?" Peter asked.

"He'll most likely drive in with a couple of his aides to back him up. He will either come to my office or go directly to the lab. As Gabby may remember he visited to evaluate progress on more than one occasion. Once there he will attempt take possession of the specimens."

"Do you think he has a court order or will he try and take them by force?" Jules asked.

"Either is possible but I doubt he will have gone through legal channels. I suspect he won't want to risk public scrutiny. It isn't clear to me what his superiors know, if anything, and if he were to involve the judge advocate general's office the whole situation might get much more complicated for him and Scott doesn't like complicated.

"If he attempts to push his way through our security people are prepared. I want to get there before he does so we can minimize the damage."

"I don't know about the rest of you, but I'm very worried," Gabby said. "How far do you think he will go?"

Gabby, surprised Michael didn't offer his thoughts, wondered whether he was deferring to Arthur with his superior knowledge of the situation with Scott or if he had decided to keep his counsel for the time being.

"If you're asking if I think he might resort to threats or even violence, I wouldn't put it past him," Arthur said. "Until recently I thought he was your average run of the mill megalomaniac. But after our last encounter, I'm not so sure."

"And you think there's no chance we can reason with him like we did with you, Arthur?" Gabby asked.

Arthur smiled. "Reason? That's a nice term for it. No, I don't think so."

"I meant to say: could we explain the Ulysses Treatment and hope he'll see the potential in it and back off in the short term?"

"The general isn't given to long explanations or what he perceives to be delaying tactics. When he wants something, he expects to get it. We can try but I don't hold out much hope.

"Now those explanations come from my rational mind and my experience with him. In my connection with him just now, well, it's difficult to describe. As best I can tell he is seething with betrayal. He doesn't truly trust anyone so I don't think anything we can do will help."

"So we have no alternatives?" Gabby asked. "I hate to think what will happen should the Achilles retrovirus fall into his hands."

"We have a vault in the basement of building A equipped with electrical power. We can transfer the specimens for safekeeping. What do you think?" asked Arthur.

"I guess that's the best we can do for now," replied Gabby.

"Why don't you destroy the specimens?" Peter asked.

"Technically they are government property," Arthur responded. "We would have to get the Army's permission. In addition, we need to dispose of them properly and I don't think we'll have the time right now. After we hold off Scott we can go to his superiors and plead our case. When we get to BDT I'll go with Gabby and Michael to the lab. Jules and Peter, you are welcome to come with us."

"Peter, how far along is the processor? Do you think you can make it work?" Michael asked.

"I wish I could tell you. At this point it looks like a Rube Goldberg contraption. It's still in the prototype stage so I'm not sure what it'll do. I'll have to reconnect the components first. Why?"

"When you get back to your lab, if you could, please hook the thing up to the BDT servers; we may have need of it."

"You bet," said Peter. "I hate to admit it, with everything else going on, but I'm excited to get into the lab and try this thing out. There are a couple of components I didn't have at uncle Jules' place that I have to get at BDT."

"Can't wait to get started?" asked Jules.

"Guilty as charged," admitted Peter. "But I don't want to miss the action."

"I think we'll get along fine without you, at least for a few hours," Gabby replied marveling at how they had all become very close in the past few weeks. And she wondered what was in store once they all had the Treatment, and then the rest of humanity; at least those who elected to make the leap.

With the planning out of the way, Michael took Gabby's hand and asked, "So, are you feeling pregnant?"

Gabby laughed. "With the weather and then all the strategizing I forgot the most important thing of all. I'm feeling fine. A little on edge. No nausea, at least not yet. Beyond that, I couldn't be happier but now that you bring it up I'm starting to feel pretty nervous." Gabby paused for a moment, thinking.

"Michael, the retrovirus, it might affect the baby. The Treatment would have changed the DNA in all your cells, not only your brain."

"It'll be okay," Michael reassured her. "But this baby will be different. Imagine being born into these abilities. Our child will be the first of a whole new generation of human beings: a more aware and evolved animal than the Earth has ever seen."

"These kids will give new meaning to the term, 'generation gap'", Peter joked.

"Peter, it's not funny," Gabby shot back feeling very protective of the new life growing within her. "It's one thing for us to walk down this path. We don't have a clue how to nurture these new children. It's going to be trial and error. It's hard enough to raise a child under normal circumstances."

"Gabby, I believe they will teach us," Michael began. "Our child will be born into a world in transition but a world which they'll have a hand in crafting."

"You know, when I was pregnant with our first child I was thinking about setting up and decorating a bedroom, all the cute clothes I would buy. Now, it's become so much more complicated."

"But you'll have a connection with our baby which no one has ever had before. While these children will be so far ahead of us, at the same time it will change how parents and children bond. Now we'll all have a chance to grow together."

Gabby sat back, thinking, a look of consternation crossed her face.

"I want to come back to the question I asked earlier," Gabby said. "I know I sound like I'm beating a dead horse, but what's the worst case scenario? At least if we anticipate it, we can deal with it."

"And that would be?" Peter asked.

"General Scott comes in with an armed cadre and forces us to hand over the Achilles retrovirus. Arthur, under those conditions I don't believe your security staff will be able to stop him. I fear he may take the specimens anyway he can."

261

"If that's the case, I don't see how we can prevent it," admitted Arthur.

"It doesn't matter how much firepower he brings, we don't have a choice", said Michael. "We have to stop him."

"I don't see how. Think about it. What's the worst that could happen?" asked Jules. "He takes the retrovirus, administers it to his troops. The flaws become apparent and he takes the blame. If the catastrophe blows back to us we can explain how he stole the specimens before we were ready. It would be unfortunate for his test subjects, but I don't see how we can stop him.

"I don't think putting ourselves in harm's way will help. If he's going to take the virus and has to go through us to get it, he'll merely consider us collateral damage and we won't accomplish anything. Even if he takes the Achilles virus, our Ulysses project might face a setback but I don't want to see any of us get hurt."

Michael stared straight ahead indecision written across his features. Finally he spoke.

"I've been debating whether to say anything. I haven't told you the whole story."

"What do you mean? What whole story?" Gabby asked.

"This isn't only about us. This isn't only about protecting a few unwilling recruits. There's much more at stake here. Gabby, the Ulysses retrovirus works on the higher centers of the brain, and the Achilles virus works on the more primitive portions of the brain, correct?"

Gabby nodded.

"Michael, what are you getting at?" asked Jules.

"I didn't say anything before because I hoped it wouldn't come to this. We are locked in a struggle here. We see it as a fight between us and a bully bent on domination. But there is much more at stake.

"During my contact, if you can call it that, there was one thing I learned which I was reluctant to share with you. Through the Ulysses Treatment we can bond with other life forms out there who have also been through the transformation; a community of sorts. But there is another league, another group. For whatever reason that group has augmented the more reptilian portions of their brains in a fashion similar to the Achilles virus. Gabby, you talked about a hyper-aggressiveness you saw in a significant portion of the test animals. That was no accident."

"This other culture, if you will, is also bent on domination. On some worlds they are the only power, their hive mentality making resistance and free will all but impossible. On other worlds, it's the Ulysses group and it isn't unusual for there to be conflict when the two arise together. That battle must be avoided and also one of the many reasons I have been advocating for broader dissemination of the Ulysses Treatment. We must stop Scott at all costs. We have no choice."

"Michael, is this the knife's edge you were talking about?" Gabby asked.

Michael nodded.

"Gabby, please don't think I'm laying blame, but, for good or ill, my injury and your research set events in motion from which there can be no return. We're actors in a drama that must play out. There's no turning back the clock, no going back to the way things were.

Gabby sat back in her seat staring at nothing. *What have I done?*

No one spoke again until the pilot announced, "We've started our descent. Please fasten your seatbelts. We will be landing soon. The frontal system that produced the blizzard up north is coming through here, too. We'll be contending with high winds and heavy rain. It's going to be a bumpy ride down."

Soon the cabin, jostled by the winds, dove into a gray nothingness. Before long large rain drops pummeled the hull of the jet. The plane bucked thrusting the passengers against their seat belts bumping along uncontrollably for what seemed like an eternity.

All of a sudden Gabby felt the bottom drop out from under them. She gasped as her stomach rose in her chest and her heart exploded. She looked desperately to Michael as she clutched the arms of her seat in a vain attempt to ground herself.

And just as suddenly the plane leveled off as the pilot said "Sorry about that folks. We hit an air pocket. We should be fine from here."

As the airplane emerged from the clouds they found themselves in a storm as fierce as the one they had left. The plane landed without incident and taxied to the private terminal they had departed from only a few days and a lifetime ago.

Chapter 30

The wind and rain whipped at the travelers as they carried their luggage into the terminal. Once inside Michael announced, "We need to get moving. Scott's close."

Jules was talking on his cell phone. "You go ahead without me", he announced. "I have something I have to do."

Gabby stopped.

"Jules, what are you doing? We may need you," she protested.

"I can do more good here. Keep going," Jules practically shouted urging them to move quickly.

A car and driver waiting for them pulled away as soon as the door closed. No one spoke on the drive to BDT; outside the car the wind and rain buffeting the speeding vehicle.

As the car pulled up to the security gate Arthur rolled his window down and the surprised security guard waved them through. They stopped first at Building C and Peter got out.

Before he closed the car door Peter added, "Good luck. I'll get this thing hooked up as quickly as I can.

He shut the door Peter ran up to his lab while the car continued to building E.

Fumbling with the security code next to the lab door Peter finally got in and set the box down on a workbench. He arrayed the eleven components of the BRIDG processor and set about hooking them together along with two other modules he found underneath one of his benches. Feeling the pressure to get the BRIDG online quickly Peter worked as fast as he could, connecting and testing each component in turn. He then hooked up a power supply to the apparatus.

When he pressed the power button he immediately fried one of the modules; blue smoke and the acrid smell of burning plastic and metal filled his nostrils.

"Damn. That shouldn't have happened. I know I have another one of these around here somewhere."

Peter rummaged around on the shelves behind him and found an acceptable substitute. He wired the new component into the circuit and this time nothing burned when he powered up. He hooked the BRIDG up to a network card and held his breath as he plugged in the network cable accessing the BDT servers.

Over in building E the employees milling about on the first floor were shocked out of their day-to-day routine by the sight of the determined parade of Arthur, Gabby, and Michael; their coats still dripping from the rain outside.

Many of the employees in the building knew Gabby had been fired. To see her walking, head held high beside Arthur, who rarely visited Building E anyway, shocked them out of their daily routine, some stopping in their tracks wondering what was up. The trio paid no attention to them, rushing to the elevators.

They reached the fourth floor and ran the short distance to Gabby's old lab. Gabby and Arthur marched into the lab ahead of Michael. Seeing Gabby working in concert Arthur Paulson pushed Karen into a deeper state of confusion.

"Gabby what are you doing here?" was all she could say. Gabby's lack of response forced Karen to realize how in the dark she truly was. She couldn't help but wonder whether her new job might take a turn she didn't expect.

If Karen was thrown by the advent of Arthur and Gabby; she certainly didn't know what to think when Michael followed close behind. Karen and Edgar had met the wheelchair-bound Michael at office social functions. Karen, frozen in place, said nothing, stunned beyond comprehension.

Edgar, on the other hand, smiled broadly, walked over to Gabby and said, "You did it! You actually did it!"

Gabby stopped. "Yes, we did. And you helped make it possible. Now, we need to move my Garden over to Building A. Can you help us?"

"Of course," Edgar's replied as he set about preparing the wheeled tanks for safe transport. "They'll be alright without power for a little while."

Michael walked over to Karen. "Don't worry. You just need a little patience. You'll be happier with Gabby back."

Looking at Edgar, he added, "You two are going to be very busy." The four of them left Karen standing forlornly in the doorway to the lab; completely disoriented.

As the elevator made its quick trip back to the first floor with one additional person and the two tanks containing the Achilles specimens Michael said, "Get ready, Scott's here."

The elevator doors opened but they saw no one. As they wheeled the tanks through the lobby toward the door leading outside they saw a group striding purposefully from the parking lot toward the front door of the building.

Gabby identified five people dressed in Army fatigues and one civilian. At the head of the column marched General Scott; and beside him, Bob Arnold.

At the same moment Bob pulled out his ID card to gain access to the building Michael and Arthur cringed, in unison, as if hearing a painfully high-pitched whistle.

"What is it?" Gabby shouted.

"Peter must have hooked up the BRIDG", Michael said through his pain. "I don't think he has it quite right yet, but we can make it work. Arthur, I assume you have the passwords?"

"Got it", Arthur responded.

The door to Building E did not respond to Bob's entry card. Gabby realized Peter must have connected the BRIDG processor to the BDT security servers.

The General turned to Bob and they appeared to be having an argument. Abruptly Bob stepped back; two of the uniformed service men stepped forward, weapons raised, and fired shattering the glass.

"Stop right there," barked General Scott as he strode into the foyer. "That is United States Government property and I am taking possession."

As if on cue, the two men in fatigues who shot through the glass raised their firearms, pointing them at the group. The other two soldiers stepped forward to take the tanks. Gabby guessed they were technicians.

No longer appearing to be in pain Arthur confronted the interlopers.

"You don't want to do this, General. These specimens aren't ready for use. There are serious side effects we haven't figured out how to control."

Bob looked at the general, "He's bluffing."

"I figured as much. Stand aside Paulson."

Bob, eyeing his adversaries, saw something out of place and suddenly exclaimed in recognition, "Wait a minute. You're Michael Neumann!"

Pointing at Michael he turned to Scott. "That man, General, Dr. Neumann's husband, he couldn't walk the last time I saw him. She's found a way to reverse his paralysis. That must be the other project she was working on! General this verifies Achilles will work."

"Perhaps." The General appeared to be considering his options.

"Dr. Neumann I'm taking you and your husband into custody. The Army will want to know what you've done here. There is more I need to learn before I determine what to do with you."

Michael took a step forward. "General, don't. We haven't done anything wrong. You will be better served not to hinder us."

"Sergeant, I issued an order. Take those two into custody," the General commanded.

As the soldier stepped forward, weapon raised, Arthur moved to stop him. In the struggle the gun went off.

The muzzle pointed directly at Gabby.

Michael shouted, "No!" and reacting with astonishing speed placed himself between Gabby and gun taking the bullet full in his chest.

Gabby screamed, "Michael!" and dropped to her knees beside him cradling his head in her lap.

The bullet had entered his chest in the upper left quadrant near his heart. Gabby didn't need to be a doctor to know Michael was in mortal danger, blood from his wound soaking his shirt.

And then she heard the sound of many feet running.

"Stand down, General."

Gabby looked up and saw what looked like a platoon of men in black with FBI in white lettering emblazoned across their chests aiming their weapons at the General and his staff. At their head stood a man she didn't recognize.

"General, I am Deputy Director Harrison Gage of the FBI. You have shot an unarmed civilian and are engaged in an illegal seizure so again, I am telling you, stand down and surrender your weapons."

"I don't answer to you. This is a matter of national security," the general shot back, though more tentatively than he would have liked.

"No, but you answer to him."

Gabby heard Jules Allen's voice and saw him step forward with his cell phone and hand it to the General who took it and placed it to his ear.

"Yes, sir. Sir, I . . . Yes, sir."

General Scott, indecision written across his features if only for a moment, handed the phone back to Jules and instructed his men to relinquish their weapons to the FBI agents as paramedics rushed into the building with their equipment.

"This isn't over", threatened Scott jutting his chin at Arthur.

"Yes it is, General. If you look around you will notice all the security cameras trained in your direction. They caught the entire incident in the event we need a record," Arthur said.

The interchange between Scott and the others had taken what seemed like an eternity to Gabby and when she looked down at Michael his eyes were open and he was looking up at her.

"I'm okay," he said in a voice weak with trauma.

"No you're not," she replied, her voice wavering. "You've been shot. You're bleeding. It looks like he hit a major vessel. Hold on."

"It's okay," Michael repeated. "I stopped the bleeding."

"What do you mean, you 'stopped the bleeding'?"

270

"Remember, we talked about how I could regulate my immune system? You of all people should know the clotting mechanisms in my blood arise from my bone marrow, just as the cells in my immune system do. I accelerated the coagulation process. Perhaps my undergrad science background is paying off after all."

The paramedics who entered the building behind the FBI now swarmed over Michael, attaching monitors and starting an IV. Gabby moved aside to let them do their work as Jules walked over with Harrison Gage to make sure she and Michael were all right.

"How's he doing?" Jules asked.

Gabby, arms folded over her chest, her slacks stained dark red with Michael's blood, stood looking down at him.

She turned to Jules, "He'll need surgery but he should be fine. I'm so glad you arrived when you did. You saved the day again. Mr. Gage, thank you so much. But, how did you know?"

"Jules contacted me yesterday and alerted me to what might be going down thinking he might need our help. I activated the SWAT team from the local office." replied Gage.

"That's why I stayed behind at the airport," Jules added.

Gage walked over to where Michael lay on the stretcher.

"So, this is Michael Neumann. You look pretty banged up."

"I've been better," Michael replied, smiling wanly.

Jules added, "Harrison and I were friends in college and we've kept in touch over the years. When we learned of Scott's plans yesterday I called him and explained the situation. He contacted the Army Chief of Staff."

Gabby looked at Jules out of the corner of her eye.

Sensing her question Jules replied, "Yes, he knows. I had to tell him; and, as Michael said, this will be much bigger than any of us".

"I don't have to put anything in my report about the Ulysses Treatment, if that's what you're concerned about. But perhaps you can brief me later today."

Gabby nodded in agreement.

As the FBI agents escorted Scott and his team out, Bob Arnold stopped, turned and inquired, "How did he move so quickly? I've never seen anything like it."

Arthur, who had been calming the waters among the observers walked over to where they stood.

"Well Bob, as it turns out the Ulysses Treatment, that's what we're calling it, achieves similar results to what we were hoping to develop with the Achilles treatment but with a whole different set of positive consequences. Ironic, isn't it?"

Arthur turned to Harrison Gage while Bob and the others were led out.

"Hello, Harrison. Thanks for coming. I really appreciate it. It's been a while."

"Good to see you Arthur," Harrison held out his hand to shake Arthur's but then paused. "There's something different about you."

Arthur smiled broadly, "Yes there is, Harrison. Why don't I take you back to my office and explain the whole thing."

And with that Arthur Paulson escorted Harrison Gage out of the building. As they exited Peter burst through what was left of the main entrance and ran to where the paramedics were finishing their work.

"Word is out all over the campus," Peter announced breathless from running. "Are you okay?"

"I'll be fine. A little surgery and I should be back to normal. Your invention worked but I think it needs a little fine tuning."

"Yeah, well, the circuits burned up not long after I hooked it up to the servers. It's going to need a lot of work. I'm glad to see you're okay. We can't lose our fearless leader."

"I'm not your leader, Peter, merely a catalyst. Each of us is in our own way, don't you think? Gabby took the initiative to find the cure. You and Jules paved the way and now with the new processor you will take our use of this technology to undreamed of heights. We joked before about Gabby winning the Nobel Prize. We may have two winners here today. None of this would have been possible without each of us. No, I think I'm simply a catalyst."

"Perhaps that's what a leader is," Jules suggested. "In any event, Peter, we need to let Michael and Gabby go. I want to visit with Harrison, but first, let's get over to your lab and see what's cooking.

"No Jules, not you, too."

"Where do you think Peter got his appalling sense of humor? We'll come to the hospital later to see how everyone's doing."

"I guess I'll see you at the hospital then," Peter added as he left the building with Jules.

The paramedics were preparing to wheel Michael out to the waiting ambulance when Michael asked them to wait for a minute.

"How are you doing?" he asked as he reached for Gabby's hand.

"I should be asking you the same question, but it's been a hell of a day," Gabby admitted. "On balance things turned out well. We'll be able to destroy the Achilles specimens. We have a few bad actors out of the way. And, most importantly, we are going to be parents. Not all bad."

"I agree although the getting shot thing hasn't been so pleasant."

"Did you know or suspect this would happen?" Gabby asked.

"Yes. This could have gone a number of ways, but I knew it was a real possibility. I expect we'll be out of the line of fire for a while."

"So where do we go from here?" Gabby queried ignoring his pun.

"I believe I'm going to the hospital. Would you like to come with me?"

"I'm glad to see your sense of humor has returned. You've been awfully serious lately."

"I'll have to do something about that."

Gabby smiled indulgently. "You didn't answer my question."

"I know. Peter will create a clean working model of the BRIDG prototype. In the next few weeks we'll begin testing its capabilities. Meanwhile, once you've nursed me back to health and taken the Treatment, you can get about mass producing the Ulysses retrovirus and figure out how to streamline the induction.

"Arthur, with Jules' help, will be tied up finding ways to bring both to the populace in general. As you can imagine we'll face considerable conflict coming from multiple directions. But if we're prepared we'll prevail."

"And what are *you* going to do, Mr. Catalyst?" Gabby teased.

Michael's face turned serious, "I have one more blog to post. Then," he was smiling again, "then we'll see. Maybe I'll be a full-time father."

"That would be great," Gabby said, "but I have the feeling that won't be all. We may be gaining a better world but we have lost as well. We can never go back to what we had before.

We had a nice life, you and I. I had visions of raising a family and quietly growing old together with all the joys and heartaches which come with that life. It would have been enough for me but that future has been lost to us forever.

"I believe we're doing the right thing here and I've resigned myself to the fact. All that matters now is wherever this new path leads we will walk it together."

As the paramedics wheeled Michael outside to the waiting ambulance, Gabby walked alongside the stretcher continuing to hold his hand.

The rain had stopped. The sun poked through the thinning clouds throwing its rays across the rolling BDT landscape. An indefinable crisp smell heralding the coming of winter permeated the air, but the promise of spring waited just around the corner, and come the summer . . .

Unbiased Opinions of the Clearly Confused

Today's Message

I concluded my last blog lamenting the fact that we are hardwired for self-destruction and pain. Ultimately, I wondered whether we are at a dead end in our civilization, such as it is. Pretty dark stuff. I have much to say today so please bear with me.

Our five senses tell us we are separate and alone, and yet we crave the companionship of others. But what if we are deceived by our senses? Maybe we're missing something? What if we are not truly separate? What if the craving results from a perception deep within us, recognition that, in fact, we are all connected?

Now, if I were you I would be thinking, Samsa has gone off the deep end, the porch light is out and no one is home. Pick your metaphor. But, I have not come to this conclusion out of some psychological or philosophical rationalization; quite the opposite.

I had, we all have, good reason to be disillusioned. I don't need to recount all the words I've written so far. Many of you will be familiar with Plato's metaphor of the cave. We live in a world with little light, a dark world as a friend of mine would describe it. We face a wall and see only dim shadows reflecting our movement and assume those shadows are what is real.

I've come to the realization I wasn't correct in my thinking, but I wasn't wrong either. I missed the point. I have been asking the wrong questions.

We spend our lives debating loyalty to the tribe vs. freedom, capitalism vs. socialism, man vs. machine, science vs. religion, the material vs. the spiritual. We think in a binary fashion like a computer. The answer must be a 0 or a 1, there are no other values.

What if we possessed the faculty to see, to perceive our world in a different way? What if we were to truly emerge from the cave in the bright light of day? What if we could grasp that we are all connected to one another, that we are a part of something greater?

Many believe this is the case. But what if we actually perceive it, know it in the same way we can taste an apple or a see a chair and know it for what it is?

I have kept my identity secret all these years because, like you, I had many things to say but didn't crave recognition for saying it. You have responded; my discussions have resonated across continents and cultures.

I was a paraplegic. I was slowly dying. My wonderful and profoundly gifted wife developed a treatment, a cure. I can now walk again. But that's not the whole story. Her treatment had other effects. It increased the capabilities of my brain in unimagined ways. I can perceive, react, and think at a more subtle level. Some have called it intuition or wisdom. Mystics of all religions have experienced it. Albert Einstein said,

"To know what is impenetrable to us really exists, manifesting itself to us in as the highest wisdom and the most radiant beauty, which our dull faculties can comprehend only in their most primitive forms – this knowledge, this feeling, is at the center of all true religiousness."

I now see with far greater clarity than I was capable of before. I can "see" the connections among us and I am affected by them.

And I am not alone. Others have taken the Treatment with the same results.

Right now, many of you reading this are thinking, I don't want to tamper with Nature or mess with God's creation. It's your choice. But realize we are already connected in this creation. The Treatment makes it possible to see and embrace the experience.

I began this latest series at a crossroads with no clear path ahead. The path is now well lit. Dream. If you don't heed and pursue your dreams, you do so at your own peril. You hold your destiny in your own hands.

  Before you think this is sheer fantasy, my name is Michael Neumann. You and I already share a Connection.

I have been asking,
HOW CAN I BE SANE IN A MAD WORLD?

Would you like an answer?

Samsa, no more